W9-AFM-386

THE EAGLE AND THE CROSS

Books by

Prince Hubertus zu Loewenstein

THE CHILD AND THE EMPEROR

THE LANCE OF LONGINUS

THE EAGLE AND THE CROSS

THE GERMANS IN HISTORY

ON BORROWED PEACE

CONQUEST OF THE PAST

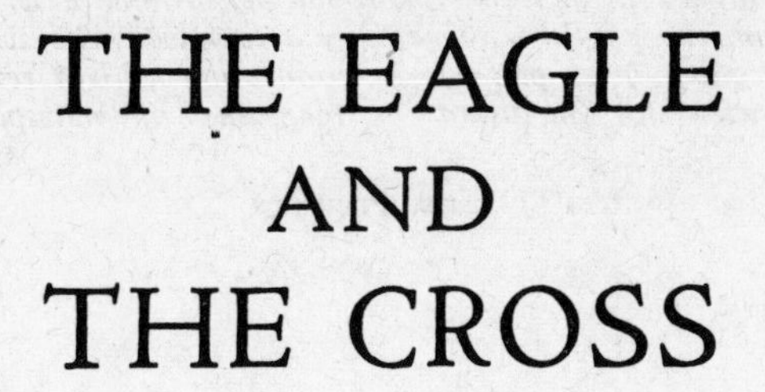

THE EAGLE AND THE CROSS

BY

Prince Hubertus zu Loewenstein

THE MACMILLAN COMPANY
New York 1947

First Printing

PRINTED IN THE UNITED STATES OF AMERICA
BY J. J. LITTLE & IVES COMPANY, NEW YORK

PATRI BERARDO VOGT, O.F.M.

SANCTI FRANCISCI DISCIPULO

NOBILISSIMAE ANIMAE CHRISTIANAE IMITATIONIS DIGNISSIMO

BEATI DUNS SCOTI EMINENTISSIMO SCHOLARI

ANNIS NOSTRIS IN TERRA NOVA

AMICO CARISSIMO

INTRODUCTION

LIKE a sunbeam, St. Eusebius said in his *History of the Church*, Christianity has spread over the face of the earth.

At the start, it was an earth overshadowed by the wings of the Imperial Eagle—a realm of peace, in which the barbaric state of tribal and national warfare had given way to a universal system of law, and to a feeling of a greater, supranational community.

It was not until the nineteenth century that the European-Mediterranean world again enjoyed such harmony and prosperity or such an excellent system of roads and communications of all kinds. In many respects even this modern period has lagged behind the cultural and technical achievements of the Roman Republic and the imperial age.

In the realm of the spirit, within the pagan world, the philosophy of Greece had done much to prepare the human mind for the reception of Christian truth. Also, at the time of Christ, knowledge of the inspired books of the Old Testament was no longer restricted to the Hebrew people.

Not without reason, therefore, has it been held that the *Imperium Romanum*, perhaps the proudest edifice of righteous government ever seen, was providentially willed, so that its body might serve as a symbol of the still wider community of all in Christ and, so that, through the means developed by Roman genius, the message of the Word might reach peoples and nations of every race and tongue.

It is a misconception to believe that "the new creed" appealed, at the start, almost exclusively to slaves and to the lower strata of the people. We read in the Acts of the Apostles that St. Paul, on his first missionary journey to Cyprus, won the proconsul of the province, Sergius Paulus, for the Faith. It is also assumed by many, among them Leopold von Ranke, that Gallio, proconsul of Achaia, consul in 53-54 A.D., who protected St. Paul during his visit to Corinth, drew close to Christianity. Gallio was the brother of the philosopher-statesman, Lucius Annaeus Seneca. And in the Epistle to the Philippians we read that all the holy ones send their greetings, "especially those of Caesar's households."

As to Seneca himself, the Christian tone and the high ethical content of his writings have caused many Church Fathers, notably St. Augustine, to claim him for Christianity. Significantly, it was believed at a very early time that there existed an intimate exchange of views between St. Paul and Seneca. The earliest extant manuscript of this "correspondence" dates from the fourth century.

The Emperor Tiberius Caesar has been called by Theodore Mommsen the most efficient of all Roman rulers. He kept the provinces in excellent shape and, a righteous and strict moralist, he saw to it that the laws of the Empire were administered with equity. It is probable that as part of the control he exercised over the provincial governors, he insisted on receiving careful reports about their conduct and accounts of all major cases which came before their tribunals. Following the lead of Ranke and Mommsen, in recent years a number of noteworthy American studies have established Tiberius Caesar's august place in world history.

Even Tacitus and Suetonius—the chief and at times vicious detractors of that great servant of the state and of the designs of History—bear, if read carefully, witness to his nobility of mind, his constitutional ethics, and his efficient administration.

That a Redeemer was expected by the pagans, too, is a matter of historic record. Virgil's Fourth Eclogue has always been cited as the clearest expression of this hope and expectation. But we may also find traces of that same feeling among the Celtic and Germanic peoples.

Even during the period of Christ's public ministry many reports of His works and signs must have reached the capital. Traders and travelers of all nations journeyed between Judea and Italy, and soldiers and officers of the imperial legions acted as carriers of messages on all matters of importance. After Christ's death, Tertullian tells us in Chapter XXI of his *Apology*, Pontius Pilate submitted a detailed report to Tiberius Caesar. This same information is contained in the apocryphical *Acts of Pilate*, dating probably from the early second century. The story of Captain Thamus of Alexandria is contained in Plutarch's writings.

Thus, the story of *The Eagle and the Cross*, though entirely fictitious, is yet projected against an accurate historic background. In particular, I have kept to historic reality in all matters of time and circumstances, such as the Sejanus conspiracy, the role of Herod Agrippa, the character of Caligula, the names and offices of the Cornelii in Germany and Italy, the deposition of Pontius Pilate by the legate of Syria, the Emperor's grandson, etc.

Several of the important minor characters, the reader will have no difficulty in identifying.

In my description of the actual attitude of the Emperor Tiberius towards Christ, I have followed Tertullian's famous account, as contained in Chapter V of his *Apology*. I should like to quote the more significant parts:

"There was an ancient decree that no god should be consecrated by an emperor without the approval of the

Senate . . . It bears also on your case, because among you a god's divinity depends on man's decision. Unless a god please man, he shall not be a god at all; in fact, man must be gracious to god! It was in the age of Tiberius, then, that the Christian name went out into the world, and he referred to the Senate the news which he had received from Syria Palestine, which had revealed to him the truth of Christ's divinity. He did this exercising his prerogatives in giving it his endorsement. The Senate had not approved beforehand and so rejected it. Caesar held to his opinion and threatened danger to accusers of the Christians. Consult your histories!"

Tertullian, born ca. 150 A.D.—barely fifty years after St. John's death—was a trained jurist and lawyer, and a thoroughly educated man of brilliant mind. His reference to the "histories" is to the Acts of the Senate, the "Congressional Record," as we might say. They were kept in the public archives of the state and formed an important source of historical knowledge, consulted and used, for instance, by the historian Tacitus. It would be strange if a man like Tertullian should make himself vulnerable by quoting from those official records, if it could easily be proved that they contained no such entry!

Tertullian's account is repeated by St. Eusebius and, of course, by the medieval historians, most notable among them Bishop Otto von Freising, whose world history, entitled *The Two Cities* has recently been made available to American readers in a splendid English translation.

That the Romans looked upon themselves as extremely "modern" is a well-known fact. But though the Roman Empire was believed to have been established for all time, men like Seneca may have sensed the trembling of the ground beneath the superstructure of culture and progress—just as today there are not a few whose minds are filled with anxiety as to the coming cataclysm menacing our own proud, and yet so hollow, secular civilization.

Material on sleeping cars, central heating, the banking system, the publishing business, the knowledge of electricity, the atom, the continent beyond the Atlantic, may be found in the sources. In short, there is no item of this or a similar nature in the narrative for which I do not have proof furnished by original documents.

Yet all these amusing parallels with our time do not exhaust the problem. Rather have I seen the central question in the conflict between divine planning and human ambitions, in the unfathomable relationship between grace and free will, and in the age-old struggle within the soul of man: not to despair of Providence, even if outward circumstances and defeats seem to make for doubt and hopelessness.

The journey of young Marcius through the world of the Eagle and the Cross—a journey, which again and again forces him to utter his anxious question, "Where am I going?"—is also a journey of the soul, in its development toward God.

It is historically not unlikely that Hibernians were found in the Roman army. Certain national traits never change; then as now the Hibernians were a valiant fighting people given to adventure as well as to great strength of faith.

Finally, I should say that I have carefully consulted Julius Caesar, Tacitus, Suetonius, Dio Cassius, Velleius Paterculus, Josephus Flavius, and Pliny the younger. There are also several instances, in which the language of Virgil, of Horace, of Ovid, of Seneca, as well as of other philosophers, orators, statesmen, writers, and thinkers of the Greek and Roman ages is woven into the text. Particularly Seneca's main sayings, pertaining to his philosophy of government, and his religious views, many of them breathing a Pauline and Augustinian spirit, are taken from his actual writings.

In addition to the original sources, I have made careful use of the standard works and specialized studies of that great epoch which saw the dawn of Christianity and the rise of a realm without end.

THE EAGLE AND THE CROSS

CHAPTER ONE

A YOUNG MAN on a dapple-gray horse approached the southern gate of the Galilean town of Capharnaum. The receding shadows of the night fluttered behind him like the folds of his soldier's cloak, while a warm wind blew the thinning purple veils from the awakening land.

This was the second morning to find him so early on the road. But to a man in the saddle, day and night, like the trees and the villages at the wayside, passed almost unnoticed. His dark hair fell unkempt upon his forehead, and his eyes looked tired. Though his legs were firmly clamped to the broad flanks of his horse, the loose reins showed that the good heavy stallion of Belgian breed was now in command.

When they had come within four or five miles of the town, the sound of the unshod hoofs began to change. Instead of the limestone and basalt, which had alternated with stretches of hard gravel, a long ribbon of asphalt lay before them. On its smooth surface, still wet from the night, it mirrored the contours and the colors of hedges and tiny inoffensive clouds.

The young man slowed down. "Where am I going?" he said, wondering. A few minutes later he stopped and dismounted. His legs felt stiff as, uncertain, he walked to the next milestone. Hewn out of its gray granite, a gilded eagle spread its wings over the name of the ruling Emperor: "Imperator Claudius Tiberius Caesar, five times Consul, Pontifex Maximus, Tribune of the People." In smaller letters it was explained that three years before, in 783 After the Founding of the City, this road had been laid out with material furnished by the tetrarch Herod of Galilee and Perea from his workshops at the eastern border of the Asphalt Lake, also called the Dead Sea.

"I thought they used this stuff only to tar ships," the young man reflected. "Now I'll have something new to tell when I get home."

Under the inscription was an arrow: "Antiochia, three hundred miles. Rome, via Byzantium, Aquileia, two thousand five hundred miles, via Tyrus, Creta, Neapolis, one thousand six hundred."

"That's a long distance–" the young man said anxiously.

He sat down on the milestone. "Don't go too far!" he told his horse. Then, as if he were awakening from a half sleep, he opened his eyes wide and with a feeling almost of surprise, he became aware of his surroundings.

"This is a beautiful day," he said. In the distance there was a blue streak of the Lake Gennesareth, and behind it the sun was beginning to rise. Its rays were strong and mild and the whole world seemed to respond to its glow.

The young man sat quiet as if he were listening to the song of the light. Haste had spurred him on his ride–a ride through rain and night, while phantoms and shadows had galloped behind him. Now, with inexplicable suddenness, his whole being opened to the joyful colors in the winding brook, from which his horse had finished drinking, to the glints of blue and red sparkling on the blades of grass, and to the green thorns and tiny leaves of the bushes. Bees and birds and opalescent dragonflies came by; they sang and hummed, until the worlds of light and tone merged in a single harmony.

"It's just a spring morning, people would say," he thought. "But it must be more than that. I am sure my friends would feel the same."

His eyes blue as cornflowers, with a lively green spark

in their depths, were veiled by remembrance. Then, like tidings of hope and happiness, which he could feel but not understand, the world streamed back into his mind.

"And it's only the beginning of April," he thought, marveling at the yellow and purple figs upon the nearby trees. The land, almost like a carefully planned garden, sloped down to the lake, its surface close to seven hundred feet below the level of the Mediterranean Sea.

"There seem even to be a few date trees around. I wonder what they'd say at home if I climbed one of them." He smiled. "I am afraid they wouldn't believe me, even if I brought a handful of dates along."

He took off his cloak and called his horse. "It may mean a little detour," he thought as he jumped into the saddle, "for an hour or so. But since I have made good time–" Then he left the asphalt road and descended a winding pathway towards the lake. The closer he came the more he felt as if he had entered a field of contest, where nature's noblest children might vie with each other. All the seasons had put forth their worthiest representatives. Peaches, called "Persian apples," apricots, the "apples of Armenia," cherries, which since Lucullus had discovered them on the shores of the Black Sea had spread out to many provinces, the Punic pomegranate, and hazelnuts from Pontus stood close to the native fig and olive trees. Between them, and creeping from stem to stem, vines with countless little grapes promised an abundant harvest.

Doublewinged golden and blue butterflies glided through this enchanted garden, and the blossoms of almond trees and of mimosas exhaled their perfume.

"Today I'd like to do something great!" the young man thought. What it might be did not matter. But it would be at least some solemn oath of fealty to a leader, a friend or a cause, such as youth likes to swear when the weight of happiness becomes too great to be borne alone.

He leaned forward. "Did you know that I love you?" he said to his horse. He meant it, but had he been alone, he would have told it to the next tree, to a wild lily, or to a bird. He might even have said it to the quick waves of the little brook, which, chattering and excited, hastened through the flower-covered meadows.

Now he had reached the edge of the cultivated zone. A broad girdle of fine white sand lay before him, and behind it stretched the blue waters of the large oval lake.

Again he dismounted and, followed by his horse, walked down the firm beach. The water was crystal clear, but of a tingling coolness. "No swimming yet!" he said. But, with the delight of a small boy, whose parents have told him that it was too early in the season, he waded in, until his knees were covered. He bathed his face and arms, and then, once more astride his horse, proceeded at a light trot toward Capharnaum.

Soon he could see the moles of the large inland port; many flat barges approached and left it on their way to and from the country east of the Jordan. They were heavily laden with merchandise, which from this important focal point of the near East eventually was reshipped to Nineveh and Tyrus, to Rome, the Ganges delta, Alexandria and many other places.

Four or five fishing boats were just coming in. Two others were already beached. Apparently the men had been trawling all night, and now they stood in a little group, while some helped their friends to jump ashore.

The hoofbeats of the horse made them look up. They seemed surprised at seeing a Roman here so early in the morning. And, quick-eyed, they also noticed that tied to the saddle there was a centurion's staff, though the rider wore the equipment of a simple soldier!

The young man felt their glance. He waved his hand in greeting. An urge to talk to the men overcame him. He halted, and slightly embarrassed—for it was an obvious pretext—asked whether one could enter Capharnaum from the lakeside or had to return to the asphalt road.

"That isn't necessary," a middle-aged man in a blue linen tunic answered in broken Latin. "Just go on. At the port turn left."

"Do you know the house of the place commandant, the centurion Gaius Cornelius?"

"It's up on the hill. It has a portico, and there are two acacia trees in front of it. You can't miss it."

"You've never been here before?" another of the fishermen cut in. The whole group had drawn closer together. "What's the matter with them?" the young man wondered, but he no longer felt embarrassed. "Never," he said aloud. "Now I have come all the way from Jerusalem—"

"From Jerusalem—" the man in the blue linen tunic repeated. "When did you leave?"

"The night before last."

"On the eve of the Sabbath?"

The young man nodded. Now they looked at him questioningly, with anxiety in their eyes. He too had become serious, and his vision seemed to withdraw into the past.

"Thank you for showing me the way," he said in a low voice.

"Will you be staying with the centurion?" someone called after him.

"For a few days perhaps." Looking over his shoulder, he saw that they had laid down their fishing tackle, and had made ready to walk to the town.

"In the name of the Emperor!" the young man said, when he was challenged by the legionnaires on guard at the gate of the port wall. This was password enough. Perjury in the name of the gods, it was said, is punished by heaven, but to misuse the emperor's name would be treason on earth.

It was not easy for the young man to make his way through the streets about the water front. Many Orientals lived there, and though it was only eight o'clock bazaars and shops were crowded. During the worst cloudburst one could have gone dry-footed through this section, for the sidewalks were covered by arcades, a whole maze of them.

"Where do all these people come from?" the young man wondered as olive-skinned Persians, little yellow men with slanting eyes and thin, drooping mustaches, and dignified Indians with glass jewels big as eggs on their turbans again and again blocked his path.

"And what a noise they make!" he thought again, amused. His horse was now in the midst of a dense crowd of Jewish-Egyptian boys who were shouting to each other in an unintelligible slang of their own. Other boys and young men of uncertain racial origin were milling through the arcades, holding out samples of all the things one could buy in the shops. Apparently they constantly got into fights with their competitors.

The young man stopped his horse for a few moments to listen to a Greek *rhetor* clad in a shabby mantle, who with cool, greedy eyes and egregious gestures proffered his art and invited the passers-by to profit from his recitation of the famous addresses of Demosthenes.

"Vital to all candidates for public office," he shouted in the intervals of speechmaking. The young man dropped a little coin into the *rhetor's* basket, and continued his ride.

But at the next corner he stopped again. There were snake-charmers surrounded by screaming and giggling negro maids, who were taking time from their marketing. Children who should have been in school by now listened eagerly to fairy-tales and adventure stories told by old Arab sages. Many coppers, Roman *asses* or of native coinage, which their parents had given them to buy lunch, clinked on the pavement.

"I wish I could understand those stories," the young man thought, "they seem to be very interesting." But he breathed more freely when he reached the Jewish quarter, where a large Hellenistic synagogue caught his eye. Finally, still higher up came the Greek and Roman section. On its edges, in streets with much green in the middle, there were hundreds of houses, for one or two families. Each had a porch, with rocking chairs and swings, home-made tables and gaily painted stone and clay amphora for wine and oil. These must have been the homes of old soldiers who had received imperial land grants. Their flower and vegetable gardens had a tidy, well-kept look.

Like most other provincial towns, this one too ambitiously tried to imitate the great city of Rome. When he approached the forum, the young man could see the exact replica of several of Rome's main temples. Of course, they were smaller and built of cheaper material, with the exception perhaps of the temples of Jupiter, of Divus Julius and of Divus Augustus, for the cult of the Caesars who had departed from this earth was considered by the government as very important to Roman authority and prestige in the outlying provinces.

At the southwestern entrance to the forum stood a large monument of the reigning Emperor, an excellent reproduction of a Roman masterpiece. Its simplicity only increased the quiet austerity of the imperial features. On the Emperor's head there was a wreath of gilded laurels. With a detached glance in his eyes, which seemed made of living marble, he rested on the curule chair. He was clad in the citizen's toga. Its smooth folds fell over his shoulders like white wool. There was no doubt about it: Tiberius Caesar wanted to be represented as nothing but the highest magistrate of the Commonwealth. There was no shrine or altar with burning incense anywhere near it.

"Yet people say that he aims at divine honors," the young man thought, as he rode slowly on.

A few minutes later he saw the two acacia trees and the house with the portico. He tied his horse to a wooden post, and, taking his staff along, he walked up a graveled parkway to the main entrance.

Two steps led up to the open vestibule, which was decorated with arms of all kinds. Their owner must have been in many campaigns, for there were trophies from Africa and Gaul, from Pannonia, Moesia and Germany. "Found in Britannia; origin unknown," were the words on a little tablet beneath a long Celtic sword.

"I think I can identify that!" the young man thought, smiling, and walked to the wooden, two-winged door at the end of the vestibule. Above the door was an oblong stone shield, which showed in mosaic a white lentil flower and three red seeds, the coat-of-arms of the ancient and noble family of the Cornelii Lentuli.

He pulled the handle of a bell and was admitted. "Official business, only for the place commandant!" he said somewhat too gravely, when a soldier, probably the centurion's orderly, asked his name and the purpose of his call.

"Will you wait here?" the orderly said and showed him into a small, simply furnished reception room.

"I wish my friend had told me more about the centurion," the young man reflected. " 'Tell him what happened, and he too may have a few things to tell you'—that's all he said. He always referred to him as 'my colleague,' not as 'my friend.' So I'd better size him up before saying much," he resolved. Just then the centurion Gaius Cornelius Lentulus entered, unattended.

"You wished to talk to me?"

The young man stood at attention. "Sir, I am on my way to Italy with a message for the Emperor."

But the centurion was not impressed. He was over six feet tall, and his cheeks and chin were covered by a rounded gray beard. His hair too was gray. His eyes were strong and severe, but not unkind. His mouth seemed formed to command as well as to express words of dutiful obedience. He was wearing a pale-blue military tunic, which left his knees free. But even had he worn other clothes, none could have failed to recognize him as a career officer of good breeding.

"Where is your garrison?" he asked with noticeable distrust.

"In Jerusalem, sir."

"Who is sending you to Italy? His Excellency the Governor?"

"No, sir."

"Your commanding officer?"

"No, sir."

"Who then gave you leave?"

"Nobody gave me leave, sir," the young man said, more and more disconcerted.

"How dare you then—" His eyes assumed a hard blank look. He made a move toward the door.

"Let me explain, sir," the young man said quickly. "I am no longer in His Majesty's army. I am being sent to Italy by the centurion Longinus, Company D, Third Syrian Legion."

Cornelius' expression changed. "Oh, by my colleague Longinus!" Then his suspicion returned. "For what purpose?" he asked.

"That, sir, I am not permitted to reveal. But the centurion was granted by His Majesty the right to ask for a special favor. I understand, sir, this was because of his services in breaking up the conspiracy of the Prefect of the Guards, Aelius Sejanus, two years ago."

Cornelius nodded. "Yes, I know. Everyone in the army knows about it. It was a very great service to the Emperor and the People. So now finally he is making use of His Majesty's favor?"

"Yes, sir. I am his messenger."

Cornelius was still hesitant. "Have you credentials?"

The young man took a small object from the inner pocket of his leather cuirass. He held it out in his hand, two wooden tablets, fastened with strings and a seal. Officers used such tablets to write messages on the inside, which was covered with wax.

"It's his seal," Cornelius said. "What else do you have?"

A green sparkle of impatience flashed in the young man's blue eyes. "This," he said rather curtly, and showed his staff.

Cornelius examined it closely. "Yes–I recognize it," he said. There were buttons on it, and apparently it could be elongated. It was the invention of a Corinthian swordcutler, and not part of the general army issue. It was widely known that the centurion Longinus had bought it at a considerable price.

"He once showed me how it worked," Cornelius went on, but before he could press the buttons, the young man had taken the staff from him.

"No, sir," he said firmly.

Astonished, Cornelius looked at him. There was a decisiveness in these words, such as he had not expected of a young man.

"Who are you?" he asked, uncertain.

"My name is Marcius Armaghensis."

"And you belonged to—"

"The Cohort Antonia, Second Syrian Legion. Your own legion, sir."

"You are not Roman?"

"No, sir. My home is Armagh; there I am called Marke, just as my father is."

"In what province—?"

"There is no Roman province where Armagh lies," Marcius interrupted. Such questions were familiar to him. "All Romans ask them," he thought. "They believe the whole world is theirs."

He smiled. "Sir, to give you a full answer: Armagh lies on the Island of Hibernia, which is beyond the sea. It is far outside the orbit of the Empire. I am returning to my parents as soon as my mission is completed."

Slowly, the poise of this rather strange dark-haired lad had penetrated the hard military shell of the commandant. His distrust began to vanish.

"You understand that I had to ask these questions," he said.

"Of course I do. I should be asking some myself."

"What do you mean?"

"Sir," Marcius replied with an impish twinkle in his eyes, "all I know about you is that I was told to pay you a visit and find out from you about the sailing of the next government boat."

"There is no message for me?"

"Only this: 'Tell my colleague at Capharnaum what you

know, and in turn, he may have a few things to tell you.' That's what my friend Longinus said."

"It doesn't make much sense. Unless—" He stopped. "Why was he not more explicit?" he asked after a while.

"We parted in a hurry," Marcius said, suddenly serious.

"How long have you known the centurion Longinus?"

"For less than a week, sir."

"Yet he entrusted you with the mission of carrying his request for the imperial favor to the Emperor—his only and most jealously guarded treasure?"

This was said with no suspicion, only with astonishment. He seemed to feel that something of great importance was going on, while he was still groping in the dark.

"During that week, sir," Marcius replied, "he and I have gone through many unusual events."

"Won't you tell me about them?" Cornelius asked kindly. He had to repeat his question, before Marcius responded. The young man's face had turned pale, and in vain did his lips try to form words.

"I can't, sir. Not yet, if you don't mind."

"You must be very tired; won't you rest for a few hours?"

Marcius smiled bravely. "Not too tired, sir, but if you think I should—" He staggered as he got up. "I am so sorry, sir. I have been in the saddle most of the time since I left Jerusalem."

"I'll have some breakfast sent up to your room," Cornelius suggested, but Marcius had no desire to eat. "All right. We'll have lunch or dinner when you are rested. My orderly will show you upstairs."

"Thank you, sir." On the staircase he turned. "Please, sir," he said, "don't forget my horse." Then he followed the orderly to the upper floor.

CHAPTER TWO

THE WINDOW of the guest room opened on the portico; it had glass panes and calico curtains with a blue and white pattern. Several chairs stood in the room, a large wardrobe, a chest of drawers, and a bed. To the right of the entrance was a bookcase with some of the Greek and Roman classics, Herodotus, Homer, Thucydides, Livy, Caesar, Virgil, Horace, and Ovid. But there were also several recent novels, adventure and detective stories, and some lighter poetry. Solemn scrolls were reserved for the important products of the human mind, while the less serious works were written on individual leaves of papyrus bound in leather or in thin wood.

"They look like flat boxes," Marcius thought. "They'll never be popular with the sophisticated; a book which is easy to handle they'll think no book at all."

All the furniture was of rosewood, which gave the room a bright coloring. There was a small bathroom adjoining, with a built-in tub and a shower.

"What a hospitable house," Marcius thought when he noticed an ample supply of Spanish soap, tooth powder, combs and brushes, and large cotton towels. Even a night shirt, a fresh tunic, sandals and slippers were laid out.

The warm water and the faint lavender perfume of the soap took the stiffness from his limbs, but he also became conscious of how tired he really was. Yet, when he laid his head on the soft pillows sleep drew away from him. The more his physical tension relaxed, the more his inner restlessness grew. Scenes and images passed through his mind, most of them belonging to his earlier years, as if he were shying away from his more recent memories.

Like all young men of his age he thought at times that he was very old. But now the feeling of being alone in the midst of a limitless world began to overwhelm all the grown-up notions of his twenty years.

"If everyone distrusts me so, I'll never reach home!" And while a Galilean morning wind billowed the curtains at the open window, he thought of his own island, where people did not know of all these modern inventions and devices which he had seen of late. But it was very green, with forests of fuchsias, and it was set in a deep-blue sea, like a throne of freedom outside the vastness of the hard and cruel world which lay beneath the wings of the imperial eagle. There were five kingdoms on this island, and one of them was ruled by his father. They must all have come to Hibernia as one tribe, one single great family. When, no one knew, but it must have been a long, long time ago. Originally, the priests said, the people had dwelt between the Danube and the southern slopes of the Alps.

"After they were driven out of the Great Garden into which death could not enter?" he had once asked, when he was a small boy. But the priests could only answer that very little was known about that garden or when it was lost.

In the course of the many civil wars which, until the days of Caesar Augustus, had shaken the Roman world, a host of political exiles and refugees had reached Hibernia. Many of them had been schoolteachers and philosophers, who passed their cultural heritage on to their descendants. King Marke saw to it that the best among these men were entrusted with his son's education. So it happened that young

Marcius not only learned Latin fairly fluently, but also acquired a certain notion of the huge Empire which many of the Hibernians viewed with a certain distrust and apprehension.

Sixty-eight years before Marcius' birth the armies of Julius Caesar had first set foot on the island of Britannia. Carried across the channel by eight hundred transports, a wave of steel and of triumphant eagles swept on shore, mightier than the tides of the Ocean by which the Empire had been thought to be bounded forever.

Ever since Marcius had first heard about this constant menace to Hibernian liberty, he had intended to enlist in the Roman army, so that he might get well acquainted with the customs and the art of war of the world conquerors. But perhaps his departure from home was also prompted by his inarticulate longing for the Great Garden. It was supposed to lie far to the East, and sometimes in his boyhood dreams he had hoped that he might find the hidden entrance.

On his seventeenth birthday he had landed at Iuliobona at the mouth of the Sequana river. He had enough coined money in the pockets of his leather breeches to bring him to Lutetia Parisiorum, a lovely Celtic town, hardly larger than his native Armagh. In two small bags which he wore around his neck, he carried twenty-five ounces of gold dust.

His next station was Lugudunum, where the Rhône is still filled with the blue waters of Lake Lemanus, and with all the freshness and gaiety of its mountainous birthland under the eternal glaciers of the Rhaetian Alps. The imperial prince Claudius, the younger brother of the late Germanicus and a nephew of the Emperor Tiberius, had been born within its walls. Of this, the citizenry of Lugudunum was very proud, for Claudius had acquired the reputation of being a great scholar and one of the most learned men of the Empire.

A permanent garrison of twelve hundred men was stationed in the town, but Marcius soon became tired of the boast that with this handful of soldiers all Gaul was held in obedience.

"I suppose they are part of the Seventeenth, Eighteenth and Nineteenth Legions?" he asked the recruiting officer, with an innocent smile, after he had been sworn in for three years' service in the army of the Emperor Tiberius. But this was not the right remark at all! Those had been the legions which had been defeated by the Germanic Duke Arminius, in the great battle in the Teutoburg Forest. Never afterwards had their numbers appeared in the Roman army.

Soon after his induction Marcius' unit was marched down to the ancient Greek city of Massilia. There a smelly troopship was waiting, and after an uncomfortable voyage they reached Sidon and were assigned to the Second Syrian Legion.

Six weeks of basic training, combined with sketchy instructions in politics and history, followed. Then Marcius and his company were sent into action on the frontier. Under the able command of the legate of Syria, Lucius Vitellius, many bloody engagements were fought with Persians and Parthians, and the losses sustained by the legions were considerable.

Marcius, brave, a good horseman, and quick-witted, was soon popular with his comrades and superiors alike; it was a great distinction that a year and a half later he received a transfer to the Cohort Antonia, the crack regiment, which guarded the city of Jerusalem.

"I didn't like it at first," he reflected, as his gaze followed the dark and lighter designs of the inlaid wooden ceiling of his modern Roman room. "I'd rather have stayed with my old pals. But then—"

Before his mind arose the Temple with its many outer and inner courtyards, its arcades and cloisters. The golden and marble cupolas soared high into the air. Every morning this had been the first thing he saw when reveille was sounded in the huge Fortress which overlooked the Temple grounds.

His service was not too strenuous and so he had much time to visit the city. It was completely different from Lugudunum and the places out East. He had already seen gardens and palaces, and stones pregnant with the aura of the centuries, but in Jerusalem everything seemed to assume a more solemn aspect. The whole city was like one great courtyard around the Sanctuary. And yet nowhere could he discover shrines or the statues and effigies of gods and men. There were not even any pictures or figures of animals such as he had seen everywhere else on the public fountains, on columns, and on the walls of houses.

His amazement grew when he heard that there had been bloody rioting every time the authorities had tried to carry the imperial eagles into the city.

"An unruly, puffed-up people," one of his fellow-legionnaires explained, "and wicked too. It's only because they have connections everywhere that the government doesn't crack down on them as it should."

"They are atheists," another said.

"Atheists?" Marcius wondered. "What about the Temple?"

"The Temple! When Pompey the Great entered it in 690, do you know what he found? A naked stone!"

"But don't they believe that there is a place for the soul after death? I have heard them say so."

"A barren sort of Olympus that would be! Just like their earth—no dryads, salamanders, or undines, no gods of the fields, rivers, woods." He made a gesture of feigned horror. "I wouldn't like to live up there, any more than I do down here, if the Jews had their way."

There was a soldier in this group who had kept silent so far. "They are not atheists; they believe in One God," he now said. "I know. I was born in Caesarea."

Since that day Marcius' interest had become intense. What at home was only a faint and undefined belief, told to a select few, was this the creed of the whole Jewish people? And then, soon, something else was to happen—

He was walking through the outer courtyard of the Temple, which was open also to non-Israelites, when he perceived a Man. His words Marcius could not understand, but they sounded as if they could be spoken in no other manner. Around His clear forehead authority seemed woven like a halo. A thought, the meaning of which he did not understand, entered Marcius' mind: "Even the sun and the stars conform to His harmony."

Many people were listening, friends, probably disciples. Shyly Marcius wanted to leave, when the Man raised His eyes, and an instant long their full glance rested on him.

From this moment on, Marcius followed Him wherever He went. He walked behind Him through the streets. He went across the Cedron valley, east of the city, where the Man taught on the meadows and under the olive trees. Once, when he obtained a three-day pass, he even followed him over the Jordan into Perea. There, once more, the eyes of the great Teacher rested on him.

But there were also weeks when he could not find Him anywhere. Then Marcius was unhappy and felt that every day without Him was lost and empty.

The ever-increasing multitudes referred to Him as the "Son of David"; others called him the "Son of Man." But more and more people said that it was He who would bring the remission of all guilt and lead the Jews and all nations back to the Great Garden, which had been closed at the beginning of time.

More Marcius did not know until a week ago. Yet he believed. He believed with a power that did not need signs and arguments. He believed because the eyes of the Son of Man had rested on him, and because it could not be otherwise. He was answering the simple call of his heart, wide open to faith, and the whole longing of his youthful soul.

He would have liked to cling to these memories. But drawn perhaps by the murmur of mournful prayers, the diffused voices of a group of men, assembled in the atrium, his mind, weakened in its resistance by half sleep, moved closer to the events of the most recent past.

"His Excellency the Governor, the Illustrious Knight Pontius Pilatus, has called in several out-of-town companies," he was told by his commanding officer. "As you are familiar with Jerusalem, you will serve as adjutant to one of their leaders."

"Anything particular happening, sir?"

"It's Easter week. There may be the usual troubles with the Jewish factions. They are always quarrelsome during their feast day. The officer to whom you will report may be put in charge of the security service. It is the centurion Longinus, Company D, Third Syrian Legion."

It was a very fortunate assignment. The centurion Longinus proved to be the first Roman with whom Marcius could talk as man to man. They became friends almost at once, even though Longinus was thirty-five, very old in the eyes of a boy aged twenty.

Shortly after they had met, they walked up the many steps of a winding staircase in the highest watchtower of the Fortress Antonia. From its top one could see much of the country on the other side of the Cedron valley.

It was a beautiful day, all blue and gold, and the sun seemed wrapped in veils of silken azure. Thousands upon thousands of a joyful multitude went out of the city, with flowers, palms, and olive twigs, to meet a man who was riding on the colt of an ass. Marcius could not see the features of the man clearly, but his heart told him who it was. His feelings changed into certainty when Longinus, who had been born in Judea of Roman parents, translated the words of the greeting into Latin:

"Hosannah to the Son of David, hosannah to him who comes in the name of the Lord."

But that week, so joyously begun, moved toward ever-greater darkness. Before Marcius' eyes, treachery, intrigue, cowardice, suffering and unbelievable humiliation were enacted. Yet, above all this there stood the heroism and the sovereign freedom of the Victim—sold by a perfidious disciple for the price of a slave, mocked, scorned, tortured by the mob, dressed in a mantle of shabby scarlet, and yet forcing even the skeptical and wavering Governor to admit His royal dignity.

Marcius and the centurion Longinus drew close together during that week, even though they looked at the events with different eyes. For the Roman it had been a trial for an offense committed against the Emperor's and the People's sacred majesty, until his sense of justice revolted, and through guilt and error the hand of Grace led him toward Marcius' faith. "The Romans too must have had memories of the Great Garden," he had thought, as he watched Longinus struggling against the world in which he had been brought up, and dreading to accept what his soul's innermost nature tried to convey to him.

When the darkest of all hours had passed, Longinus asked him to go to Rome on his behalf. It was this mandate which released Marcius at once from all further service in the imperial army and which placed all traveling facilities at his disposal. The message to Tiberius Caesar, which could be divulged to none but the Emperor himself, was written on the wax slate between two tablets which Marcius had shown to his host; he had learned the contents by heart just in case he should lose them.

Then, before a sleep of exhaustion overwhelmed him, there arose in Marcius' mind the last of all these images:

He saw three crosses, which faced the sinking sun, and a sky glowing in all the shades of red and purple. Nailed to the tallest of the three, which was planted on a skull-shaped rock, was He. His eyes were veiled by the blood which flowed from His forehead, adorned by a threefold crown of thorns. Blood flowed down from His pierced hands and feet, and from a wound in His side which the centurion Longinus had struck with a thrust of his lance.

But before the eyes of the Crucified had lost their sight, Marcius thought that once more their gaze had found its way to him—

CHAPTER THREE

MARCIUS COULD still feel this gaze when he awoke. He drew back the curtains. It was late afternoon. A group of men were just leaving the house. Among them he recognized the fisherman in the blue linen tunic with whom he had talked that morning. "That's strange," he thought. "How can they go into the house of a Roman? In Jerusalem they would not even enter the paved courtyard of the Governor for fear they might defile themselves." He waited until they were gone and then went downstairs.

Gaius Cornelius greeted him cordially. "Your good horse has been taken care of," he said.

"Thank you, sir. Now I should be leaving soon."

"The *Isis*, under Captain Thamus of Alexandria, is sailing tomorrow from Caesarea. You can't make it."

"I could always try, sir."

"Impossible. They leave early in the morning. Besides, you must think of your horse."

"I should not have slept so long," Marcius said, remorsefully.

"Don't worry. The shipping agency told me that there will be another sailing two weeks from today. It's the *Neptune*, a very good and modern ship. It goes from Tyrus directly to Neapolis." His voice had a tone quite different from that of their earlier conversation. "Why don't you stay at my house meanwhile?" he asked.

"May I really, sir?"

"I hoped you would accept. While you were resting I sent word to Jerusalem to have your belongings forwarded to the port." He cut short the young man's thanks. "Now I want to talk with you," he said and showed him to a large room in the rear of the main floor. Its entrance from the atrium was shut off by a thin curtain. The opposite wall had a folding door with two wings, which opened toward the peristyle, an inner garden encompassed by a double range of columns. A fountain, with three shell basins, two of them overflowing, stood in the middle of the peristyle.

"I know now what happened," he began. "A dispatch from the Governor arrived in the early afternoon. He seems to have sent word to all the garrisons. His Excellency is obviously worried about possible unrest."

"His Excellency always worries," Marcius said bitterly.

Gaius Cornelius turned his face toward the garden. His gray-blue eyes betrayed no emotion, and his hands lay quietly in his lap.

"He is my military superior," he replied. After a pause he added, "Of course, I know only the bare facts. Perhaps you can tell me more."

Marcius went to the door and stared visionless at the fleeting rainbow ribbons in the fine spray of the fountain.

"I will try," he said, and turned to the officer. His speech was halting as he began, and he stumbled over words which he had used a hundred times. After a while he began to talk faster, as the stream of facts broke forth, carrying him along by their own power.

"The centurion Longinus was in charge of the security service," he said. "He wanted to protect the court against the pressure of the mob. But his orders were constantly countermanded. The Governor was more afraid of what the Jewish factions might write about him to the Emperor than of the mob itself. So the centurion put me in charge of a special platoon to watch over the safety of the prisoner. They might have killed him during the trial, sir, there was such terrible hatred."

Gaius Cornelius sat motionless. Not one gesture showed that this report touched him in his innermost being. Only when Marcius stopped or struggled with an expression, he gently told him to go on.

But even after the report had passed on to new scenes, some of Marcius' sentences seemed to remain visibly inscribed in the air, as on a slate of marble.

". . . the scourging column," he had said, "the floggers were like beasts, short-legged devils from an Egyptian slave tribe, with bulky arms and no forehead."

". . . I could not stop the soldiers when they pressed a crown of thorns on His head."

". . . I thought the earth would shake from the battering of the hammers when they drove in the nails. Later the earth really shook. It must have been because of that."

". . . No wonder the sun went blind for hours when blood covered His eyes."

". . . When He died, the primipilar Abedanarius, who was in charge of the death watch exclaimed, 'Truly, He was a just man–He was the Son of God.' Silently to myself I repeated those words."

When the short dusk of the south had almost given way to the shadows of the evening, Marcius was still talking. And Gaius Cornelius still listened.

Finally, when darkness filled the room, Marcius closed his report. He said that during the first night rain had overtaken him, but that he had ridden on, without sleep, without thought. Then, early in the morning, when the sun rose behind Lake Gennesareth, it had seemed to him as if the fangs of death, which had been close to his heart, had suddenly been broken.

"Most of His disciples come from the shore of this lake," Cornelius said. "Now a disciple has come to it."

"Oh no, sir," Marcius replied almost timidly. "I am not a disciple. I only followed him."

"Did you know that He was at Capharnaum many, many times?"

"I heard about it, vaguely."

"But you have heard Him in Jerusalem?"

"Yes, often. What He said I did not understand."

"And yet you believed?"

Marcius was silent. Then, struggling with himself, deciding whether he should bare his most cherished secret, he replied: "He has looked at me. On Golgotha He looked at me for the third time."

Cornelius came close to him. "Marcius, will you be able to repeat in front of others what you have told me? Some of His friends came to see me this afternoon. They would like to hear from somebody who was there."

Marcius nodded. Then a thought seized him. "Into this house, sir–?"

"Yes, Marcius. May I ask them to come?"

The young man hesitated. "This was not what I meant." He stopped. "Into this house–" he went on. "Did He come here when He was at Capharnaum?"

A lantern had been lit in the garden. Its flickering gleam danced on the flagstones and the fountain, and a thin streamlet trickled into the room.

"Into this house–?" Cornelius repeated. "No, Marcius. But when my servant was dangerously ill, I sent friends to Him with the message: 'I too am a man subject to authority and have soldiers subject to me; and I say to one "Go" and he goes; and to another, "Come" and he comes, and to my servant "Do this" and he does it.' With this message went a plea for help."

His voice grew stronger. "Marcius, I was not worthy that He should enter under my roof. But He said the word, and my servant was healed."

The man in the blue linen tunic, whose name was Elon, came to the house on the following day. A large group of his friends accompanied him, and there could be no doubt that Marcius' report would spread at once all over Galilee.

When Marcius was alone next morning, Elon came again, He had already talked to Jairus, the chief elder of the local synagogue.

"There will be a special service on the eve of the octave of Easter Sabbath," he said, and asked whether Gaius Cornelius and Marcius could attend.

"I should love to come," the young man replied. There were almost five hundred synagogues in Jerusalem, but he had never dared to enter one. "If I may–" he added, blushing.

"Of course you may. Many gentiles come. It's only from the Temple that they are excluded."

During this conversation Marcius also learned that it was his host who had donated the synagogue, the new Hellenistic building which he had noticed upon his arrival.

"Gaius Cornelius is a good and just man," Elon said. "He loves our people, and therefore he stays at Capharnaum. With his wealth and his family connections he could have become a legate or a Senator a long time ago. He grew up as a pagan, but he has been waiting for the Kingdom just as much as we."

Such words were new to Marcius, but they agreed with the inarticulate language of his heart.

"I'd like to say something," he said, with a schoolboy's diffidence. "We Hibernians also have heard about the Great Garden. One day, our priests say, we may all return to it."

"That is very strange," Elon said. His weather-beaten face showed how hard he was thinking. "That's it!" he continued, "Gaius Cornelius told us that some of the Greek philosophers also spoke of such things. He said Pythagoras, Socrates and Plato–"

"But our priests did not get it from them. On the contrary, perhaps." A certain pride came into his voice. "We have a tradition that Plato learned his wisdom at Druid shrines."

"I wouldn't know about that," Elon replied, slightly embarrassed. With a grain of sententiousness, such as Marcius had noticed in a good many Israelites, when religion was being discussed, he went on, "Anyway, it would not matter. In the Great Garden, which we call Paradise, all peoples received the same revelation. Some may have preserved a memory of it, even though their minds became warped by superstitions because they worshipped false gods."

"Something that your people never did?" Marcius asked, with an impish twinkle.

"We always rallied from our errors," Elon replied gravely.

"Perhaps you can help us to do the same," Marcius said as they parted.

When Gaius Cornelius returned from duty, Marcius repeated to him a few of Elon's remarks, and he would have loved to continue with such conversation.

"We will get around to it," the centurion said, "but first–"

Then he brought up various matters of which Marcius had not yet thought although they were very important for the completion of his mission. There was, for instance, the question of money.

"I will gladly give you all you need," he said.

Marcius shook his head. "Never!" he replied, and explained that he had saved almost five hundred sesterces.

"That won't last very long. In Neapolis, your lodging alone will cost you three to four hundred sesterces a month. In Rome it would be even more."

"I can move to a suburb."

"Which suburb? Pompeii? Herculaneum? Salernum? My dear boy, you don't know what you are talking about. Most probably the Emperor is in Capri, and there are only luxury places along that whole gulf. You may have to wait for weeks."

"I still have twenty ounces of gold dust," Marcius said, brooding. "I think it will be all right for me to use it now."

"You'll get a better price here than in Italy. They are having an economic crisis now and coins are scarce. There is a wave of bankruptcy all through the West. The Emperor just created a credit fund of a hundred million sesterces."

"But I can't walk around with bags of silver."

Cornelius smiled. "We'll settle that. Let's go first to the office of Titus Pomponius Atticus."

"Is he a jeweler?"

"No, a banker."

"You know him personally?"

"There is no 'he.' The old man died over sixty years ago. He did much of the banking and investing for Caesar and Cicero. It's his firm that I mean. It has branches the world over."

"Then they won't bother with such a trifle."

"Leave it to me. Besides, for a banker no money is ever a trifle."

The office of Titus Pomponius Atticus Heirs was in the Greek section of the town. "Taberna Argentaria" was lettered over the door. In the front window, nicely arranged on blue velvet, lay gold, silver, copper, nickel, and brass coins from all countries. There were also a few odd-looking leaves, with letters and signs running from top to bottom. "That's Chinese money," Cornelius explained.

"Why, it's just paper! It can't be worth anything."

The centurion had estimated that Marcius' gold dust would sell for about a hundred aurei, or ten thousand sesterces. This was no mean sum of money, yet, with prices up in Italy, and the young man's obvious ignorance in financial matters, Cornelius feared that it might not be quite enough. So, under the pretext of calling on the chief clerk, he went behind the counter and whispered instructions to add seventy aurei from his own account.

Marcius was far too bewildered by the questions he was asked to notice any change in the value of his gold.

"Sir," the chief clerk inquired, "how do you wish the money? Travelers' checks made out in your name or a letter of credit?"

"Well—just money, Roman money, I suppose."

"Thirty aurei in cash, the rest in a letter of credit," Cornelius intervened. "I'll explain to you afterwards," he said to Marcius.

So, a few minutes later, the young man was handed a beautiful parchment with many seals and signatures which he could present at all branch offices of the firm.

"Don't lose it," Cornelius said, and then they walked out into the afternoon sunshine.

CHAPTER FOUR

A LARGE PARK, with many exotic trees, separated the Greek business district from the Roman quarters. Most of the people who strolled along seemed to know their place commandant personally. Friendly greetings were exchanged and there was an air of mutual respect and sympathy. In Jerusalem things had been quite different. There the Jews avoided the Roman officers; they always looked the other way or pretended not to see their conquerors at all.

A green bench, standing in a circle of fine sand, faced a dreamy pond alive with ducks and white and black swans. "Let's sit down for a while," Cornelius proposed. He took a wood-covered tablet from his pocket. "We must make a list of people whom you ought to see. The first whom you may meet is the Praeses of Campania, Marcus Cocceius Nerva. He is an imperial privy councilor, Minister of Roads and Public Works, and Consul Designate for the second half of this year. Then, there are a few of my cousins. Corsus Cornelius Lentulus has just been appointed Prefect of Rome; his brother Gnaeus is a prominent Senator and was a friend of the younger Drusus, the late son of the Emperor. Of course, both are now getting along in years. Another cousin of mine is Cornelius Lentulus Gaetulicus, the legate of Upper Germany. His daughter was engaged to Sejanus' son, and an informer seized upon it. But His Majesty turned a deaf ear to the accusation of conspiracy and reinstated him in his command. Gaetulicus' father-in-law, Lucius Apronius, is Legate of Lower Germany."

"I would be very happy to meet them," Marcius said, and wondered how he would ever tell so many Cornelii apart. "But should I really waste their time?"

"They may be very interested in what you have to say. The legates may be useful on your journey home. The Prefect and the Senator can make your way easier while you are in Italy. I'll write the letters before you leave, also the one to Nerva, although he is no relation of mine." He closed the tablets. "There are many intrigues around His Majesty, so it's important for you to meet loyal people."

"There is much talk about the court—"

"I know there is. One of the worst schemers is a certain Herod Agrippa. He hopes to be made King of the Jews, so naturally he will be most unsympathetic to your report."

"A brother of the 'fox,' as my friend Longinus called him, the tetrarch of Galilee and Perea?"

"No. He is a son of the tetrarch's halfbrother Aristobolus. His sister, the infamous Herodias, is married to the tetrarch. But the two men hate each other. Therefore Herod Agrippa is always siding with Pilate against his uncle and brother-in-law."

Marcius sighed. "If I ever unravel the Herod family!"

"Don't try. Herod the Great was married ten times. Most of his descendants are cross-related through countless marriages with the sisters or divorced wives of their closest kin. And of course murder, the killing of sons, brothers, husbands and wives, has cursed this whole family from the beginning."

Marcius shuddered with horror and disgust. "My friend Longinus often wondered," he finally said, "which was worse: the old Herod or the tetrarch."

"There isn't much to choose," Cornelius replied. "And Herod Agrippa is true to the family tradition. He is an ambitious, dishonest and depraved adventurer. A year ago he cheated his creditors out of three hundred thousand sesterces. He secretly sailed for Italy, but the Emperor found out and made him pay his debts. So he borrowed the money from Antonia, His Majesty's sister-in-law. Recently he raised a million. Nobody knows just how."

"His credit still seems to be good, though I wouldn't lend him a copper. Why in the world does the Emperor put up with him?"

"The Emperor is very loyal," Cornelius said in an embarrassed tone. "Salome, the sister of Herod the Great, was a very decent woman and an intimate friend of His Majesty's mother, the late Livia Augusta. His Majesty is very devoted to his sister-in-law. She first warned him of Sejanus' conspiracy."

"But doesn't the Emperor know that Herod Agrippa is a schemer?"

"He is beginning to find out. Herod seems to be using his money to corrupt Gaius Caesar, the Emperor's grandnephew. He arranges banquets for him, games, garden parties, luxuries of all kinds. He must be gambling on the chance that Gaius will surely repay him if he becomes emporer some day."

"Gaius Caesar Caligula—the 'Little Boot'?"

"That's his nickname. He was born in an army camp, and his father was Germanicus. That makes him very popular with the legions."

"What sort of a person is he?"

"He is only twenty-four, so it is difficult to tell," Cornelius said evasively. "Apparently, Herod Agrippa is putting ideas into his head which might be all right for Oriental principalities, but which are alien to our traditions. The Emperor's grandson, Tiberius Caesar, called 'Gemellus,' because he had a twin brother, might be a much better choice. He is fourteen now but a boy of very noble character. This one can tell already. Decently he received the title Princeps Iuventutis."

"Perhaps the Emperor no longer knows what would be best to do. He must be getting rather old–"

Cornelius frowned slightly. "His Majesty has never needed a physician in his life."

"But people say–"

"You must never listen to 'people.' For years there has been a whispering campaign against the august person. Since the Emperor moved to Capri, to have more leisure for his work, the slander has grown worse. The stories which his enemies tell are appalling. Roman society will still be gossiping about him two thousand years from now."

"So you don't think–"

Cornelius felt that there was no malice in Marcius' doubts.

"I am telling you the simple truth," he replied. "The Emperor is the most virtuous, the wisest and the most efficient ruler Rome has ever had. 'The Prince is the first servant of the State,' he said in the Senate, and that has been his philosophy of government always. Never have the provinces been better administered, never has there been a more efficient central authority. Besides, the Emperor is a great soldier. 'Nought is there that the Claudian might will not achieve,' Horace could write of him forty years ago. 'A wonder to behold in martial combat,' the same poet said of him in another of his Odes. Tiberius Caesar and his brother Drusus pacified the frontiers and brought the Alpine provinces Rhaetia and Noricum and the whole of Pannonia into the

Empire. Julius Caesar reached the Rhine. Tiberius Caesar has reached the Danube."

"But he ought to recall Pontius Pilate!" Marcius exclaimed. "That man is a disgrace."

"I shouldn't be surprised if he did."

"Well, I'll certainly make it hot for Pilate when I see the Emperor," Marcius said a little wildly.

Cornelius did not reply at once. He looked at the procession of swans gliding through the water as though drawn by some invisible power. "This young man must be judged by different standards," he thought. Of course, his own opinion of Pilate had never been favorable—a courtier, who had wormed his way into high position. Now, since he knew what the Governor had done, he had only contempt for him. But no Roman would ever have made a threat like the one Marcius had just uttered.

Cornelius tried to change the subject. "Why don't you bring your father to Capri?" he asked. "The Emperor would certainly receive him. He might even make him 'Friend of the Roman People.' "

A spark of boyish mischief shone in Marcius' eyes. "That would be a great honor. But wasn't there once a Germanic king, Ariovistus? Under Caesar's consulate, the Senate gave him the title 'Friend.' And what happened shortly afterwards?"

"You must have read Caesar's *Commentaries on the Gallic War* with better attention than many a Roman schoolboy," Cornelius said, with friendly anger. To himself he silently wondered, "Can't I make him understand what Rome really is?"

"You have told me about the discord in Hibernia," he went on. "Why not have a peaceful, united island, governed by its own rulers, but protected by the Emperor?" He noticed that a flippant reply seemed to tremble on Marcius' lips and forestalled him. "Please don't say it; it's too obvious!"

Yet Marcius had already realized that Cornelius had something to say which he should not brush aside.

"So far you have only seen the harshness of Roman rule and you have become witness to a most shameful violation of justice. You must see the other side of the picture too. Once the world was torn by war. Now, virtue, strength, and fortune have built a hearth for all nations. 'Where the Roman conquers, he dwells,' is an old saying. And that is something to be proud of; it is not just the sword and the war horse that have pacified the world, but rather the threshing ox and the ploughshare. Earlier men drifted on a wild ocean, now there is a place of anchorage for all."

"My friend Longinus told me that," Marcius replied, startled. But then he paused—Longinus was the son of a humble family of peasants and soldiers. Naturally he would submit to the official lore of the Empire, without questioning the facts. But Cornelius? Marcius knew by now that his ancestors, as consuls, praetors, senators, as generals and judges, had served the Republic since the days when the first Junius Brutus had ousted the tyrant Tarquinius Superbus. Surely, he must have peered behind the façade of power and splendor!

More important still, when Longinus had praised the Empire he was living in the world of his native gods; all their talks had taken place before the Great Evening had descended upon the skull-shaped rock. Cornelius, who now spoke with such glowing restraint about the mission and beauty of Roman power, belonged to a different world entirely; he had followed Him, and he had not felt worthy that He should enter under his roof—

"I must ask you something," Marcius said hesitantly. "How

do you reconcile your views—with—with what you and I have seen?"

"There is no contradiction." Cornelius leaned forward and with his staff drew lines in the sand before their bench. "This is a rough sketch of the Empire," he explained. "The oval is the Mediterranean Sea, the boot is Italy, and the triangle at its tip is Sicily. The square is Hispania." He drew more lines. "That's the Rhine and the Danube. Down here is Africa. No one knows exactly how far south it goes. But there are rather interesting stories about that strange continent. About five hundred years ago the Carthaginian explorer Hanno sailed sixteen days and sixteen nights along its western coast, until he reached a green cape. People think that if he had gone on, he might have landed in Arabia or India. But he was frightened by huge forest fires, and at night he could hear the beating of countless drums, scattered voices, and the sound of flutes and cymbals. Because of the tremendous heat it seems that the natives sleep during the day and come out only after darkness falls."

"I'd love to go down there myself!" Marcius interrupted.

"It would be fascinating, wouldn't it? But there are other places, nearer and yet very interesting too. Now take the Nile. Its sources must be somewhere in the heart of the ancient kingdom of Ethiopia. A tribe of dwarfs that have no ears and almost no mouths, but with huge, paddle-like hands, is supposed to live at the sources of the river. To make the Nile recede, after it has brought its fertilizing earth to the Egyptian valley, the dwarfs press their hands on the springs of water. Sometimes they are mischievous, and then Egypt has a drought."

"Do you think that's really true?" Marcius asked.

"I don't know; it may be just a yarn," Cornelius replied,

smiling. He shifted his staff to the left. "Here is our province of Africa Proconsularis. South of it is Gaetulica, which my cousin pacified–hence his surname. Further down are the Garamantes, and the Troglodytes, who live in caves of salty rocks. Herodotus says that the cattle of the Garamantes move only backwards, while the Troglodytes eat snakes."

"Brr–snakes! I'd rather live with the Garamantes. It must be fun to take one of their oxen by the horns."

"Here to the left is Mauretania where stands Mount Atlas," Cornelius continued unperturbed. "The ancient Greeks thought it was not a mountain, but a Titan who carried the skies on his shoulders."

Marcius suppressed his question, but his excitement was growing visibly.

"These are the Pillars of Hercules, and beyond opens the immensity of the Atlantic Ocean," Cornelius went on explaining. "It is like a huge desert of water, but it too is about to be charted. Some sailors I have talked with claim they have heard the sun splutter and hiss when it plunged into the waves. But you know how sailors are!"

"Has nobody ever followed the course of the sun?" Marcius asked, his cheeks flushed. "Perhaps the Great Garden–"

"Andalusian merchants once reached a group of islands several hundred miles from the North African coast; they thought that they had found Homer's Elysium."

"If they had, they wouldn't have returned, and then no one would have heard about it. But perhaps they were terrified by the roaring of the abyss, just as Hanno was by all the fires and the drums."

"Well, the abyss–" Cornelius repeated thoughtfully, "I am not so sure about it. The Phoenicians, who were good navigators, tell a story that some of their men, three hundred years before the Founding of the City, got much further than these islands; they speak of an enormous continent with gigantic streams flowing into the sea and of red-skinned men dressed in beautiful feather robes."

He looked towards the western sky where the sun was sinking.

"There is a promising young writer and philosopher in the Emperor's entourage, a native of Hispania. His name is Lucius Annaeus Seneca. I shouldn't be surprised if you met him. Recently he published a play called *Medea.* It contains some rather remarkable lines." He turned to Marcius. "But perhaps you don't like poetry?"

"I do—though in school they kill the most beautiful verses, you know, by studying the syntax."

"It's the same in our schools. So you see, Rome and Hibernia have something in common."

Marcius was still at an age when it appealed to him greatly to hear a mature man criticize the artlessness of teachers. Now, Cornelius seemed much younger to him. "Do let me hear those lines!" he begged, smiling.

"In future years, centuries from now, when the mysteries of the ocean are revealed, a land will appear which is still unknown and navigators will discover new regions. Then Thule will no longer be the land farthest away."

"So he knows about Thule," Marcius said, amazed. "It lies far to the north of my country. Few people have ever been there."

"Your country is up here," Cornelius replied, without noticing the slight shade of worry in Marcius' voice. "Now we are almost through with our map." The staff jumped. "Armenia, the Black Sea, the Euphrates, the Ganges, where the trees are so high that an arrow can't fly over them." He dug a little hole in the sand. "And this is the place where you and I are sitting."

"Of course, there are still quite a few countries which aren't Roman yet," he went on, "but even so, the Empire is rather big the way it is, don't you think? About two and a half million square miles, with a hundred million people. They talk a hundred or more tongues and belong to almost as many different races. Yet to keep the peace, we need only twenty-five legions, most of them stationed on the frontiers. With their auxiliaries hardly three hundred thousand men—"

Marcius' eyes focused on the few dashes which marked his island. Fear, coupled with defiance, had drowned out his interest in the strange nations and climes of which Cornelius was speaking.

"Why do you want still more, when you already have so much?" he said.

"We really don't," Cornelius replied in a matter-of-fact tone. "Caesar Augustus laid down our future policy: no further expansion, unless for purposes of defense." Now he noticed the harassed young face. "I have upset him," he thought. "He is worried about his little country."

He put his hand on Marcius' shoulder. "Let me explain what I mean," he said with paternal tenderness. "You have very important news to convey to His Majesty, haven't you? In the old days brigand kings, pirates and bandits would have been everywhere. There was no common currency, no transportation system, no legal protection. Today it is different. Soon you will ride again on a broad safe road. In Tyrus, a fast comfortable ship will be waiting, with nothing and nobody to stop its course. A universal language is at your disposal. Wherever you are you move upon the soil of well-established justice."

Marcius' eyes opened wide. "But, Cornelius, is comfort so important? Is it worth the high price that has been paid for it?"

"I am not talking about comfort. I am talking about your message. Perhaps one should not overrate its importance. I would certainly be the last to fill you with false pride. When the time has come, others will carry the fullness of the tidings. And you are not of their number, you are not an apostle. Still, your report has its meaning. It is part of the Great Design. During the last three years much news of what has happened in this country must have reached the Emperor and the people of Rome. Now you can fill out their knowledge in greater detail. A stream of truth is irresistibly breaking forth, and eventually it will reach the very frontiers of nature."

All distrust had vanished from Marcius' open boyish face. "I think that now I see what you mean," he said.

"Do you really? Then look at this again." The staff glided over the sketch in the sand. "Here is Gaul, with its somber Druid cult. This is Germany with its endless woods. Here are the wind-lashed plains of Pannonia—here the rugged mountains of Thrace. All this and infinitely more must be reached, on Roman roads and through all the countless channels which we have built."

"Under the wings of the Eagle," he added after a short silence, "the Cross will grow like a tree, until it shelters the peoples of the world."

There were deep folds in Marcius' forehead, as when a schoolboy ponders over a weighty problem.

"So you don't mean dominion?" he said.

"I do mean dominion but not for its own sake. Do you remember how Virgil expressed it?"

"Virgil?"

Cornelius nodded. "In the sixth book of the Aeneid." And then, as if they were rhythmic prose, he quoted the great Mantuan's famous verses:

"Roman, be thou mindful of swaying the peoples with dominion.
These be thy arts: to impose the customs of peace,
To spare the vanquished and to humble the proud with might."

Spoken artlessly and yet with strength, it sounded like a creed, a philosophy of life. It was the same spirit that vibrated in the clarion call of the tubae and in the sparing commands and the sharp marching rhythm of the legions.

"Do you want to hear more?" Cornelius asked, and before Marcius, swayed by his friend's words, could answer, he continued:

"This is the hero, of glorious Caesar's race,
Whose touch shall re-create the golden age.
Beyond the Garamantes and the Indies shall his realm extend,
Even to lands beyond the boundaries of the stars–"

He made a gesture as if he were closing a book. "Beyond the Garamantes and the Indies," he repeated. "Unlike the mighty kingdoms of old, Assyria, Babylonia, Persia, we have never destroyed the peoples' legitimate customs and liberties. But we have made them conscious that they are one family, parts of a nation above all nations." He sat erect. "Do you think, Marcius, that what you have seen on this map has no meaning for the future? Do you think that such an empire could ever have been established unless it were through the will of God?"

"No, it could not!" Marcius replied. But then the spirit of opposition rose again in him. "No realm has ever been established without the will of God, and each has had its day."

Cornelius did not answer. He rose, and silently they walked to the edge of the park. There he stopped. "Each realm has had its day in history," he said slowly. "But our day will be the harvest of time."

CHAPTER FIVE

THE JEWISH SECTION of the town was tense with excitement on the appointed evening when Marcius went to the synagogue. He was alone, for a courier had arrived from Caesarea and business might detain Cornelius for some time.

The crowd filled the rectangular center space almost to capacity. In the gallery, women and young girls, their heads and faces covered with dark veils, seemed to have been waiting for hours. The air was drenched in mournful silence. Shyly Marcius started to take a seat in a back row, but Elon discovered him and ushered him to the front.

Before him, on a platform, stood a seven-branched candelabrum. The mild and living glow of its wax candles fell upon the holy ark which contained the sacred scriptures. Cornelius had told him about them and he longed deeply to read them himself. They spoke of the Great Garden, into which death could not enter until sin had broken the gates and angels with flaming swords had driven the first parents of mankind out into the harshness of the world.

It was precisely one week since darkness had covered the whole land. Then, Marcius' eyes had been resting on the three crosses. They faced towards the West, and like a gigantic warrior in full armor Orion had kept watch; the diamonds in his belt had sparkled brightly, and his gleaming sword was pointed menacingly toward the earth.

Marcius shuddered as he remembered those hours. Could

the coming of darkness have meant that the Great Garden had once more been closed, and closed this time forever—

His thoughts were still on Mount Golgotha while the opening prayer was intoned. Some of the words sounded familiar, and he thought that he must have heard them in Jerusalem. *Shehma Israel*, "Listen, oh Israel!" he understood, and *Adonai Elohenu*, the solemn invocation of the One Lord.

Now Marcius noticed that many non-Israelites had come. Cornelius' servant was there and with him forty or fifty soldiers from the garrison. Some Greeks were also present and men of various other nationalities. For their sake, according to the announcement of a functionary of the synagogue, the Aramaic texts which Jairus, the chief elder, was to read would later be translated into Latin.

During the half hour that followed, it seemed to Marcius as if a powerful hand were pushing aside mountains and centuries and opening new vistas to his gaze. So this was what had happened in the Great Garden! Oh, why did Adam and Eve ever listen to the cunning serpent!

"I will put enmities between thee and the woman," Marcius heard, "between thy seed and her seed, and she shall crush thy head."

This was the first promise that the evil one should not triumph forever. Marcius gripped his chair, and in his ears roared the sound of pouring rain and the moving waves of the deep. In Hibernia, too, there were faint memories of the great flood, but they did not know what happened when the water receded: in quiet beauty, a rainbow spanned the gap between heaven and earth and a new race of men went forth into the world.

Hopefully Marcius raised his head. Were not the seven

flames before the ark like seven different colors, blending into a single light?

Then, with the prophets as guides, the journey continued. The heart of Marcius was troubled with fear for little Isaac who was visible to the eye of his mind, as he heard how the Patriarch of all promise ascended the mountain to place his son upon the altar of the holocaust. But fear was changed into joy. "Lay not thy hand upon the boy." The Voice spoke, and like an echo rolling out of paradise there came the message that in the seed of Abraham all nations would be blessed.

Yes, there would come a great king, whose scepter would be held forth over the lands and the seas and the islands. Pillars of cloud and fire and thundering prophecies accompanied the elect through sand and desolation, and the Voice Itself announced its commands from the summit of the awful mountain. Yet the weary journey seemed endless, and the old enemy had lost none of his power. Now Jairus told of man's new corruption, and how the earth shook from the hoofs of Assur's hordes, the sanctuary fell and the chosen people were carried into slavery.

When Jairus had finished reading, a servant approached and handed him a scroll. This he slipped into the long sleeve of his ministerial robes, and then he left the platform.

In the pause that followed, Marcius noticed that Cornelius had arrived. He tried to catch his eye, but the centurion was too absorbed in his own meditations. A desk had been placed in the center aisle. There Elon stood and speaking for the people, continued the service. His voice was less strained than that of Jairus, but there was great strength in his rough Galilean accent. The choice of his texts revealed the purpose for which the congregation had been convened.

"Tribulation is very near, for there is none to help me," Elon said. "Many calves have surrounded me: fat bulls have besieged me. They have opened their mouths against me as a lion ravening and roaring. I am poured out like water: and all my bones are scattered."

A shade of disapproval stole over the faces of some of the elders. Reproachfully they looked at Jairus, who had taken his seat on the front bench. But he did not respond. The little scroll lay in his lap, and his lips moved silently with Elon's words.

"My heart is become like wax melting in the midst of my bowels," the reading continued. "My strength is dried up like a potsherd and my tongue hath cloven to my jaws: and thou hast brought me down into the dust of death—"

Now Marcius no longer needed an interpreter. For him the words reverted once more into the images which the inspired psalmist had translated into words. These verses, every syllable, every letter, had been enacted before his eyes one week before.

"They have dug my hands and feet: they have numbered all my bones. And they have looked and stared upon me: they parted my garments among them and upon my vesture they cast lots."

Did not the others perceive it too, all those who had listened to the report, and those to whom it had come by word of mouth?

In place of the ark arose, with arms outstretched in a gesture of implacable love, a Man—His hands and feet pierced by nails. And a tablet above His head announced the coming of a new covenant.

Marcius lowered his eyes, but the vision was within his soul; he would go on seeing it even if all light were extinguished.

"With Thee is my praise in the great church," Elon said. "I will pay my vows in the sight of them that fear him. The poor shall eat and be filled."

"To whom does it apply?" Marcius asked, and immediately the answer came: "All the kindred of the gentiles shall adore in his sight, for the kingdom is the Lord's and he shall have dominion over the nations."

Jairus rose from his seat and walked to Elon's desk. A servant tried to hand him a book of prayers to conclude the service. He made a gesture of refusal.

He looked towards the ark. "There the words were enshrined," he said, "but we did not understand—"

The congregation seemed like a great shell, in which the faintest murmur of the sea sounds on, even after the waves have been turned into dry land.

"As was written by the prophet Isaiah," he continued, fighting with the turmoil in his soul. " 'I will give you the holy and sure promise of David.' Brethren, we thought that this referred to a great ruler, and for generations we have waited for the rise of his banners."

As the congregation listened, as if to take into its mind and its ears every word not for themselves alone, but also for those who might be standing beyond the walls, Jairus' voice went on at quickened pace: "A great ruler indeed. The heir and hope of the tribe of Jesse, through whom the captivity will be turned from Jacob and Israel will be made the light of the nations."

Almost unnoticeably a ripple went through the congregation. In the gallery the prayers of the women, which had seemed to be draping the very walls as with dark veils, halted and then began to take on a different tone. It was as if young hands were timidly reaching for brighter flowers, while the maids of the household were still braiding a wreath of mournful purple.

"We need not look for another," Jairus said firmly. "He who was to come has walked in our midst. It was He of whom David has said in the fifteenth psalm, 'Thou wilt not suffer thy Holy One to see corruption.' "

He took the scroll from his sleeve. "The message which I received is signed by Joseph of Arimathea and Nicodemus, members of the Sanhedrin." His eyes began to rove over the Latin script, like fingers groping over letters engraved in marble.

"Very early in the morning, on the first day of the week, when the sun was just risen—" he read. Irresistibly the words moved on, until before the eyes of the listeners the empty grave, filled with light, seemed to open, and the message, which had first been given to the women and the disciples, took shape: "He Who was crucified has risen. He is not here. Behold the place where they had laid Him."

In the great stillness that followed, in the gallery a child's voice of tears and exultation gave the answer. Jairus looked up.

"Brethren," he said, choking, and closed the scroll. "I should have known. He who raised my daughter from the dead must be the Lord over life and death."

It was no longer the synagogue with its chorus of chants and jubilant prayers to which Marcius was listening. It seemed to him, that in the first dawn of an awakening morning he was standing beside the road. Closer and closer there came the sound of unshod hoofs until out of the receding shadows of the night there emerged a dapple-gray horse with a young man in the saddle. At the next milestone they stopped, and the young man dismounted. He turned his face toward the east, and then Marcius recognized the young man's features as his own . . .

Behind the blue streak of Lake Gennesareth the sun began to rise. Its rays were strong and mild, as they are only in Spring, when morning clothes the world in the raiments of an early noon. The whole of creation responded to its glow. . . .

And while the glints of blue and red sparkling on the blades of grass, the bees, and the birds, and the opalescent dragonflies, the trees and the little brook, these and all creation returned to him as he had seen them on that morning and he suddenly knew: that had been the hour.

Then, as even these images dissolved, his soul withdrew farther and farther along a mysterious path, until the Message to which he had listened became one with the fact of which it had told, the Resurrection. In it from now on, all generations of men would participate.

A strange and unexpected sound penetrated his mind, and he looked up, still uncertain of his surroundings. Before the ark stood one of the elders. His words sounded like the tinkling of impure metal, but as they struck the congregation, its silence echoed back like the tolling of a heavy bell.

Aghast, Marcius glanced at the speaker. How did anyone dare to bring a note of discord into an hour like this? The man's thin beard trembled, and in his tiny, narrow-set eyes was an evil look. Now he waved to the translator, and, gathering his cassock about him, he returned to his seat.

"So that our brethren and foreign guests may not be misled," Marcius heard the translator say, "here is the true story, as vouched for by the authority of the High Priest himself. Remembering that this deceiver had said, 'after three days

I will rise again,' and for fear that the last imposture would be worse than the first, the High Priest obtained guards from the Governor to watch the sepulchre. Yet, precisely what had been foreseen happened—the soldiers have given testimony that while they slept, the disciples of the condemned blasphemer came and stole his body."

The stillness deepened, till it seemed the vortex of a maelstrom, where the swirling waves laid bare the rocks and the shadows of the abyss. In the faces of some, disappointed hopes were changing into hatred. They left their seats, and slowly, menacingly, moved toward Jairus. All this was so sudden that Marcius did not grasp its meaning until he saw that Gaius Cornelius had risen from his chair. The centurion surveyed the turmoil. His straight, lean figure stood out like that of a commander on the field of battle. All looked at him, expectantly, and even the insults muttered by Jairus' enemies died down.

"If the soldiers were asleep," Cornelius said quietly, "what could they have seen? If they saw nothing, what is the value of their testimony?"

"The Governor's most recent dispatch fully confirms brother Jairus' report," he went on, without raising his voice, "even though His Excellency is unaware of the meaning of his own words." He made a wide-embracing gesture. "For over four thousand years you and the whole of humanity have been waiting for this very day."

A Hebrew word, taken up by all the Israelites, rose like a chant of love. In this one word, which meant Redeemer, there was gathered as into a single jet of flame all the age-old longing for deliverance. When the fire had again descended into the hearts of the people, like a fountain into its overflowing basin, Gaius Cornelius continued: "*Dignum et justum est gratias agere Filio Patris, qui propter nos homi-*

nes et propter nostram salutem, descendit de caelis et incarnatus est."

Slowly, but irresistibly, the new creed expanded over the rectangular center space, and rose up to the gallery, until the hearts of all, open to receive it, overflowed with its message, audibly transformed into the language of the people:

"It is truly meet and just to render thanks to the Son of the Father, Who for us men, and for our salvation, came down from heaven and was incarnate."

Cornelius lowered his head: "*Crucifixus etiam pro nobis: sub Pontio Pilato passus et sepultus est.*"

Again, their voices trembling with compassion, the people responded in the vernacular tongue: "He was crucified also for us, suffered under Pontius Pilate, and was buried."

Cornelius paused for the space of a heartbeat. Then, in a firm voice, he gave testimony to the great triumph over death and darkness: "*Et resurrexit tertia die, Deus Verus de Deo Vero—Mundi Redemptor, Altissimus Dominus, Jesus Christus.*"

And once more, joined by the whole congregation, now carried along to the fullness of conviction, there came the Aramaic answer: "The third day He rose again, very God of very God—the world's Redeemer and Lord Most High, Jesus Christ."

CHAPTER SIX

TWO DAYS after the tidings of the Resurrection had come, Marcius was standing not far from the marble statue of the Emperor Tiberius Caesar, when his attention was caught by the shining eagles and ensigns of an approaching unit. It was Company D, Third Syrian Legion, and at once he rushed forward to greet his friend, the centurion Longinus.

But nowhere could he find him. A senior standard-bearer was in command. The man recognized him at once and yet pretended not to notice him; he even hurried his steps so that all the soldiers had to march faster.

Marcius could not talk to men in a closed column. "Perhaps they will stop at the end of the Forum," he thought, and kept pace. Finally he was almost forced to run.

When the standard-bearer and most of the ranks had disappeared behind the Temple of Augustus, Marcius caught the eyes of a young legionnaire, whom he remembered well. Up on Golgotha, he had been among the men who formed his special platoon, and together they had sunk to their knees—

"He has been demoted—deprived of his command," the legionnaire whispered without stopping. "He's going to be courtmartialed for having used subversive language, criticizing the Governor." He fell back a few steps. "But the real reason probably is that he confessed faith in the Son of God."

"Who condemned him?" Marcius asked under his breath.

"The Prefect of the Praetorian Guards, Flavius Sabinus. He has hated our commander ever since he helped to break the plot of the Prefect Sejanus."

"Can he not appeal to the Emperor?"

"No. In military matters the Governor is the highest court of appeal. If he still had his special favor, it would be different. But Flavius knows that he gave it away when he sent you to Italy."

Other soldiers began to notice the conversation, and the young legionnaire grew silent. A few moments later, he and all the ranks had vanished behind the Temple.

Pale, unable to make up his mind, Marcius remained standing where he was. Around him the busy crowds swirled and hummed, but he did not hear them. Finally he pulled himself together and went back to Gaius Cornelius' house.

"I shall try my best," the centurion said, "but I am not too hopeful."

"It is an outrage without precedent!"

"It is. I know those spiteful praetorians. They all stick together, traitors and 'loyal' alike. Marcius, I am afraid we won't see him again, even if the Emperor himself should order an investigation. Men blacklisted by praetorians usually succumb to an 'accident.' "

"He must have known that he would be arrested as soon as he had used up his imperial favor. Of course, he must have known! Oh, why did I not understand! I should have refused to act as his messenger. I should have forced him to go himself–!"

"Perhaps he wanted to stay at his post. He was a very conscientious man. Or possibly he wanted to atone for his guilt. We cannot judge."

Marcius in his report had truthfully said that one of the Romans took his lance and with it opened the side of the Crucified. But he had felt unable to say that this Roman had been his own friend, the centurion Longinus–perhaps, because he could not have explained the great struggle that must have torn his friend's soul, his fear of the Victim, through Whom the world of Rome's mighty gods would be turned into dust. And though he knew in his heart, he could not have made it clear to others that Grace had used his friend's very guilt to change it into salvation–

Gaius Cornelius had known of Longinus' action for some time, but he had understood Marcius' reluctance to discuss it, and so he had kept silent.

But now–and for this Marcius would always be grateful–he showed him that he knew.

"The blood and the water which touched Longinus' forehead must have opened his soul," he said. "His wisdom may be greater than ours–"

Shortly before Marcius had to leave for Tyrus, Cornelius came back to this conversation. "Longinus' case has a general importance. If belief in Him can be construed as disloyalty to the State, this conflict will shake the foundations of the world."

"But Longinus was never disloyal! He was the Emperor's most faithful servant."

"Of course he was. But entirely new standards of loyalty may develop. Let's assume that a living Emperor might claim divinity."

"Isn't it bad enough that the dead do?"

"It isn't quite the same, Marcius, though many people are confused on the point. Caesar's and Augustus' titles are 'Divus,' not 'Deus.' Strictly speaking, 'Divus' only expresses a grateful piety, a reverence toward their immortal souls, which are believed to continue their work for the Commonwealth. The danger which I see is the deification of a man—"

"Tiberius Caesar? I thought he did not—"

"Oh no, not Tiberius Caesar! As long as he lives everything is all right. Once a servile Senate did offer him divine honors, statues, temples, incense. 'To accept such worship would be arrogant and vainglorious,' he replied. It is one of the noblest letters in the Latin language, Marcius; you ought to read it in full! 'I desire posterity to remember that I am but a mortal, discharging the duties of a man,' the Emperor went on. 'I will be content if I may fill the highest place worthily. Enough and more than enough will men render to my memory if they believe me worthy of my ancestors, thoughtful of your interests, unflinching in dangers, undaunted by enmities which I encounter in the public service. There shall be my temples in your hearts, my fairest and most enduring images. For stone-built monuments, if posterity turn their judgment into hate, are but dishonored sepulchres.' A tranquil spirit and, after his death, honor and kindly recollection of his name, only for these has he prayed."

In recent days Cornelius had begun to talk more freely about the imperial house. Yet he still hesitated for a moment before he added: "I have been thinking of Gaius Caesar. Should he become Emperor—"

"The Little Boot a god?"

"It is fantastic. But it may happen, with his unbalanced mind and Herod Agrippa's influence. Now we have a lawful constitutional Principate. What we will have then, nobody can foretell. From Oriental despotism to blasphemous claims of godhead is only one short step. It has happened before, throughout the eastern tyrannies."

On their last evening, Cornelius talked with him until deep into the night. He told him about the men whom he had seen around Him, and what they had been doing. "There is a sacred rite waiting for you—of water and of the spirit," he finally said. "The Mystery of Baptism—the door to all things."

He pointed toward the peristyle, where the lamp's reflections danced on the rising and falling fountain. "If you come down tomorrow, early in the morning, Elon and some of the disciples who have returned from Jerusalem will be here too—"

As they parted, Cornelius handed him a round leather case about ten inches in diameter. It contained a dozen or more scrolls. "I wrote down what I know about the Master—" he explained, "His words and deeds alike, things which I have witnessed, as well as what some of His friends and disciples have told me about Him."

"It is only a human work," he cautioned in reply to Marcius' enthusiastic thanks. "But others will come whose narratives of the Redeemer's life will be free from error."

Marcius' feelings were in a turmoil when he left the house and when once more the broad road extended before him. These weeks at Capharnaum had meant so much, and now every mile which brought him closer to the port was a farewell. It was Duty which drove him forward, of that he was well aware. But it was Love that bound him to these shores, and with the first reach of the wide Mediterranean Sea rising before his eyes, that sea which he was now to cross, he asked his anxious question: "Where am I going?"

It was this very question that was to accompany him throughout his journey—

Comfortably stretched out on his wicker deck chair, Marcius listened to the splash of the waves and the cries of the sea gulls. The ship, driven toward Neapolis by sails and by a hundred and twenty oars, vibrated slightly, and he could hear from deep down in the hull the monotonous voices of the overseers who were directing the rhythmic strokes of the men on the rowing benches. An umbrella protected him against the sun, and between meals Phrygian stewards, with odd red caps on their heads, served him stuffed olives, pickled onions, artichokes, and cups of delicious chicken broth.

This leisurely life had been going on for almost three weeks, and by now the good ship *Neptune*, a twelve-hundred tonner with a top speed of ten knots, had become a world of its own. When he peered over the railing, out at the white crests of the waves, he sometimes felt as if he were moving through uncharted space. At such moments he wished that the voyage might continue forever, and for deeper reasons than that it was restful and pleasant and very different from the experience he had had on the noisome troopship, which three years ago had taken him from Massilia to Sidon.

But soon he would arrive at his destination, and each time he thought of it, he felt a pressure in the pit of his stomach. Back in Judea, the idea of seeking an interview with the Emperor had been quite simple. Capri was so far away that it seemed unreal. Now, every hour was cutting down the distance as the ship plunged forward, leaving a foaming wake behind.

Slowly, the inevitable arrival had pushed its way above the horizon of his thoughts, and the more it began to overshadow everything else the more he tried to cling to this voyage, and to forget that it was transitory.

Everything connected with it had been exciting. When he had reached Tyrus, the *Neptune* was already lying in the port, and his luggage had been brought on board. A cabin was waiting, and the skipper had given orders that he should not be molested by all the hunters for tips who were swarming over the three decks. So far so good. Then he had asked what provisions had been made for Pomponius.

Marcius chuckled every time he thought of the incident. "For Pomponius?" the chief purser had asked, perplexed. "I am sorry, sir, but we are booked to capacity."

"Pomponius does not need a cabin. Any decent space will do. You don't expect him to swim all the way, or do you?"

"But——"

"Pomponius comes along, and I warn you: he needs a special diet! . . . Pomponius is my horse," he had finally explained. "Don't you think the name suits him?"

"Perfectly, perfectly!" was the half-relieved answer. And so the good broad stallion was hoisted on board and given a stall on the lower deck.

"I am glad I am not alone," Marcius reflected, as he watched the bluish streak of the Campanian coast grow nearer. "He at least will be glad when this voyage is over."

As the sailing had been delayed for two days, he had found time to do some shopping. He bought purple wool, a silver bracelet of fine Persian filigree work, coral chains and earrings with moonstones for his mother. For his father he bought a beautiful sword of chased Damascene steel. Its handle and scabbard were inlaid with pale ivory leaves, and its red leather scabbard belt was strewn with many tiny symbols of the rising sun.

"But what can I give to the Emperor?" he had wondered, when he roamed through the noisy bazaars. "What can anyone give him?" It was a real stroke of luck that he did find just the right thing.

A merchant had arrived from the eastern edge of the world. Apparently he had completely miscalculated his prices and his expenses, for now he was bankrupt, and his whole merchandise had to be auctioned off, to satisfy his local creditors.

"No wonder that nobody wants his paper money!" Marcius thought as he watched the hapless stranger, who, resigning himself to fate, was attending this painful procedure. Only when a bag of white silk which was sewed shut and weighed about half a pound came up did the drooping mustaches of the poor Chinese man betray some excitement. "Very very valuable," he muttered. "The first *te* to come to Ta-Tsin."

Ta-Tsin, the Great Tsin, was the name which the Chinese used for the Roman Empire, and quite obviously in the eyes of the man from Liang-tschu its inhabitants were nothing but uncouth barbarians.

"This bag," the auctioneer explained, "contains dry leaves, to be boiled in water. When it is given to women, the brew will loosen their tongues. When it is taken by men, it makes them amiable, pensive, sociable, philosophical. It is the morning and evening drink of the Grand King of Sinae. Worth twelve aurei——"

Somebody laughed. "If it tied my wife's tongue, I'd pay fifteen."

Marcius saw his chance. "One can always give things which are new and unusual," he thought.

"Three aurei!" he shouted, ignoring the suppliant and contemptuous look in the eyes of the unfortunate owner. "Three and a half!" somebody else said, probably an employee of the auctioneer, and then Marcius got the precious little bag for four aurei.

When he left, the Chinese man came rushing after him. As if he feared some horrible desecration to his native product, he broke forth in a stream of half-intelligible instructions. He begged, implored, finally adjured Marcius never to boil the leaves, as the auctioneer had said, but to pour boiling water over them. "And promise, first to warm the pot!" he said. He stopped. "How can you? You don't have a decent pot in all Ta-Tsin!" he said disdainfully. He glanced furtively about to see whether anyone was looking. Then quickly he opened his silken kimono, and from the region of his well-rounded belly he produced a package. Wrapped in rushes and soft paper, it contained a pot, such as Marcius had never seen before. But to discern that it was beautiful and completely unique was not difficult. On a surface of milk-white enamel it showed dark blue ornaments, and one large and many small dragons of the same color. On the bottom, probably as trade mark, there was a tiny deep-blue onion. No doubt, the Chinese man had been hiding this gem from the hammer of the auctioneer. Now he handed it to Marcius. "One spoon for each cup, one for the pot!" he said gravely. "That's the rule!"

"But how much——" Marcius stammered.

"Among educated and gentle people one hundred aurei; it comes from the state factory in Canton. Among those, over there–" he pointed politely at the auction room, but Marcius felt that he himself was by no means excluded, "a price so shameful that it would break the pot's heart."

"You mean you want to give it to me?" Marcius asked, astonished.

"May the youngsters of the Great Dragon devour you if you ever use the pot for anything else!" the man said and withdrew to the door. When Marcius made an effort to thank him, his expression became even more sour than before. "And may the Great Dragon himself come upon you," he whispered, "if you should ever take your *te* with milk or cream. Only the black-skinned, low-caste Indians do that."

Still bewildered by this experience, Marcius strolled

through various stores, pondering the question of his new wardrobe. He could no longer dress like a legionnaire, and as a foreigner he could not wear a toga. So he bought a dozen civilian tunics of Egyptian linen, underwear of the same material, one long and two half-length woolen mantles, Greek style, and a waterproof black cape, called sagum, which left his arms free. For more formal occasions he purchased a blue Macedonian chlamys, fastened at his right shoulder by a silver clasp. Brown shoes, with long leather thongs up to the knees, completed his transformation into a young traveler of non-Roman origin.

All these preparations had kept his mind busy until the hour of the sailing was at hand. But when he looked down upon the port, he realized again how much he left behind in that country which probably he would never see again—

Marcius sat up in his deck chair, and glanced across the silvery rippling waves to the clearing coast. A few land birds had already found their way to the ship, and the skipper had passed the word along that by tomorrow morning all luggage should be ready to be taken out of the cabins.

"Longinus," he thought. "My friend—I won't forget you!" and now the speed of the boat did not suit his taste. "I wish it went faster!" he reflected while his mind returned to the hour of departure.

When the ship had begun to loose its moorings, he had cast a last glance towards that land of destiny.

"The face was turned toward the West—there lies Rome!" The word flashed through his mind, and then he remembered a skull-shaped rock, and how the last rays of the sun had woven a robe of gold and purple around the shoulders of the the Sufferer. Every trait was engraved indelibly in the tablets of his soul. And, while his thoughts still wandered back, through the last great cry of agony and consummation, there echoed the Message which he had received in the synagogue at Capharnaum.

Marcius got up, and looked at the coastline. Now one could already distinguish hills and bays and a few white spots of houses and whole villages. The sight no longer frightened him, as he went down into his cabin to make ready for his future tasks.

CHAPTER SEVEN

"NOW WE TWO are on our own," Marcius said to his horse, as they left the pier. He had been warned by his fellow-passengers: every arrival in Neapolis is something of an ordeal, a mixture of beauty, commercialism, exultation about the wonders of this fairest gulf on earth, and bewilderment about the people who inhabit it.

"After the gods had created Neapolis," one had said, "men no longer desired to enter the Elysian Fields. Neapolis, they felt, had more splendor and was certainly easier to reach. So, quickly, the gods created the Neapolitans—"

But, surrounded by shouting, screaming, arguing boys, each waiting for a tip, the one because he grabbed his luggage, the other, because he did not, Marcius held his own. "You can't outwit a Hibernian," he said, laughing, and he finally even brought a certain order into the wild melée. In a droll procession, singing and goodnatured, the boys carried his large and small trunks to a cart which belonged to the Taberna ad Vesuvium.

Cornelius had given him this address. "Most taverns are unsatisfactory," he had explained, "but the Vesuvius may be the most reasonable."

Marcius did not feel like going to his hotel at once. "First we want to get firm land under our feet, don't we, Pomponius?" he asked. And so it was not until evening that he returned to register.

"Twenty sesterces a day for room and board," said the *copus*, the fat owner, with a servile smile.

Marcius made a grimace. "I'll pay you ten sesterces, and you keep your board!" Thereupon the *copus* swore that such prices would land him in the poorhouse and that young men nowadays were heartless and inconsiderate. After more protestations, they settled upon Marcius' offer, and he was given a room, not too good, not too comfortable, but far better than the one which the *copus* had originally set aside for him.

He took Pomponius to a nearby stable. Then he went upstairs and unpacked for the night. He also made sure that the locks of his big trunk, in which his precious staff was hidden, had not been touched.

The room had a small balcony—certainly the most redeeming feature! He pushed open the wooden door and stepped out.

A board promenade separated the tavern from the bay. To the left, on an egg-shaped islet, stood a mighty fortress. Far to the right a high ridge slanted down to the cape called Posilipo, the Greek word for 'Sans-Souci,' taken from the name a certain knight, Vedius Pollio, had chosen for his luxurious villa. That man had been infamous for his cruelty: to get good fat *murenae*, he had cut up slaves and thrown them into his fish ponds.

Behind the fortress, in the auxiliary naval port, there was a small forest of masts, and still further beyond Marcius could see the vineyard-covered cone of Mount Vesuvius. Along the entire coast noble villas stretched out like a string of pearls, a worthy necklace for Neapolis, the ancient queen of the sea. This gulf, a lovely crater filled with sparkling water, and the whole land around it seemed made to bring soothing happiness and tranquillity to the human mind.

A soft wind brought gusts of perfume from oleanders, roses and mimosas, which mingled strangely with the salty air of the sea. From down at the beach came the clear voice of a young fisher boy. "*Dulcis Neapolis–Oh sol' beatum*" he was singing–a popular song with a sweet melody.

When the last verses had drifted away, there came from a barge out in the wide bay, single notes, struck from a mandolin touched by a nonchalant hand, and a duet of love floated toward the land.

Marcius' heart responded to the sounds with nostalgic longing. He shielded his eyes. In his mind another gulf replaced these southern shores–a rocky and stern coast, where wild waves, like the hoofs of galloping horses, beat against the walls of the crevasses into which the sea had forced its way. A few miles outside the white breakers, almost inaccessible, lay the small island of Lundy. Since time immemorial, its people had been under the same paternal scepter. Now the heiress was a child of sixteen. It was four years, almost to the day, since Marcius had rowed through the treacherous waters off the western Britannic coast–

Would that child still be waiting? He smiled, and the duet of love sounded to him like an answer.

A paper lantern was attached to the stern of the little barge. It was still twilight, and his eyes could not follow its circling path over the waters. As his gaze tried to cling to the red drop, which moved ever farther away, something which was neither sea nor sky came into his vision. At first it looked like a triangular sail of pale purple, perhaps that of a large schooner trying to make port. But it stood still, and suddenly he realized what he was seeing: the silhouette of Capri, the imperial island, the throne of all earthly power.

In the morning, when the *Neptune* had passed through the narrow strait between the isle and the Cape of Sorrentum, he had been down in his cabin and at the purser's office, where he had settled a few bills. So he had missed the sight, which now struck him with the force of a discovery; it was as if his eyes, without warning, had beheld in actuality the Majesty before which the whole orbit bowed.

And while Marcius glanced across the waters, time glided along almost unnoticed by his spell-bound senses. He was standing on the balcony of his shabby tavern, staring at the island of dominion, when night settled down over the melodious gulf. A strong, mild light flared up on the horizon. "The full moon," he thought for a moment. It was so bright that it bridged the miles of water and painted stark shadows of the trees on the pavement of the promenade. But it was not the moon. The light came from three rays which streamed from the rotating cupola of a lighthouse on the northwestern tip of the island. Marcius counted the rhythmic turns of the movement. It was so novel and fascinating that it made him forget his worries about the forthcoming audience. "I'll wait for another turn," he said to himself, when Posilipo, the white villages at the foot of the Vesuvius and the egg-shaped island were lit up by a ghostly glow. An hour later he was still watching and waiting for the next rotation.

"I should have reported to the Praeses of Campania. Cornelius was very definite about it," he remembered as he lay down. "But today it would have been too late." The truth was, of course, that he had completely forgotten his instructions. "I'll go to see him first thing in the morning," he decided, feeling a pang of conscience. But now he was so tired that not even the light of Capri, which shone through the open door of the balcony at regular intervals could prevent him from falling asleep.

Marcius dressed carefully next morning, and for the first time he put on his blue Macedonian chlamys with the silver clasp.

A drawbridge connected the fortress islet with the mainland. Through the officer of the day Marcius sent the letter of introduction which Cornelius had written to the Praeses of Campania, and was shown into his office a few minutes afterwards.

"I am glad he is not a praetorian," Marcius thought. Every army man had an instinctive dislike for that special élite guard, a highly paid and privileged clique first established by the Emperor Augustus.

The Praeses received him with great politeness. He even seemed to have expected him. "I would have been at your disposal last night," he said, with slight reproach in his voice. As soon as the *Neptune* reached Neapolis, its captain had reported that a young man, Marcius Armaghensis, a former legionnaire who claimed to be traveling in the Emperor's name had been on board. Because of these special circumstances, the case had been submitted to the Praeses within the hour.

Marcus Cocceius Nerva was a man of over sixty, with a fine, hooked nose. His cheeks were sunken and he looked ailing. His gray eyes did not focus but were completely parallel, as the eyes of impartial judges sometimes are. There was no ambition in his glance. In his long and brilliant career he had seen many things, and as a Stoic he had long ago recognized life's vanity and illusions.

"You would like to see His Majesty as soon as possible?" Nerva asked. His attitude, unlike the original reaction of Cornelius, did not seem to show suspicion. This fact Marcius felt, and he also understood that the Praeses wanted to leave it to him to explain the purpose of his journey.

He made it short. "Sir, I am the messenger of the centurion Longinus, Company D, Third Syrian Legion. He helped to break the conspiracy of the Prefect of the Guards, Aelius

Sejanus. Thereupon His Majesty granted him the fulfillment of a special wish."

"Can you tell me what it is?"

Marcius blushed. "I wish I could, sir. But I can't. It's not that I don't trust you–"

A shade of a smile passed over Nerva's face. Nobody had ever said such a thing to him. "All right, I won't insist."

"Thank you, sir." He gathered his courage. "Could I–when do you think, His Majesty–?"

"You unfortunately have just missed him. The Emperor left Capri very early this morning. He is going to Rome. This is the first time in almost seven years."

"Oh, but that's terrible!"

The Praeses thought for a while. "You don't have a carriage of your own?"

"I have a horse, Pomponius. I brought him along from Jerusalem."

"Let him rest for a few days. You can leave him in the care of the Fortress while you are gone."

"To Rome?" Marcius asked with rising hope.

The Praeses nodded. Speaking seemed to tire him unduly. "You could take a sleeper tomorrow afternoon. It should get you to Rome on the following evening."

"A sleeper, sir?"

"The imperial mail service operates them. I trust you will find it comfortable. I will send you a passport and a ticket reservation, if you give me your address."

"Taberna ad Vesuvium."

"I'll remember it. If you should happen to miss His Majesty in Rome, you may meet him in Antium. Do you have friends in Italy who could advise you?"

"No friends, but a few men whom I ought to look up," Marcius said, and wondered why, in spite of the Praeses' courtesy, he felt so depressed. With an effort he mentioned Cornelius' letters of introduction to his cousins.

"They may all be in Antium. The season is just opening."

There was nothing more for Marcius to do beyond expressing his thanks. The Praeses made a tired gesture. His face was of unusual paleness. Politely he conducted Marcius to the door.

"What I wanted to ask you–" he said. "Wasn't that a very abridged version of the origin of your mandate?"

"How do you mean, sir?"

"Your friend's home garrison is at the Syrian border. You were a legionnaire in the Cohort Antonia. You met in Jerusalem. Were there any special events which brought you together?"

"It was the Jewish Easter week, sir. I understand that it is customary to call in out-of-town garrisons during that time. The Jews are a very unruly people, sir." Suddenly, a flash of understanding seemed to strike him, and his face lit up. "How do *you* know what happened?"

But the Praeses did not respond. As if overcome by dizziness he sat down, and several seconds passed in silence. "Two weeks ago another ship, the *Isis*, arrived in Neapolis," he said in a low voice. "Its captain, Thamus of Alexandria, asked to see me. Later he was granted an audience by His Majesty. He told a strange story, an ominous one, a story of somber portent. Would you know whether it has any foundation in fact?"

"If I knew what Captain Thamus said–"

"You left two weeks after he did. So you would know whether there is anything to his report, even if you don't know his precise words." His strength returned. "His Majesty has been greatly disturbed. Perhaps you can set his mind at peace." He looked at the window which was high above the sea. In the background, wrapped in the haze of morning, stood the triangular silhouette of Capri.

"When the *Isis* approached the Syrian coast, there was a chorus of voices, coming from the upper regions of the sky," the Praeses went on. " 'The Lord of Nature suffers'— Thamus could hear distinctly those words. Then, the voices seemed to be everywhere. Many of the sailors also heard them. Some said it sounded as if their own souls were speaking out aloud. A few hours later—"

"A few hours later, sir—"

" 'The Great Pan is dead, the Great Pan is dead!" the voices announced."

"What does that mean?" Marcius asked.

"Pan may signify the Universe. A young philosopher in His Majesty's service, Lucius Annaeus Seneca, interpreted it this way: the divine principle of the world has become extinct."

"I think I know better," Marcius said joyfully, but then he noticed that the Praeses, in spite of all his efforts, was unable to listen. Apparently his strength had been completely spent.

"You must go now," he said in a toneless voice. "You are young, the centurion's favor gives you a unique opportunity. If you desire the vanities of life, grasp the moment! Don't let the chance you have when in the imperial presence slip by!" The grip of his hand was feeble. "Be wise, my friend, enjoy the fleeting hour!"

Dazed, Marcius left the fortress and walked down to the beach. "What a strange man, entirely different from Cornelius!" he thought. "Why didn't I tell him that Longinus is in prison? Perhaps he would have set him free." Once more the whole scene passed through his mind. "No," he concluded, "it was impossible to mention it. His thoughts were elsewhere. He would have paid no attention."

An hour later he returned to the tavern. "I am leaving for Rome tomorrow," he told the fat *copus*.

"And on what a journey!" the man replied in his greasiest voice. He took two documents from an iron safe. "They arrived ten minutes ago—a pass, I see, with His Excellency's seal, and a diploma for the imperial mail coach—even a sleeper ticket!"

Marcius after changing his dress came down again to find the *copus* still there. He seized Marcius' tunic. "Just one word, most noble youth!" he begged. He brought his mouth close to Marcius' ear. "How much longer will His Excellency—?"

"What do you mean?"

"All Neapolis is talking about it. And how we all admire his sense of duty! Imagine, holding on to his office to the last moment!" He drew back a little. "Didn't you notice anything? He has been fasting for almost a week. People say that not even His Majesty could make him change his mind."

"How's that?" Marcius asked, his curiosity awakened, though against his will.

The *copus* wagged his head. "The great and powerful have their own way. For us, the little ones, it is only to marvel and to gossip. And as the saying goes, More money, more worries!"

"What has that to do with the Praeses' fasting?"

"Patience, innocent stranger, patience! Money is also political power, isn't it? It can even defeat what genius and the sword have won. So after the Divus Julius had conquered the world, there still remained the money bags of his republican opponents, who belonged to the aristocracy. All he could do was to decree that their floating capital must be invested in Italian land, which he could more easily control. Now the story goes that His Majesty intends to revive this old law."

"I still don't see–" Marcius said and tried to untangle the matter in his mind.

The *copus* took his hand from Marcius' tunic. "Oh happy unsuspecting child!" he exclaimed, "Oh starry-eyed traveler through the wickedness of the time! Don't you know that the great have many privileges? They may even be republicans–but of course, only so long as their opinions keep a 'world view,' to use the fashionable word. Marcus Cocceius Nerva is such a republican. He is also a Stoic, who disdains life–especially after he has enjoyed all its good things! But he is still very much concerned about his friends and his cousins, the nobles, the conservative class. His Majesty's decree hurts his feelings and strikes at much that is really sacred to him. He counseled against it and predicted dire consequences, the ruin of the State. Still His Majesty insists on taking the money, so His Excellency insists on not taking food." He opened a black toothless mouth. "But he's still going strong? I am sure His Majesty went to Rome so as not to see the suffering of his most loyal friend. Such examples of duty, coupled with kindness, are what the common people need." He sighed. "Now His Majesty will soon have to make up his mind whom he wants as consul for the second half of this year!"

Marcius could stand it no longer. Brusquely he left the tavern and got his horse out of the stable.

"Let's go, Pomponius," he said. "Just you and I." He felt a chill run up his spine as he rode past the fortress. "That Praeses! He talks about the divine principle of the world. He's polite, helpful, a perfectly educated man. Yet, he is playing a mean trick on his emperor! Taking his own life–and in such a way–that's inhuman!"

All the revulsion which youth feels for death and decay seized upon him. The Praeses' office now appeared to him like a tomb. The man in it was dead though he still lived. "Well, I won't see him again!" he thought as he pressed his heels into Pomponius' flanks. "He'll stay at his desk until he drops dead. They'll call it 'strength of character,' 'duty,' 'virtue.' But it's just part of the Roman game of power, and it's a terrible game! I wonder what Cornelius would say about it!"

He began to feel better only when he had left the fortress far behind. By the time he had reached the edges of the blossoming Pompeii, he had succeeded completely in dismissing the pale and ailing man. A Greek play was going on in the amphitheatre. He found a seat, from which he could see the pinetree-shaped plume of smoke above Mount Vesuvius. It stood quietly in the brilliant air, while the chorus of the Erinyes, their hair looking like snakes, moved solemnly over the wide stage.

He stayed to the very end. When he returned to Neapolis, the first oil lamps had been lighted along the promenade, but he did not even look at the fortress on his way to the tavern.

CHAPTER EIGHT

ON THE WAY to Rome, Marcius had slept solidly throughout the night. Not even the changing of the mules at the *mutationes*, which were always twenty-five miles apart, could wake him up. But now, for the last half hour, he had been conscious of slight swinging and rocking movements of his bed. It was a pleasant feeling, quite unusual and somewhat bewildering.

The sharp grinding of the brakes snapped the thin thread of his sleep. A Negro attendant stood before him. "Next stop Tarracina, sir. May I make up your bed while you dress?"

In the front part of the coach was a little washstand, a writing desk, and a built-in wardrobe with two hangers for his clothes. The road was so smooth and the car had such good springs that he could even risk shaving.

Many times he had ridden on horseback like a flash through the night. But speed is relative; that he was traveling at six to seven miles an hour, while he slept and dressed, seemed extraordinary, and looking out of the window, he watched the trees and some suburban houses whisk by with unheard-of velocity.

"It's a fine day, sir," he heard the attendant say. "It certainly is!" he replied gratefully. The bed was already lowered, so that he could glance through the back window; the baggage car was there, swaying along behind the two day coaches, which were filled with passengers who had been unable to secure sleeping reservations.

"They'll get dining cars next!" he thought, when at Tarracina a man called out that there would be a stop of twenty minutes to allow for breakfast. With good appetite he ate unleavened bread, dipped in honey, with dried dates, cheese, and pastry. There was also a basket with fresh apples and pears, imported from North Africa.

"I am glad I could arrange things for Pomponius," he thought, helping himself to another cup of goatsmilk. The idea of leaving the horse in the care of a man who refused to take food had not been appealing. So at the terminal in Neapolis he had seen to it that Pomponius should be sent along with the next convoy of animals, coaches, and merchandise, which was due to reach Rome about twenty-four hours after his own arrival.

That terminal! The busiest place on earth! Even the firm of Titus P. Atticus Heirs had a branch office there. A good thing that turned out to be, for he was running short of cash. The clerk just scribbled a few remarks on his parchment, and then he again had twenty-five aurei. One fifth of this sum he took in silver denarii and sesterces, the rest in actual gold—beautiful, new-minted coins. Instead of the Roman she-wolf on the reverse, they had the words "Pietas et Clementia" and the head of the late Empress Livia Augusta. "They were struck in memory of the illustrious Mother of the Country," the clerk explained respectfully.

Marcius also found time to write to Gaius Cornelius, telling him about the voyage and his experiences with the Praeses of Campania. He asked his friend to reply in care of the station master in Neapolis, who would forward the mail to Rome.

In the carriage, he was given a road map and, shortly after he had settled down on a soft couch, the whole train began to move along the broad coastal road, the Via Domitiana. The tomb of Virgil at the rim of the city was marked by an asterisk, and then there was a note: "Crypta Neapolitana, built by Marcus Cocceius Nerva." An instant later, the daylight vanished, and instead, the light from countless lamps was reflected from the smooth tiled walls of a huge tunnel. Ventilation shafts at numerous intervals provided for enough fresh air.

It was an uncanny experience even for a fearless young man. "If that mountain came down on us—" he thought, when on the second lane a train of horses, mules and cars came thundering by, making for Neapolis.

The tunnel was a mile and a half long. On narrow galleries it was patrolled by men from the city fire brigade. "They would notice it if rocks or water broke loose," he comforted himself. But his enthusiasm did not fully develop until his car had re-emerged into the sunlight. "I wish I had known about it when I saw the Praeses. I would have asked him how he did it!"

Shortly before they reached Puteoli, a city of over a hundred thousand inhabitants, the largest seaport of the whole west coast, there was another strange sight: a huge natural amphitheatre, with dozens of swirling smoke columns breaking from the ground. "The burning fields," the Negro attendant whispered softly. "It's the forum of the god Vulcan."

Of course, there was no such god, but a superstitious fear from his pagan days crept over him, and he was glad when they had passed the ghostly place.

Huge moles, each supported by twenty-four pillars and twenty-five arches, protected the inner port of Puteoli. From the road house, where the passengers stopped for half an hour, the view stretched out to the great naval station of Misenum, at the tip of the peninsula. Hundreds of warships of all sizes and types rode there at anchor.

"Isn't it wonderful?" an elderly lady commented. "And to think that we have a two-ocean navy now! My son-in-law says Ravenna is just as busy!" Marcius was not so sure whether he really liked the sight. "If those battle-wagons set out for Hibernia . . ." he thought, but wisely he kept his fears to himself.

About dinner time they reached the southern tip of Latium. A huge trilon, erected in the reign of Caesar Augustus, marked the end of the Via Domitiana. From now on they would be on the Via Appia. "Over-all length, three hundred and sixty miles. Terminal, Brundisium on the Adriatic Sea," the map explained. With Roman predilection for large figures, the makers of the map had added that each mile had cost one hundred thousand sesterces.

A meal was served at the *mansio*, the postal road house, of Sinuessa. When Marcius returned to his carriage, the Negro attendant had changed the couch into a comfortable bed. "In Hibernia they won't believe a word of it!" he reflected when he lay down, and shortly afterwards he was sound asleep.

From Tarracina the Appian Way soared to the capital, straight, as if drawn with a ruler. Hills, brooks, swamps, had simply not existed for its constructors. Not even the Pontine Marshes had taken them an inch out of their way. Right through their treacherous ground, parallel with the road, ran a canal. The traffic of freight and passenger ships was busy, and some of the vessels were sleeper boats, operated by private companies.

"Horace in his Satires described such a trip!" Marcius remembered with the delight of a schoolboy who sees his classroom knowledge put to practical use. "It'll greatly strengthen the authority of my old teacher over his students, when I tell him about it. He'll say at once, 'You see,

Marke got much more out of his trip because he knew Horace!"

Whole passages came back: "Then the slaves bantered with the boatmen, and the boatmen with the slaves. Troublesome mosquitoes and marsh frogs keep us awake, while the boatman, filled with much sour wine, starts singing and a passenger rivals his song. At last the weary traveler falls asleep . . ."

"Well, I had a better night than old Horace did!" he thought gaily, and looked at the smooth brilliant surface of the road. "Longinus' family comes from this part of the country. 'The blessed shores of Latium,' he called it." Marcius' face became serious; his friend was deep down in some lightless cell, while he could behold all this with his own eyes, vineyards of noble name, heaving fields of wheat, olive groves, and endless orchards with ripe cherries, and tiny little pears, plums and apples.

His conscience smote him. "I am an irresponsible boy," he thought. "I behave as if I were traveling for pleasure. And it's all my friend's property—the voyage on the *Neptune*, the journey through this country, all the comfort around me. I must think of my mission, not of amusement." Nerva's emaciated face passed before his eyes. "He was kind to me, and I didn't even thank him properly."

He sat down at the desk. It contained stationery, a brass inkwell and several calamus pens. In primitive school Latin, with not too few grammatical errors, he plodded along for half an hour; then his speaking knowledge, which was much better, flowed into his writing, and finally his long boyish strokes filled two whole scrolls. "I'll mail it from the next *mansio*," he thought. "Perhaps he will still get it—"

He reclined on his couch. "That was a very remarkable story he told me about Captain Thamus." It occurred to him that perhaps the account might have prepared the Emperor for his own message. Something else occurred to him: "During the last three years much news of what has happened in this country must have reached the Emperor and the people of Rome," Cornelius had said. At the time Marcius had not fully realized the import of the remark.

During that same conversation, Cornelius had also warned him against false pride. "Others will carry the fullness of the tidings," he had cautioned him. "You are not of their number; you are not an apostle." Who they were, these "others," Marcius had been able to surmise from the scrolls in the leather box. Yet, a tidal wave of enthusiasm swept over his youthful soul—a feeling of unbridled self-importance. "I am the first to arrive—the first who knows the whole Truth."

The Truth. What it was he had never enquired. He had had a great longing, and then found its fulfillment. For him there were no problems. Everything had been given to him, as to a child or to one asleep.

Things twisted or distorted had always been distasteful to him. Why he had not even tried to analyze. He did not realize that everything distorted is untruthful, and is therefore contrary to the nature of man. He had only followed his instinct, the law, engraved in the tablets of his heart. Since the Mystery of Baptism which he had received at Cornelius' fountain, the letters of that law had become clearer. But that all this had anything to do with Truth and that Truth was the greatest of all human problems, of these facts he had not been previously aware. Now the discovery struck him with unexpected force, almost with a feeling of intoxication.

A magic wand had been given to him. At its touch all things were sure to change. "I am the only man in Italy who knows the Truth," he kept on repeating. All others were still in darkness. But soon he would stand before the Emperor, and surely he would be able to convince him. Truth is irresistible; it only needs to be made known. And since the Emperor who held supreme power, was High Priest, the Tribune of the People and the Commander-in-Chief, the altars of the false gods would crumble. Harshness and cruelty would vanish, and even the slaves would be regarded as brethren. Soon the whole world would be different! "No longer any aggression!" Lovingly his thoughts turned toward his green island, and he visualized his return. How joyously would his parents and the whole people listen to his words! "My friend, too, will soon be free!" he thought, and happiness and blessings without number would accrue to the whole human race.

Words from Cornelius' introduction to his scrolls came to Marcius' mind: "Beating swords into ploughshares." He said it half-aloud. It was the most concise formula which one could find. And while his carriage rolled closer and closer toward the great city, he added cheerfully, "Perhaps before this month is up!"

"Yes, sir, only thirty more miles!" the Negro attendant had just said, when with shrieking brakes the coaches came to a sudden stop. "An accident!" Marcius thought and jumped out. To the left, a gravelled road branched off. "Antium—fifteen miles," a signpost said. At the junction stood a *mansio*. Its station master was talking to the driver. "Not until some time tomorrow!" Marcius heard.

Fifty yards ahead, like a wall of glittering metal, stretching deep into the land on either side of the Appian Way, was lined up in double rank a company of the Emperor's German bodyguard.

"Why do they block the traffic?" Marcius wondered

anxiously. "Perhaps something has happened to the Emperor . . . ?" The figure of the commander caught his eye. He was a strong, yet slender man, about twenty-five years old. A silver helm was pressed into his unruly golden hair. With hands quietly folded, he was leaning on a long pointed shield, which was decorated with lozenges in argent and azure. Before his watchful blue eyes passed the disorder of cars, mules, horses, and excited Romans.

An instinct of racial kinship between Celts and Germans seemed to tell Marcius that he should talk to this man, even though he only had a halting knowledge of the Germanic language.

There was a whole ritual to be completed before he could get to the questions which he wanted to ask. First, he gave his name, and the names of his father and grandfather. He spoke of his clan and tribe and of the battle of Eblana, a great feat of arms which might have become known even on the Continent. Then he waited–

"My name is Luitprant," the young commander replied. He too was sensitive to some affinity of race, a common bond in a world of strangers. "I am a Suevian. We live on the Upper Danube, in Vindelicia, in the northern part of the Province of Rhaetia. My ancestor was Ariovistus, the conqueror of the Aedui in Eastern Gaul."

There was no more need for him to mention Ariovistus' end than for Marcius to say that at Eblana his grandfather had been defeated. But something else struck him as strange.

"Ariovistus' descendant serving Rome?" he said in a tone of astonishment.

"Rome? What is it? Rhaetia is under Tiberius Caesar's personal rule. So I am serving him, a great soldier. He is the heir of Emperor Julius, whose glory is sung throughout Germania Magna."

"I understand. When I was a soldier, I too served only the Emperor."

"You serve him no longer?"

"I have seen a greater ruler—"

"Greater than Tiberius Caesar? Then he must be very great!" Luitprant stated with conviction. "Could I meet him?"

"Some day I shall tell you about him. Now I must hurry to Rome to see the Emperor. I carry an important and vital message from my best friend. So will you kindly let me pass."

"Impossible. Not until tomorrow. The Emperor came through half an hour ago. The road behind him must be clear."

"But he should have been in Rome last night!"

"He traveled slowly. Four miles from the Porta Appia he stopped. There was a grim portent. A giant woman seemed to stand at the roadside, and above her head a flight of ravens came swooping down. The same omen had warned his brother Drusus not to enter Moguntiacum, the town where the Main river flows into the Rhine. Drusus entered and died."

"So the Emperor turned back?"

"There was a short discussion with his companions. Seneca advised him to go on. There was no woman, he said, only a column of fog. And he asked, what do birds know about the will of the gods and the doings of men? He is a young man without regard for tradition. The Emperor trusts him, but when Gaius Caesar Caligula and his friend Herod Agrippa urged him to proceed, he grew suspicious. 'I don't mind the ravens, but I don't like your insistence,' he said." Thoughtfully Luitprant added: "The Emperor is a wise man. He knows what Herod and the Little Boot are up to.

But he might have trusted blindly in our swords and our vigilance."

Marcius was horrified. The flight of the ravens may have been coincidence. But the words of the Emperor showed that he suspected treason within his closest circle. Could it be perhaps that the Little Boot and Herod Agrippa had been planning murder? If anything happened to the Emperor now, while his grandson, Tiberius Gemellus, was only fourteen, the purple would surely fall upon the shoulders of Caligula and then Herod would be richly repaid for his "expenses."

"Where is the Emperor now?" he asked.

"He has gone to Antium. His palace there is guarded by the praetorians, under their prefect Naevius Sertorius Macro."

"Praetorians! The right sort of people to trust!"

"Don't worry," Luitprant admonished. "Two companies of the imperial bodyguard are there also. My own unit will join them tomorrow."

Marcius no longer insisted. He shook hands with his new friend and returned to his coach. "No luck, sir," the Negro attendant said, and asked for his orders. As a guest of the state, Marcius could spend the night at the *mansio,* or eat and sleep in the coach, whichever he desired.

"I have changed my mind. Can you check my big luggage through to Antium?" He had his two suitcases brought into the *mansio,* tipped the attendant, and went in himself.

The *mansio* was constructed in the form of a cube. It was built of concrete, which was made from the dark-brown volcanic earth of Puteoli. Downstairs was a baggage room, a ticket office, and a combined dining and waiting room. In contrast to the warmth of the outside air, the air inside was cool, almost chilly, apparently because of some artificial ventilation.

His room on the upper floor was clean, practical and completely impersonal. Yet a few colorprints showing the Roman Forum, the Palatine, and the span of an aqueduct, even though they were made in mass production, lent a certain gaiety to the whitewashed walls. There was a metal field cot, a table and two chairs with striped gray and blue upholstery, a wardrobe, and a tiny wash cabinet.

He wrote a short letter to Cornelius, and another to the station master in Neapolis, giving Antium as his forwarding address. Then he went downstairs to post his mail and to have a glance at the *Acta Diurnia*, the official government gazette. In it he discovered that according to the society column both Cornelii, the Prefect of Rome and the Senator, had gone to Antium. An earlier issue, under "Court News," mentioned that His Majesty had granted an audience to Captain Thamus of Alexandria.

When Marcius had eaten supper the station master asked whether on the next day he would like a horse for the last lap of his journey.

"I'd better wait for my own. He should be here around noon."

"Very well, sir. We can flag the convoy."

CHAPTER NINE

MARCIUS DID not feel like going back to the chilly cement building. Ahead he saw the campfires of the German bodyguard. The road, for hundreds of feet, was packed with caravans of carriages which had been halted during the late afternoon. "That'll be a nice jam tomorrow," he thought, as he walked away from the *mansio* until he reached the end of the crowded lines.

During the last hour or two, before his journey had been interrupted, he had not paid much attention to things outside. Now he became aware what a strange kind of alley the Appian Way had become. On both sides of its broad ribbon, this lifeline of the Empire was framed with tombstones, and lots, though still empty, had clearly been set aside to hold the dead.

Temples, shrines, and chapels, the resting places of many of Rome's most famous families, silently looked down upon the motley crowds, upon the rulers and dignitaries, the merchants, the toilers, the citizens and the strangers, who had trodden this road since the days of antiquity. Oil lamps, their flames protected by shields against the wind, burned before many of these monuments. They threw broken shadows over the allegorical figures and the inscriptions on slabs, portals, and marble blocks. Fresh flowers, laurel wreaths and circlets of pine needles had been strewn abundantly by loving hands or by order of the grateful Commonwealth.

Above the sleepers the sky was a span of deep black velvet, such as one can see only when looking up from Italian soil.

Driven in, like the polished heads of golden nails, were the stars—the big W of Cassiopeia, the seven Threshing Oxen, the tail of the great Serpent, and Jupiter in its benign brilliancy. The gleam of the silver sash of the Milky Way and the steady light of the Polar Star brought order into the seeming anarchy of the celestial republic.

A feeling of deep humility came over Marcius. He could not have expressed it, though, and had he tried, he would have stumbled over the simplest words. His faith was straight and primitive, and many years were to pass, until in an inspired Book he might read that in the Beginning there was the Word, and that through the Word, Which was God, all things had been created.

Yet while he stood humbly under the light of these stars, he remembered the glance that had rested upon him in Judea, and finally on Golgotha. "Even the sun and the stars conform to His harmony," he had thought. Now, with great awe, he felt that the law, which was engraved in the tablets of his heart, obeyed the same order as the starry firmament above him.

"I thank you that I am alive," he said, and into his gratitude there entered the urge to pay respect to those who had gone to rest. A chain of lamps lighted the colonnades of a large memorial chapel at his right. Pinetrees were carved into the three steps of lava blocks.

On the third step he paused and looked back. Far away he could see the long-stretched pack of cars; the voices of men and animals had died down; and the campfires of the Imperial guards were but tiny sparks.

"How long has he been dead?" he asked himself. Dead. Even while the word took shape, his awareness of life, which had caused him to utter a prayer of thanks, changed to an awareness of death. Out on the Eastern frontier he had seen men dying. But death always lay on this side of the world. It may have been the end of life, yet to life it still belonged. Youth cannot comprehend death otherwise, because it is far away and outside their customary domain. Now, for the first time his consciousness had reached into death's proper sphere . . .

On the bronze portals of the chapel was a bas-relief. A young hero, his mantle flying back in billowing folds, knelt on a bull, his dagger plunged deep into the neck of his prey. "Mithra Invictus" an inscription said. There followed the name of the dead. "Washed in the blood of the bull. *In Aeternum Renatus.*"

Marcius did not know that he was looking at a symbolic figure which had come from the very cradle of the Aryan race, Mithra, the god of light and of the sun, the source of all budding life. From Persia his cult had been brought to the West by Pompey's legions. Now it was spreading all over Italy, and it had with its vague promise of immortality taken hold of many who in the midst of Epicurean materialism shuddered at the thought of the Beyond. Nor could he know that obscured, distorted, and corrupted by deceit, there yet lived in this cult a spark of the Promise, which had been given to all men and races in Paradise. But some instinct, some whispering in his blood, drew him closer to this strange place of rest.

Now, in the reddish flickering of the oil lamps, he made out the signs of the zodiac. They were aligned twice, in concentric spirals. In the outer spiral, spectres of horror were shown passing from one to another a human form, until it was thrust into a body as into a grave. The inner spiral showed the cycle reversed. Again, demons of different shape, with rays of light that looked like claws emanating from their hands, had dominion over the departing soul.

Through ordeals and torments it ascended through the spheres of all the planets, utterly stripped of its personality, it was completely merged into the soul of the world.

His ancestral memory awakened, and Marcius felt that, from the stones on which he stood, a wave of deadly cold was filtering up through his body and to his heart. "These demons must have had real power," he said, "Until–" With an effort, he tore himself away, "Until it was broken," he finished the thought.

He stumbled back to the road and to the adjoining tomb. It was less elaborate. Only a block of marble, with the name of the deceased and two lines beneath it. "Whether or not you remember me, I do not care," Marcius deciphered. "I was not, I have been, I am not, I feel no pain." With slight variations, he found the same language engraved on several more stones.

He crossed the road. There stood a temple with Ionian columns; the letters were gilt; six geniuses held extinct torches; winged phantoms emerged from caves; and snakes coiled up to strike. Some high dignitary was laid to rest there, one of the new rich probably. "Eat, drink, enjoy yourself, then join me," was the message.

Going farther and farther, Marcius lost himself in the velvet darkness of the road. "They can't mean it–" he said to himself haltingly. "It's their fear of the demons which makes them wish for nothingness."

In empty monotony and suffocating grossness the litanies of despair and cynic resignation rolled on: "I had my day –only what I had at table is mine–Death is the ultimate end, who speaks otherwise lies."

"They can't mean it," Marcius repeated, as if to reassure himself of his own faith, for from these mocking stones, which stood out in the jaws of darkness like uneven teeth, an evil breath of doubt had reached his soul.

Still he wandered on. Two tombs were different. "I hoped to still my thirst for knowledge at Plato's sacred wells," one of the inscriptions said. "Now I have set sail towards the Isles of the Blest." Over the second, a majestic golden eagle spread its wings. "Behold the symbol of eternity," Marcius read. "As long as this eagle lives, I too shall live." It was the grave of a tribune who had served in Julius Caesar's Tenth Legion, and who had crossed the Rubicon with him.

"At least they thought of glory and knowledge," Marcius reflected. "They must have had their ample share, the philosopher and the tribune, yet, still they thirst." He looked again at the Eagle. Rust had eaten itself into its claws and the long feathers of the wings. "Symbol of eternity," he said half-aloud, and a feeling of compassion overcame him for the poor soldier beneath the ground.

"Pray to the gods in the sweet air of life. Once you have passed this gate, their might is nought." The marble statue of a tender boy, fifteen or sixteen years old, rose before Marcius; the lifeless gentle frame seemed to quiver with the wailing verses engraved on the pedestal. "I died a lingering death while still the purple stripes of youth adorned my toga. May others call you just, ye gods, for I cannot."

A young mother rested not far away. "Now she is off towards the mournful fields, where love is dead, and tears are shed forever. May she receive the water of oblivion, and sleep in unawakening sleep, once she has crossed the stream in Charon's steel-gray bark."

Like a cloud of fog, unsatisfied longing, hopes never fulfilled, and horror of the pathless mazes in the land of the shadows seemed to hover above the monuments. Slowly, the vapor of death drifted over to the road towards the one who lived.

Marcius cowered down. In his ears the rushing sound of his blood mingled with the soft breathing of the sleeping land, and the thin chirping of a lonely cricket. A question rose up in his mind. He had asked it before, but now it had a wider meaning. "Where am I going?" he stammered, and stretched out his hand. "Decay. Everything is decay—"

Two days ago Nerva's office had seemed to him like a tomb. Now the tomb had widened to embrace the whole world. They all were dead, even those who still lived, for what is life if it is not eternal, and what is eternal life, if love and justice are but empty words?

The little lamps twinkled at him like hundreds of malicious eyes. There was no escape. "We hold you fast," the spectres behind them seemed to say.

Gaius Cornelius' words returned to his mind. He began to take up the argument. "You were wrong, my friend. What we see is only a mirage. The true Empire is the one under these tombstones. It longs for the food of the flesh. And the flesh is the food of the worms."

He thought of the boy in the purple-striped toga, of the tribune, sheltered by his falling symbol of glory, of the philosopher, who hoped for more knowledge, of the young mother.

They had not called death the ultimate end, but they might have wished that it were—even the philosopher, who wanted to sail for the Isles of the Blest. He too must fear the mournful fields, the demons, the cries of anguish, for Whom could he conceive strong enough to carry his barge across the perilous waters?

But have heroes not a claim against the powers of heaven?

They all were heroes. Each of them had dreaded death, yet they had suffered it with equanimity. Or did courage offer no help? Perhaps acceptance of what cannot be avoided is not true heroism? Marcius had never seen a soldier run away in the face of the enemy though none had cherished the thought that, at the end of the day, he might be one of those bleeding on the field of battle.

Instinctively Marcius put his hand upon the ground. Did it not glow from the fever dream which had burned in the blood of them all and which still entangled their souls, so that they moved aimlessly through the mazes of a lightless land, like the minds of restless sleepers smothered under heavy blankets?

The night had crept forward towards the small hours, when even the frogs and the crickets go silent and the plants and the waters lapse into slumber. This is the time in which most men are born and in which most men die.

So still was everything that even the longing deep down in the vaults and in the arteries of the earth seemed to have come to rest.

His own feelings extinguished, Marcius stared at the dark monuments. Now they looked like battlements on the crest of broad submerged walls, waiting for the coming struggle. Only the forward-moving constellations, the star-set hands of the great clock, turning around the pole of the world, showed that life continued on its course.

In his ears the rush of his blood and the noises of the night had subsided, and as his mind turned inwards, another voice began to speak. "I was so proud of my message to the Emperor," he thought. Only a few hours ago a tidal wave of elation had swept over him. In the whole of Italy he was the only one who knew the Truth. "They can beat the swords into ploughshares, perhaps before this month is up." And at the touch of Truth, the whole world would change. . . .

Now under the first attack, doubt and dejection had won the upper hand. "If this happens to me, who was a witness–" his thoughts ran on, with burning shame. "I have seen a greater ruler," he had said to Luitprant. Greater than whom? Clearly the voice in his heart gave the answer, "Greater than death, so far man's true master."

He got up, and in the middle of the road began to walk back. But he was no longer alone. With him, let in once more through a mysterious gate which contrition had opened, there were the living visions of his memories: the scenes of pain, of royal sovereignty even in utter humiliation, the skull-shaped rock, and a sky glowing in all its shades of red and purple.

"Death could not have slain Him," he thought. "It was He who slew death by freely submitting to its agony." As he walked faster, the monuments on both sides of the road seemed to be moving toward him. "The message about the True Hero. They heard it before I did. Therefore the earth shook. All under its surface were told to make ready for Life."

What did they mean–inscriptions he had read? They were empty. Those who had caused them to be written now knew better.

"The true Empire," he had thought, when a short while ago he had been arguing with his friend Cornelius. The true Empire indeed!

But when the road lay behind him, he wondered for the first time whether in this dense world of matter the conquest of Truth could be consummated by the word of a man, even if he be the Emperor, the all powerful.

CHAPTER TEN

THE CONVOY that was bringing Pomponius was somewhat delayed, so Marcius did not arrive at Antium until evening. He first rode to the *mansio*, but upon looking at his passport, the station-master showed him to a carriage. The *mansio*, he explained, was full, and furthermore it might not be too inviting a place to spend more than a night or two; in the Villa Ciceronis, which was government-owned, quarters had been set aside for him.

"How did you know I was coming?" Marcius wondered.

"We received advance information half an hour after you decided to await here His Majesty's orders."

"I thought the road was closed; and it's fifteen miles!"

"A light-letter, sir. Some call it light-telegraph, but His Majesty dislikes Greek words." There was a pedagogical note in the man's voice. "He takes me for a country yokel!" Marcius thought. "Yes, of course, I quite forgot!" he said casually, and then he asked that his luggage and mail be sent to the Villa Ciceronis.

"There won't be any mail until tomorrow noon, sir. As to your luggage, we expect it with the last freight convoy."

This was all. Marcius stepped into the carriage, while Pomponius trotted alongside. "More things they won't believe in Hibernia," he thought. "Light-letters—tele-graphos, long-distance writer, if my Greek is correct." Vaguely he had heard about it before. Capri was the center of this modern news system, extending to Rome, Brundisium,

Mediolanum, and some provincial outposts. When Sejanus was executed in the capital and his whole conspiracy was crushed, the Emperor had received intelligence of the events within a few hours. Now more branchlines seemed to have been established.

"They'll end up by flashing whole books across the Empire —dot, dash, dot, dash, I suppose." Would that be one way, he pondered, to let his father know of his whereabouts? Perhaps there might be transmitters at all the *mansiones* throughout Gaul? On a clear night the signals would be seen in Britannia. Finally, from somewhere in the West a ship could sail to Eblana, the port closest to Armagh.

He smiled incredulously. "It sounds fantastic!" But it was a pleasant chain of reflections, so why not dwell on it a bit longer? "I'll try to broach the subject to the Emperor," he concluded, now firmly convinced that service such as this was already functioning to perfection.

The brightly lit main street of the town surpassed in elegance anything he had seen thus far. He would have liked to get out of the carriage for a short walk, but he was too dazzled to tell the coachman of his intention. So only when they were caught in the traffic of the many nimble carriages or in the stream of theater-goers, late shoppers and of the ingoing and outgoing guests of expensive restaurants and night clubs, could he get more than a superficial glance at the show windows of this fashionable resort.

Fantastic firmaments of diamonds and precious stones shone in the jewelry shops, and the food stores were filled with ice-packed oysters from Gaul and Britannia, caviar from the south shore of the Caspian Sea, live rainbow trout from the Aenus river in Rhaetia, pheasants from Colchis in the Caucasus, wild asses, ringousels, red grouse, and preserved fish from the Tyras and Borysthenes, those huge streams flowing from the steppes of Samartia down into the Black Sea, and countless other things the very names of which meant nothing to him.

There were whole rows of beauty parlors and perfumeries carrying the choice products of Arabia and Judea. Also expensive furriers, shoemakers and fashion houses were abundant.

When the carriage had to wait to cross a side street, Marcius noticed with a certain relief the familiar name of Titus P. Atticus Heirs. In the same block was a store the signboard of which, topped by two intertwined M's, announced: "Maxentius Millanius, booksellers and publishers, Rome, Neapolis, Ravenna, Antium, Athens, Alexandria."

"I certainly must drop in there before I leave," he thought as the carriage moved on.

Well-kept roads with broad, shadowy trees opened before him. On both sides lay sumptuous private gardens. Illuminated fountains painted red, blue and yellow patterns on the foliage. Dance music and a solo soprano mingled with subdued laughter behind hedges and bushes.

The road ended at a wide square, and then, stretching out for three or four miles along the shore, a broad girdle of brilliant lights blinded his eyes. "Antium Beach," the coachman explained.

Some of the palaces and villas stood far out in the dark-blue sea. The long spans of bridges, edged with garlands of red and white lamps, connected with the mainland. Swift barges shot through the waves.

The Villa Ciceronis lay half a mile from the big square. It had been built about seventy-five years before, in the old Roman style, farmhouse as well as manorhouse. To protect it against real-estate speculators, Augustus after Cicero's death had bought it for the State. It had since been renovated several times and was now used for guests of minor rank and importance.

The whole site covered only one acre, but it had its own private beach. There Cicero and his friends had gathered shells and, as the great orator had expressed it in one of his letters, had become boys again. In the garden stood a huge eucalyptus and many other old trees. "I love this house!" Marcius thought, enthusiastically, as the carriage stopped in front of the main entrance, and an aged couple—the caretakers apparently—led him into the atrium.

Marcius first had a quick glance at his suite of rooms and then returned to the atrium. He sat down on a chair with a round back, and told a slave that he was hungry. He did not notice that he was not the only guest.

Soon a tray was brought in and placed beside him on a small collapsible table. It was a simple supper, consisting of soft boiled eggs, white bread, cuts of cold meat, a large wooden bowl of cucumber and garden salad, leeks and mushrooms in oil and wine, a compote of mixed fruit, cherries, apricots, and pears, and a plate with one rosy-cheeked apple. A jug of country wine and a pint of Egyptian barley beer, from the imperial breweries in Alexandria, were served with the meal.

He ate with healthy appetite, first the apple, then the eggs, finishing up with another helping of compote. The tray was as good as cleared, when the slave brought him a silver bowl to wash his hands, and some napkins of Punic linen.

"Any further wishes, my lord?" he was asked. He shook his head, irresolute what to do next, when a voice came from across the hall.

"Another non-Roman guest in our Villa Chimaera, our little house of illusions!" A man emerged from behind a reading desk. He had a pointed brown beard, a complexion deeply tanned, bushy hair, and a pair of alert dark eyes, with a slightly melancholy expression. A not unpleasant smile bared very white teeth. "Would it not be a propitious idea to share the hours of our boredom?" he asked.

"I have no objection, sir," Marcius said, somewhat astonished. "But may I enquire how you know that I am—"

"Not Roman?" the man finished the question. "A legitimate question, easy to answer." He raised the finger of his right hand, like a teacher, dealing with a weighty question. "There is a certain rule in this world, not binding in conscience, you understand, yet very strict nevertheless. It is a rule to which all conform. For many, it is even the only one, the sole directive of their lives, lawless pleasure hunters though they may be." The slave brought another chair and he sat down.

"This rule, my friend, you have transgressed," he concluded.

"I am not aware—" Marcius said, uncertain.

"I know you aren't. *Ab ovo ad malum,* from the egg to the apple—the yardstick of organized foodtaking, the law which brings harmony into the chaotic pasturing of our world rulers. An element of discipline for high and low, good and wicked, for monarchists and republicans."

"But what did I—" Marcius began, wondering and upset.

"You began with the apple instead of closing with it, don't you see? And you ended with the compote instead of beginning with the eggs. I am from Corduba in Hispania. There we begin with olives. I needed a complete re-education before I could attain to my present position, a lawyer for my bread, a philosopher for my spirit."

Marcius laughed, relieved. "That's really too bad! And you watched me all the time I was eating "

The man nodded gravely. "Observation is the acid test of

knowledge, even though in the case of a conflict between the idea and the manifestation, it is the first that counts."

"Could you say that again?"

"Never mind. The evening has just begun, and resort towns of this type, specially at this time of day, are the dullest places on earth. So one way is as good as another to introduce oneself to one's fellow man. In short, my name is Lucius Annaeus Seneca. You, my friend, seem to belong to a sister-branch of our great Celtic family of nations?"

"My name is Marke de Armagh. I was born in Hibernia. Usually I am called Marcius Armaghensis, or just Marcius."

"Hibernia–" Seneca repeated with obvious delight. "How perfectly fascinating!" He caressed his beard. "I assume, that now you want to retire to do some serious studying? Finishing your term paper, for instance?"

"No–I am just waiting for my luggage."

"The whole of life is waiting, nothing but waiting. Why not for luggage? I take it that you have just returned from the schools of wisdom in Athens or Alexandria, where you majored in rhetoric and government, with a minor in philosophy? You probably took an extra course in Latin composition, and on your school team you played–"

"I was a volunteer in the Cohort Antonia, stationed at Jerusalem," Marcius said, exhausted. But he liked the man, and found his ways and manners decidedly entertaining. "Why should I not tell him who I am and what I want to do?" he thought, and so half an hour later Seneca knew most of the outward facts of his biography.

However, he must have noticed that somewhere in Marcius' account there remained an open space, a center of great importance, which had been left untouched. "This morning the Emperor has received a report from his governor at Caesarea," he said with telling emphasis, "a rather ambiguous report, so far as I could judge from his remarks. So His Majesty may ask you a number of questions. He is very much interested in Eastern affairs." Still there was no response. More lightly he added, "Tomorrow you must write to him to submit your request for a private audience."

"Write to the Emperor? I am not even sure of my spelling!"

"I shall be glad to do it for you."

Marcius grew hopeful that he might get more aid. "I have letters of introduction to Corsus and Gnaeus Cornelius Lentulus. Shouldn't I write to them too?"

"What do you want with these old fogies, I pray?"

Marcius was stung. "They are cousins of my good friend Gaius Cornelius, place commandant of Capharnaum." With boyish spite he added, "I also have letters to the legates Cornelius Lentulus Gaetulicus and Lucius Apronius. But of course, if you don't want–"

"A real pity that those ancient worthies, the Horatii and the Curatii are dead! With a few more letters of introduction to both factions you might have reconciled them." He looked at him with friendly sarcasm. "Nobody gave you a letter to Lucius Annaeus Seneca?"

An impish green spark came into Marcius' eyes. "Sorry, sir. People must have thought that I couldn't help running into him somewhere. The whole world must know him, since he knows the whole world, they said. Truthfully, sir, I have heard your name no less than three times!"

"You have? But that is remarkable," Seneca replied, but whether he spoke with real or pretended vanity, or was actually somewhat hurt, it would have been difficult to tell.

"I even know that you wrote a play, called *Medea*. I liked those verses about the land which the navigator will discover, when after centuries the mysteries of the ocean are revealed, and Thule will no longer be the remote place of the earth." With the pride of a student who remembers his lesson, he quoted the exact words:

> "*Venient annis saeculis seris*
> *Quibus Oceanus vincula rerum*
> *Laxet et ingens pateat tellus*
> *Tethysque novos detegat orbes*
> *Nec sit terris ultima Thule.*"

"Very good, very good. You are a great charmer, my boy," Seneca said, obviously flattered. He got up. "The night is soft and soothing. Why not continue this most pleasant conversation under the branches of the eucalyptus tree?"

CHAPTER ELEVEN

MARCIUS FOUND that the expression "Villa Chimaera, the house of illusions," was not badly chosen. In the high trees the stars glittered like candles, and from the buoyant town, with all its palaces, and from the doings on the beach, which night had not interrupted, only a faint murmur reached the garden. The perfume of roses, jasmine, violets, and mimosa was in the air. In the gentle breeze which fanned the blossoms, all the thoughts of the great men who had lived here seemed alive and moving.

"Who told you that there must be a land west of the ocean?" Marcius broke the silence. He had never met a poet and philosopher before, and all his youthful curiosity was awakened.

"There are some ancient legends, even half-forgotten reports—Phoenician, Egyptian, in origin. We in Hispania always liked to look westwards, so naturally I am interested in all the tales of the sea. But my reason too could have told me that there must be still another continent. The earth is round, so much modern science has established beyond any justified doubt. What the Romans call the orbit is probably only a fraction of the universe. The legions with their armour and ensigns, the daring horsemen who traverse rivers and streams, are small things in relation to our globe."

"If the earth were round—the stories about the abyss would be just so many fables!"

"Quite. Your island lies far to the West. If a few hundred miles further out there were the terrible bottomless cataract, you should notice its suction all around your coast. But I am sure you haven't."

"On the contrary. There is a great current in the ocean, a stream of warm water, which comes from the west. Sometimes strange things are carried along upon it, for instance nuts, as large as a child's head."

"Coconuts? This is most interesting. They may have come all the way from India."

"But they drift in from the west!"

"What is the difference if the earth is round?"

Marcius pondered for a while. "I like your idea that not everything is Roman. If the thought were better known, it might make for more modesty!"

"You don't like the Romans?"

"Some of my best friends are Roman. But as a whole I find them conceited. And they always want more! The best answer might be if we Hibernians set out for the new continent."

"Halt, my friend! Who wrote those verses, an Hibernian or an Hispaniard? Don't you think that my people have a priority?"

"We are closer!"

"Perhaps a compromise will do," Seneca said, amused. "You take over the northern part, we the southern. Together we'll establish the Imperium Celticum."

"Wonderful! Then we can plan on a really grand scale and have things just the way we like them. The Roman system doesn't agree with me—a handful of citizens, the rest strangers in their own land. In our Empire everyone should be a citizen, native born and newcomers alike. And no slaves! On the new continent all must be free!"

"Slowly, oh founding youth! Is this just sentimentality or have you philosophical reasons for your constitutional ideas?"

Marcius remembered his thoughts in the carriage on the Appian Way. "Shall I tell him?" he wondered. "He may find it childish."

"I don't know whether you'll call my reasons philosophic," he said. "It's just the way I see it. All men are brethren. Therefore there should be no slaves."

"A word wiser than Aristotle's best! That overrated epigone, Plato's inferior, indeed! He taught that slavery is rooted in natural law, while in reality we are all born free.

"You say that you never went to any school of higher learning?" he continued. "No? Who then, may I ask, instilled in you such wisdom? Who told you that freedom is primarily a moral, and not a legal principle?"

"It is part of the Truth," Marcius replied.

"The Truth? Beware of generalities, my friend. We will never know more than part of it."

Marcius grew bolder. "If we knew God, would we not know the whole truth?"

"Truth is infinite. Our minds are finite. Once I watched a child who patiently tried to pour the sea into a little sand hole."

"And did he not succeed in filling the sand hole?"

Seneca sighed. "You are a born dialectician. But there are limits to your art. The distance from the sea to the hole could be measured. No one can measure the distance between men and the Divine. How then, can we know It?"

"Through Love," Marcius said, his heart beating faster.

"Love? Man's feelings for the Supreme Deity are awe and reverence. Love would presuppose a very different, a mutual relationship. How can I love, when my destiny is directed according to Necessity even if it be for my own good? For me to love God, He would have to turn His countenance to me. God would have to be Man."

"And if someone told you that just that event has happened?"

Skeptically, Seneca raised his eyebrows. "I know that certain circles think along these lines. Perhaps you came in touch with them while you were in the East? There are the writings of Moses, Isaias, Jeremias, Hoseas, the Psalms of David—"

"How do you happen to know these names?" Marcius asked in a low voice.

"What a question! Plato, our master, became acquainted with Hebrew thought when he sojourned in Alexandria. Much work has been done since. A Greek translation, called the Septuagint, has been extant now for over two hundred years. The wisdom of the Jews moves outside the realm of Greek philosophy. Yet their concept of a Mediator, an incarnate and unique manifestation of God, God's *Alter Ego* so to speak, may have influenced the Stoic notion of the *Logos,* the all-pervading and creative principle, the intermediary between God and the world. It would not be the first time that a conquered people gave laws to its very conquerors."

He seemed to wait for an answer, but Marcius, unable to cope with such expressions, remained silent.

"I am very self-centered," Seneca went on, in a completely different tone, half-jocular, as in his earliest remarks. "Didn't you tell me that there were two more instances when you heard my name?"

"Yes, of course!" Marcius said, torn away from his thoughts. "It was Luitprant of the German bodyguard who told me about your advice to the Emperor four miles from the Porta Appia."

"The candid barbarian! I am sure I shocked him by my flippancy. Germans are so much given to superstition. If they knew Greek, they would talk about a national 'ideology.'" He became serious. "His Majesty was wiser than I. The insistence of his two other companions was indeed a bad portent."

"You are a rather interesting man, why can't you get hold of Caligula and crowd out that scoundrel Herod Agrippa?"

"I like your blunt approach, and thank you for the compliment! But things are not quite so easy as they seem. If I could I would have tried long ago to mould young Gaius Caesar according to the image of the true ruler."

"Why don't you make another effort to become his teacher? It might be very important."

"A ruler needs a soul which is as healthy as his body." There was the same evasiveness of tone which Marcius had noticed when Cornelius had first talked about the Little Boot. But then Seneca became more outspoken. "A Prince must be like a physician," he said. "He must be prepared to cure evil—by force if necessary. Never should he rejoice over punishment inflicted. The people will look upon a prince who is mild, just, and free from passion as upon a benign star. But before a cruel ruler they will take flight as before a wild beast springing from its lair. Eventually such a prince will be slain like a beast."

"Some say that the Emperor's grandson, Tiberius Gemellus, would be a much better choice?" Marcius said in questioning tone.

Seneca's face brightened. "A boy of remarkable promise! *Iuvenis pudentissimus*, peerless, virtuous, filled with high ideals. He is still a dreamer in the mountains of childhood, but it is there that the gold for the laurels of the heroes must be found. Like old Cato, the Emperor has seen to it that no unseemly word is uttered in the presence of this boy. I must try to have you meet him. You are one of the few to whose company His Majesty might not object."

"But why then," Marcius asked, aware that he was treading on dangerous ground, "why then does the Emperor not make it clear that Tiberius Gemellus, and not the Little Boot, will be his successor?"

"The Emperor is hesitant, because of Gaius Caesar's popularity with the army, especially the eight Germanic Legions, and because, through his mother Agrippina, the granddaughter of Augustus, he has more of the Julian blood than Tiberius Gemellus. Also, these last two years have been a constant ordeal which left the Emperor little rest to think of the future. Sejanus' treason forced him to a severity contrary to his nature, and he has suffered greatly from it. Unfortunately his trials are not yet over. He knows now that Drusus, his only son, the father of Tiberius Gemellus, was poisoned by that same Sejanus, whom he had trusted so much. But the accomplices of the murderer have not all been discovered yet."

"The poor Emperor!" Marcius exclaimed. "I am sorry for him."

"The Emperor is above pity. He is the crowned reality, the incarnate categoric imperative of duty. Plato would have rejoiced over him, a ruler who is a philosopher, a philosopher who is a ruler! When in his best manhood years he returned from his exploits in Germany and Pannonia, covered with glory, he withdrew for seven long years to the isle of Rhodes. There he completed his education, yet he has never ceased to study. At Capri he converses daily with the most learned philosophers, jurists and scientists."

Marcius' thoughts sped ahead. "Can one talk quite frankly with Tiberius Caesar about abuses of justice?"

"In the Senate he has been called the best and most just of rulers, *conservator patriae*."

"Thank you; that's what I wanted to know," Marcius replied.

Like high shafts, rising from the depth of the earth, the dark old trees stood around him. His eyes followed their branches to the little patch of sky above. It looked as if under a thin plate of transparent marble there was a thin gray veil of silk.

"There is constant movement up there," he said, dreamily without noticing Seneca's slight disappointment that there had not been a stronger response to his discourse on high politics and the Emperor's virtues.

The older man got up. "Nothing is a better cure for egocentrism than a starlight night," he said somewhat sententiously. "It reduces man to his true proportions."

"We haven't talked yet about the third instance when I heard your name," Marcius replied, with a bit of mischievousness.

"Don't worry. I'll come to it. Something tells me that you are going to stay here for some time."

CHAPTER TWELVE

WHEN MARCIUS entered the breakfast room, shortly after sunrise, Seneca had already left the house. But he had kept his word; a letter to the Emperor was awaiting his signature. It said that he, Marcius Armaghensis, son of King Marke in Hibernia, sought an audience to lay before the Majesty of the Emperor and the Roman People the humble request for a special favor promised to the centurion Longinus, Company D, Third Syrian Legion, after the crushing of the Sejanus' revolt.

"It will be dispatched at once," the slave said, when Marcius had signed the letter.

The garden was still covered with dew. Crocuses, chaste lilies, and gladioli were opening their chalices, and an old rosebush, with hundreds of blossoms between dark-green leaves, spread out like the apron of a young mother, playing with her children. The mimosas were still half-closed, but the violets and the jasmines had already shed their slumber.

No grown-up people were around, but on the beach adjoining that belonging to the Villa groups of boys were frolicking in the sand. Deeply tanned, with white hairlines on their foreheads, they were building walls and castles, until some sulky slaves told them that they were trespassing on private property. "A shame not to let them play!" Marcius thought and signified to ten or twelve of them, that they could move over to his beach.

Their Latin was not easy to understand, a mixture of local

dialect and boys' slang. The name of the town they pronounced as if it were "Anzio." Mostly they seemed to be speaking about the summer, a series of forthcoming ball games and what a shame it was that vacation would not start before July.

"Let's hope the teacher doesn't find out that we're here," one of them said. So, Marcius noted, playing hookey was as popular among the Italian boys as it was among Hibernians!

"You've heard the story, haven't you?" a blond thirteen-year-old asked. "In arithmetic, the other day, Pamphilius, that old scare-crow went completely mad. 'Dionysius over there in the corner is disturbing the class!' he groaned. We all started yelling, 'But sir, Dionysius isn't here, he's sick!' 'When he gets here, he will disturb the class,' the man said!"

"They are all the same. Guess they never were boys. They were born schoolmasters."

"Let's defy the tyrants!" a chubby fellow said, with the pathos befitting an oration on the virtues of Harmodios and Aristogeiton, those celebrated youths who had slain Hipparchus, the Athenian despot. "Let's announce to the wild sea that among the boys of this country the longing for liberty is strong!"

They all started singing:

"What have you against us, you school-teaching villain
Detested by girls and by boys,
That before crested cocks break the silence,
Your blows raise such horrible noise—"

"That'll teach them a lesson," the blond boy said, whereupon they settled down again to their sand castles. To Marcius, they paid not the slightest attention. "At least they don't take me for a schoolmaster!" he thought with satisfaction.

After a while a somewhat older boy, whose slick black

hair was pasted to his head, suggested something else. "The investigation game" he called it, but at first Marcius did not understand what it was about.

"I'll take the part of the consul Memmius Regulus, who conducted the original show," the boy announced. His fingers, with flat nails, pointed out his younger comrades. "And now let's see, what each of you can be–"

"I won't be Sejanus, no, I won't!" a little fellow said, wincing.

"Shut up," the slick-haired "consul" snapped. "Today we'll deal with Sejanus' friends and co-conspirators."

"That's the most disgusting thing I've ever seen," Marcius thought as the meaning became clearer. Some of the boys had to act as secret agents, informers, and accusers. They dragged the others before "Memmius Regulus," and the "Indictments" came forth. "I saw you with Sejanus the week before last–No? you're a liar!" "You brought offerings to his statues!" "You said, he ought to be Emperor!" Here again was the whole sad chain of deadly accusations from the real trials which for the last two years had brought so much unhappiness upon the country.

The "verdict" was always the same: "Fling him from the Tarpeian Rock!" Slowly this game lost whatever outward fun it may have had. The "convicted" boys stood trembling and frightened in a row, while the "consul's" gang, with kicks and abuse, expended all their cruelty.

The blond boy defended himself cleverly: "I was a friend of Sejanus' and his wife–so what? The Emperor was their friend too!" But it did not help him. "Give him a real whipping first!" the "consul" shouted.

Now hate, passion, all the low instincts, kindled in the boys by the bad example of the grown-ups, rose to a fury. Some of the smaller ones cried.

"Perhaps his parents really were friends of the Sejanus couple!" the slick "consul" sputtered. "I'd better tip off the police; it's a patriotic duty!"

Marcius turned to the group. "You ought to be ashamed of yourselves!" he said sharply.

"Mind your own business!" the "consul" retorted.

One of his aides made a sign. "Careful! He stays at the Villa. He's a guest of the State!"

"Oh well, it was just a game, nobody takes it seriously," the "consul" said in a conciliatory tone. "All right, boys, let's get on!"

"No, you won't, not with that dirty game," Marcius said with mounting anger. "Not if I can help it!"

Like a beaten cur the slick-haired boy slunk away, and the group broke up. Four or five followed him, the others stayed with Marcius.

"Now he'll surely try to play a nasty trick on my parents," the blond boy whispered.

"I'll make certain that he doesn't," Marcius replied, and he followed the "consul" a few steps. "Get this straight! These boys are under my protection! I've come all the way from Judea to see the Emperor!" The "consul" mumbled an excuse and made his escape.

"Laying it on thick, but it'll help," Marcius thought, and returned to his group. "Now, boys, let's have some real fun!" he said gaily, and ran into the water. The fine sand sloped down very gradually. Two hundred yards out even the smaller boys could still touch bottom.

He had not been in swimming for some time so, carried on warm rippling waves, Marcius went out a considerable distance. The boys were still waiting when he returned almost an hour later.

"That was fine, the way you handled the 'consul,' " the blond boy said gratefully. "I am called Publius Quirinius, after my father. He's a town councilor. What country are you from?"

"You guessed that I am not Roman?"

"With your funny 'R?' "

"I am from Hibernia. You've probably never heard of it?"

"Of course I have! We had a politician here who came from Hibernia."

"I'd like to meet him!"

"He isn't here any longer. In the last mayoralty election, when he ran for the fifth term, he overshot the mark. He promised his voters seventy thousand jobs. But there are only twenty thousand wage earners, and people got frightened at so much work ahead. So a fellow from northeastern Italy came along. He promised higher pay and lower taxes. He got in, and the Hibernian went home. This country wasn't green enough for his taste, he said."

Marcius laughed. "You've only yourselves to blame, if people do such things!"

He was still sitting surrounded by his small companions, who were listening with attention and exclamations of surprise and feigned incredulity to his stories about the wide world, when shortly before noon Seneca appeared on the beach.

"I was on my morning visit when your letter to the Emperor arrived," Seneca said, as they lay down in the triclinium, the small dining room adjoining the atrium. "I added a few words of explanation. His Majesty was very gracious. He may receive you tomorrow at a private audience, followed by an informal supper. Should Herod Agrippa be there too, you will, as son of a sovereign foreign king, have precedence over him. He won't like it, but he is only the grandson of a client-king."

"So soon?" Marcius said anxiously. The question of protocol did not interest him in the least.

"Yes, unless His Majesty should not feel well. We will know by tomorrow morning. He has had upsetting news."

"Upsetting news? Political?" Marcius asked.

"Partly political, but mainly personal. One of his trusted friends died last night, the Praeses of Campania, Marcus Cocceius Nerva."

"Oh, I am sorry," Marcius said, tears coming into his eyes. "I can't tell you how sorry I am."

"You knew him?"

"I met him in Neapolis. He too mentioned your name. Last night it was too late to talk about it."

"Why not do it this evening, under the eucalyptus tree?" Seneca replied.

As Marcius left the triclinium a slave approached him. "Mail for you, my lord," he said.

It was a letter from Nerva. "My young friend," it said, "I enjoyed your courtesy in writing to me. I have not failed to inform His Majesty of our little talk. May I still hope that you will be able to corroborate Captain Thamus' narrative? The Emperor would certainly appreciate it. And if you are wise, my friend, do not forget my advice! Vale."

Marcius spent part of the afternoon in the beautiful library of the Villa. Countless scrolls were stacked in the cases of birchwood, each with a little red tag attached, giving the names of the author and the work. But there were also many flat, boxlike books. "So the sophisticated have taken to it after all!" he reflected. Valuable illustrated volumes and collectors' items with Marcus Tullius Cicero's *Ex Libris* were among these treasures. Other books were dedication copies, with the autographs of Julius Caesar, Pompey, and most of the great writers and poets of Rome's golden age of literature.

"I am an unerudite boy," he thought. "All I know are some names and a few things we read in school." He wished that he could spend months and years under this high ceiling, guided perhaps by someone who could tell him what was essential. "Seneca? It would be wonderful!" Yet his feelings were somewhat mixed.

The conversation with the philosopher had occupied Marcius' mind deep into the night. His luggage had been brought in by the servants' entrance, and because he was nervous, he had spent a whole hour unpacking. But his thoughts continued even when he finally lay down.

If he ever got into a conversation on the events which had really mattered in his life, he might not even be able to explain them properly. Certainly, Seneca would cover him with learned terms, taken from Platonic and Stoic philosophy; and he knew the Hebrew Scriptures as well!

Yet, something about the man was strange. There was a cleavage in his character, an inconsistency between word and personality, which Marcius sensed, without being able to explain it. "It is the idea that counts," he had said, but he was at the same time certainly ambitious. Or was it perhaps that he felt it necessary to play up to the great and powerful in order to achieve his philosophical ideals?

"His mind is like a sponge," Marcius thought. "It absorbs everything. His curiosity seems to be boundless. But I shouldn't be surprised if he held the whole world in contempt —even the mighty men, whom he says he admires so much."

What Seneca had told him about virtue, fortitude, the duties of a ruler, all these things were very beautiful, and while listening to him, everything was fascinating, brilliant, and one would like to hear more. "But after a while much of it melts away," Marcius reflected. "I wonder why." A new thought struck him. "I know what's the matter! He has no love! He gave me a long description of it and what it 'presupposes.' But somehow he didn't quite know what I had been talking about."

A friendlier sentiment emerged. "I am unjust. He's a bit of an actor, but he is decent and he has a kind heart. If he doesn't know yet what love is, perhaps I should tell him what happened in Judea. Then he might understand how much–" His thoughts paused for a moment, "–how much God has loved the world," he concluded.

He put the books back on their shelves and looked out of the window. Sunshine filtered through the air like golden wine and overflowed the chalices of the flowers. "I can't concentrate now," he thought, and the library in which he had just longed to spend months seemed to him like a classroom on a summer day.

"Pomponius hasn't had any exercise. Perhaps I can pick up some of Seneca's writings. Then I'll know better what kind of a man he is."

The broad, heavy stallion, with a good-looking, well-dressed young man in the saddle, caused some excitement in the midst of the elegant carriages on the promenades and in the shopping center of the town. "Why do these people stare at us?" Marcius wondered. "Have they never seen a dapple-gray horse?" A few blocks from the office of Titus P. Atticus Heirs was an empty lot. "Park your horse here! Half a sestertium an hour, three sesterces all day," a poster read. "Don't get impatient, Pomponius," Marcius said, and decided to continue on foot.

First he went to the Maxentius Millanius store and purchased some of Seneca's works and a book called "The

Hibernian Question—How to Solve It." The title page explained that it was written by a staff reporter of the *Acta Diurnia*. He asked that the parcel should be sent to the Villa Ciceronis.

The shopping fever seized him. An hour later he had purchased half a dozen silver plates, some silken kerchiefs, two silver saltshakers, and a whole set of tableware of beautiful red-glazed pottery from Tuscany. For his father he bought a water clock. It cost a whole aureus.

His purse was almost empty when in a side street he discovered a small and rather shabby-looking jewelry shop. Only a few old coins and some brooches with semi-precious stones were in the window. "Sell your valuables here. Discretion guaranteed," a tablet said.

"I can look around and pay later," he thought and pushed aside the curtain of strings of multicolored glass beads. The small, vaulted room was dark as a cave. An old hunchback, crouched on a three-legged stool was polishing a water pitcher made of pewter. He smiled when Marcius wished him a good afternoon, but seemed not too anxious to do business.

"I want something nice," Marcius said.

"Yes?"

"Something really nice—for a young girl."

"The same old story," the man said, bored.

"Do you want to sell it to me, or don't you?"

"Sell you what?"

"Oh, a ring, a necklace perhaps, something with a stone."

The little man left his three-legged stool and began to fumble in a drawer under the counter. "He looks like a friendly gnome," Marcius observed to himself.

"Where does the fair lady live?" the man asked. "In Rome?"

Marcius' blue eyes were veiled with longing. "Out in the sea, miles from a wild coast, there lies an island," he said. "It is called Lundy. Rocks and racing waves protect it well. But they could not stop my boat."

The gnome's hands seemed to have found their object.

"So she need not be afraid to wear Domna Apicata's gem," he whispered in a sad voice.

"She need not be afraid of anything," Marcius replied.

With a hasty gesture the man tossed a little box on the counter. "Quick, take it!" He moved back to his three-legged stool. "Twenty aurei," he said over his shoulder.

"He must be insane," Marcius thought, and unwrapped the box. The hunchback looked at him, aghast. "What gods do you think are protecting you that you dare—" Furtively he glanced at the entrance.

"I want to see what it is, even if I can't spend twenty aurei," Marcius said lightly.

"It is worth two hundred." The gnome came around the counter and shoved Marcius behind a black curtain in the back of the store. A flickering oil lamp was burning on a small table.

A subdued shout of delight and amazement came from Marcius' lips. In his hands he held a cameo ring, the apotheosis of Augustus engraved in a chrysoprase, an inch and a half in diameter. The translucent stone was of a pale apple-green. On both sides it was held by seven prongs of yellow gold, inlaid with Oriental emeralds. The many layers of the stone, each thin as a finespun veil, created a unique impression: the Eagle Triumphant, here the symbol of the Emperor's immortal genius, the myrtle-crowned figure of the great ruler, the flaming torches and the column of the temple seemed projected upon a background of limitless depth.

"The emeralds have the color of the sea around Lundy,"

Marcius thought, more and more enthralled. He was no expert on jewelry, but that this piece was beautiful beyond description, and that twenty aurei could be only a fraction of its real value, he well understood. "It must be stolen," he thought. "Therefore the man asked where it would be worn. In Rome everyone might know the true owner."

"There are a lot of rich people in Antium," he said, somewhat rudely. "Why don't you sell it for its real value?"

"Because nobody would take it."

Marcius put down the ring. Quickly the gnome covered it with a dirty kerchief. "You think it's stolen?" he giggled. "You sweet innocent fool!"

"It it's not, why does nobody—"

"Because," the man interrupted him, "there's no man or woman brave enough to buy it."

"A charm?" Marcius asked, with all his inherited superstitions aroused.

"Yes, a charm, and a deadly one too! Didn't you understand what I said? It's Domna Apicata's gem." Marcius eyes went blank. "Listen, you knight errant, with the look of a grown-up and the heart of a child," the hunchback went on, "Domna Apicata was the wife of Aelius Sejanus. She was a beautiful and virtuous woman, who loved her husband and her two children dearly." His voice became more intense. "When Sejanus was killed, and she saw the broken bodies of her boy and girl lying on the Gemonian stairs, she cried out terrible curses against the Emperor. Then she took her own life. But her revenge came later. Several months after her death a letter was mailed to Tiberius Caesar, in which she revealed that Drusus had been poisoned by Sejanus at a time when the Emperor had trusted him most—"

Marcius uncovered the ring. "And this belonged to her?" he stammered.

"It was Tiberius Caesar's wedding gift. You won't find one like it in the whole Empire. Domna Apicata had no heir, so it passed to a certain Publius Quirinius, a secret friend of Sejanus' family, who had it in keeping. He brought it to me to dispose of."

"Publius Quirinius, the town councilor?"

"You know him?"

Marcius did not reply. A wave of terror and of compassion for the lovable blond boy engulfed him. With his clever answer during the "investigation game," little Publius might have given away his parents' dangerous secret. Perhaps the slick-haired "consul" was a stool-pigeon—many young fellows were. The secret police used them to find out the political views in the homes of their classmates.

"They'll end by buying children to spy on their own parents," was the thought that flashed through Marcius' mind. "I'll take the ring!" he gasped. "It must not be found here!" He rushed to the entrance. "I'll be back in a moment!"

The warm summer evening failed to break the chill he felt. His legs shook as he walked to the office of Titus P. Atticus Heirs. "I need money," he said, trying to control his voice.

"Perhaps you would prefer to open an account, sir?" A bank clerk said. "Your address?"

"Villa Ciceronis."

"Very good, sir. It won't take more than a few minutes."

Mechanically Marcius signed a number of papers. Then he was given a little book with thirty perforated leaves, each with the name of the firm and space for his signature, and the sum of money, to be expressed in denarii, twenty-five to the aureus.

Hastily he returned to the cavelike shop. With an indulgent smile the gnome explained how to make out a check for five hundred denarii. "We needn't put a sales tax on it," he said. "The town treasurer might discover what kind of transaction it was."

"We won't stay much longer in this country, Pomponius, not you and I, I promise!" Marcius told his horse, as he was riding back to the house of illusions.

CHAPTER THIRTEEN

MARCIUS FOUND a note from Seneca saying that he would be back about an hour after supper. So when dusk came, the Hibernian sat alone by the edge of the beach and gazed toward the blue and amber of the sky. The sea was a polished sheet of metal, with two or three long-drawn shallow undulations.

"Villa Chimaera," he thought again, but now he saw in the name a wider implication. "I wonder whether the Emperor knows about all the fear and terror among his people. He probably gets only the prominent cases. But it's the pressure upon the countless small ones that matters.

"Sejanus has fallen; Macro, another chief, has taken his place. To the people it makes no difference. The means are the same."

Restlessly he drew senseless figures in the sand. "Couldn't I mention the matter to the Emperor, tell him frankly about my impressions? It's the same everywhere! Of course, one can't speak in one breath about the case of Publius Quirinius and of what Pontius Pilate did to Him—yet, somehow it is connected. 'Security of the State,' no matter what the price."

His mind turned to Seneca. Suddenly he saw him in a different light. "He can't come out with criticism—so he pours out praises. They are demands addressed to the rulers, rather than flatteries and adulations. What a terrible state of affairs it is that forces an honest man to appear a hypocrite. Of course he does it for the sake of the Empire."

The Empire—Cornelius had spoken of its transcendent design. "I'll concede it. I really do; he wouldn't have to convince me again. I am convinced. But something is lacking."

Tiny clouds blurred the quarter of the sky where the sun had set. The color of the sea changed to a dark blue. Just above the streak of clouds the arrows of the evening star pierced the sky.

"Something is lacking," he repeated. "One can feel it everywhere. I know what it is. They have no Love."

Love. Seneca had not understood the meaning of the word, and it was absent also from the whole proud structure of the edifice, even though the Empire possessed virtue and fortitude, and a well-measured justice of its own.

He started to generalize his conclusion. "What's the use of pointing out individual examples, the great and small? Even if the Emperor were the most just of men—and I don't doubt that he is—what could he do? It's in the system." He felt an inner resistance. "No; it's cowardly to think that way. What would my friend Longinus say? He didn't capitulate! He went right on. And what did He do—"

Marcius took a handful of sand. It was still warm. Slowly he let it trickle through his fingers. "It will take a long time," he thought, "more days perhaps than there are grains of sand on this beach." A whole desert of days, which must be crossed. . . .

He leapt up, and youthfully shook off his mood of depression like drops of water.

"If I only knew how to talk back to Seneca!" he thought. "He always startles me with his learned definitions." He smiled. "Perhaps I ought to go back to school and enroll for a course called 'How to converse with a philosopher.' Oh, well—"

But he felt much better as he walked through the slumbering garden to the bench under the eucalyptus tree.

"I bought some of your books this afternoon," he said, as soon as Seneca had joined him. But today the philosopher-poet did not seem interested in a conversation about the written products of his mind.

"I hope you didn't spend too much money. As a Millanius author I can get all their books at a drastic discount."

"The only other book I bought is an account of Hibernia. I have glanced through it. It's appalling. The man confuses us with the Troglodytes. He probably never came within five hundred miles of our coast."

"The perfect qualification for a staff reporter of the *Acta Diurnia.*" His tone sounded slightly bored. "If you insist, I will draw up a whole list of good books for you and provide you with an up-to-date work on encyclopedic knowledge. But not tonight." A friendly satyr's smile bared his white teeth. "Won't you tell me what His Majesty's lamented friend said about me?"

In matters of great importance, Marcius' consciousness was one of images, words and forms, rather than of independent reproduction of what had happened. To remember he had to switch back to the scenes as they had taken place in time and space.

Now under Seneca's question the vision of his mind shifted backwards, until there arose before him the office in the Castellum Ovi, Nerva's emaciated face and, high above the sea, a window showing the triangular silhouette of Capri. Haltingly he began to tell the story of the arrival of the *Isis* and the report of Captain Thamus of Alexandria about the death of the Great Pan.

Seneca shook his head in obvious wonderment. "I know that the Emperor attaches considerable importance to this story. It seems to coincide curiously with the ambiguous report he received from the Governor of Judea."

"I asked the Praeses what 'Pan' could mean," Marcius continued. " 'Pan may signify the Universe,' he replied. A young philosopher in His Majesty's service, Lucius Annaeus Seneca, interpreted it in this way: the divine principle of the world has become extinct."

"I was wrong, of course," Seneca interrupted. "If the divine principle had become extinct, it would have meant the end of all things."

Marcius' mind returned to the present. "Why do you say 'divine principle'?" he asked somewhat shyly. "God is much clearer."

"The word God is used too indiscriminately. Strictly speaking it implies a monotheistic concept, God as a Person distinct from the world, the One Supreme Ruler of the universe."

"Then why don't you say 'God'?"

"Marcius," Seneca replied, "I wish I had your faith, even though I do not know on what you base it, as you possess no knowledge of philosophy." He got up. "I will make a confession: I am no longer so young, but I am still immature, perhaps too immature to be an educator. Therefore what I say is often vague and contradictory. Take 'God' and 'divine principle' as an example. But I am willing to learn." His voice assumed a warmer tone. "From you."

And as Marcius looked at him with a somewhat puzzled expression, Seneca added: "You have received faith while you were still very young. For this you should be grateful. Faith, my friend, is greater than wisdom and reason, for it is the synthesis of both."

Early next morning a courier came to the Villa Ciceronis. He told Marcius that His Majesty had graciously granted him an audience, which would be followed by an informal supper.

A carriage would drive up to the Villa at three o'clock in the afternoon.

"So this is the day!" Marcius thought, his finger tips growing cold. He started his preparations at once. Carefully he wrapped in silken kerchiefs his *xenia*, the little sack with the dried leaves and the precious pot with the dragon pattern. He put on his best clothes and shoes and covered his shoulders with his blue Macedonian chlamys.

His eyes fell on the chrysoprase. "I had better put that into my tunic. Somebody might find it in my room while I am gone." Arrayed in his best, he went to breakfast. "I wish Seneca were here!" His excitement, however, had not impaired his appetite. "That's wonderful honey, not like the thin, pale stuff I got on my trip." He read the label. "Massiacum, valley of the Aenus, Province of Rhaetia," and he said to himself, "I must remember the brand!"

After breakfast, he sat undecided in the atrium. Through the open square space in its roof the warm rays of the sun slanted down on him and made him think of the inviting sea so near-by. "No, not today! There isn't time for swimming." Then he realized that it was barely eight o'clock and seven more hours must pass until the carriage should come to fetch him.

"I should do some thinking," he decided, and went back to his room. "There is so much in Cornelius' scrolls that I haven't read properly as yet."

When the time for lunch arrived, Seneca was still not back. Finally, shortly before two, the philosopher-poet entered the hall. He said a casual "Good afternoon!" and disappeared into his suite. It took him twenty-five minutes to change into a new white toga and a tunic with the two narrow vertical stripes of knighthood.

"The red ought to grow broader some day," he said, when

he noticed Marcius' glance. "In the good old days the quality of man pertained to freedom. Now it begins with a seat in the Senate." But by now Marcius had discovered that he should not take Seneca's ironical and self-complacent remarks too literally.

"Herod Agrippa will be most distressed," Seneca went on. "He must have felt completely sure that the Emperor would postpone the audience. So off he went, together with his high-born prospect, for some worthy little divertissement. Now neither will be back in time."

Marcius remembered what Gaius Cornelius had said when they were sitting on the green bench by the quiet little pool in the park at Capharnaum, "Herod Agrippa hopes to be made King of the Jews, so naturally he will be most unsympathetic to your report."

"Why did he want to meet me?" he asked, just to make sure.

"He, too, takes a great interest in Eastern affairs, but for different reasons from those of the Emperor." He accentuated his words, as if Marcius had by secretiveness hurt his pride. "You have not told me much. Of course, it would not have been proper for you to do so, before you had reported to the Emperor, but now I, too, am tongue-tied as to what I know. Suffice it to say that Herod receives and dispatches mail all the time."

"The Herods are all the same. They are all no good. The tetrarch of Galilee constantly writes to Capri, and always with some mischief in mind. He and the Governor, Pontius Pilate, used to be enemies. Cornelius says that the tetrarch and Herod Agrippa hate each other, and that therefore the latter always sides with Pilate against his brother-in-law. But now Pilate and the tetrarch have become good friends, so I wonder what Herod Agrippa is going to do! Some day I may tell you more, including the things I know through my friend Longinus."

"Your friend interests me. After all, it's because of him that you are here. You haven't heard from him lately?"

"He is in prison." With a sudden outbreak of temper he added, "Now, please, don't ask me, 'So you have come to see the Emperor about his release?' Everyone has asked that question. I can't listen to it again."

"Everyone has asked you that?"

"Gaius Cornelius and Nerva almost did."

"What an engaging Celtic trait! Just a slight exaggeration here and there!"

"I am sorry. I am a bit nervous today." He pushed his hand up through his hair. "Now you'll be full of malice, and I had meant to ask you a few things." Hectically he enquired whether it was proper to bring gifts into the audience room.

"Completely. May I ask what your *xenia* are? Or is that also a State secret?"

"No need to rub it in!" But he was recovering his good humour. "I have two, which I got from a man from Liang-tschu. One is a little sack of *te*. *Te* is the morning and evening drink of the Grand King of Sinae. Taken by men, the brew makes them amiable, pensive, sociable, philosophical. Given to women, it loosens their tongues."

"Don't mention that to the Emperor. Many of his troubles are due to the loose tongues of women."

"The other *xenion* is a pot. There are large and small dragons on it. On the bottom is a tiny dark-blue onion."

"The trademark of the state factory of Canton!" Seneca said with genuine pleasure. "That is a very valuable gift indeed!"

"Are you serious?"

"Absolutely. I know porcelain of the kind only from

books. There is probably no such pot in the whole imperial household or in any Roman household."

"I am terribly glad!" Marcius said. "But I must tell the Emperor how to make the *te* just right." His spirits drooped again. "What I really meant to ask you—how shall I behave?"

"Just be yourself. Don't follow a fixed program. Talk as you would with your father. The Emperor will make it easy for you." He smiled. "I have told him that you are a slightly high-strung young man. The Emperor is not only a wise and paternal ruler; he is a gentleman." He looked at the water-clock in the rear of the atrium. "The carriage should be here any minute. Are you ready?"

Marcius rushed to his room. His heart beating loudly, he took the two parcels, Longinus' wooden tablets, and the centurion's staff which he had carried from Jerusalem to Tyrus. When he joined Seneca again, the carriage had just stopped before the main entrance.

CHAPTER FOURTEEN

IT WAS a long drive. After they had passed the large square, the carriage rolled along a raised three-lane promenade, which paralleled the garden fronts of the beach villas. "Is it here?" Marcius asked Seneca, as a building of special splendor came in sight.

"No. That belongs to the banker, Lucius Caecilius Jucundus," Seneca replied. "But this–?" "No. That's the house of a former tax collector. The man who lives in the next made his money in the shipping business." He pointed out a few more. "That one has a new owner, a grain merchant; he made five million sesterces in three months, due to the depression. His neighbor has silver mines in my homeland. And that's the place rented by our dear Herod Agrippa." He noticed how tense Marcius was. The young man sat stiff as a ramrod with the staff pressed firmly between his knees.

So Seneca continued to make conversation in a light vein, even though the replies were forced and at times almost automatic.

"If you really want to eat luxuriously," he said in a bantering tone, "you absolutely must visit Herod Agrippa. His kitchenmaster is a wizard. He knows all the tricks by which to change every dish into the appearance of something else. This is considered a great art. You are served a pheasant, and it turns out to be a wild hare. You take cabbage and discover it's a mackerel. On some solemn occasion a whole roasted wild boar was brought in. Contents: oysters, conger eels, lobsters, sea urchins, green peas, mussels, boned mullets, olives, Gallic snails, shark fins, shrimps, all in a medley, and smothered by a brown sauce."

"Was it really good?"

"It was expensive. One hundred aurei!"

"The very thought of it makes me sick. I hope we won't have such a dish tonight."

"You needn't worry. The Emperor's meals are usually very simple. He believes in the old Roman saying that with different ingredients one should be able to produce a whole dinner out of a pumpkin. There are fifty ways to prepare pork, he once told me; each is all right, if it allows you to recognize the pork. But one thing is certain. Tonight we will have cucumbers. His Majesty eats them every day."

"Is it here?" Marcius asked, distracted.

"Goodness no! This is the villa of an insurance and real estate broker. His father was a slave of Maecenas. He himself became a freedman at the age of fourteen. Now he has amassed a fortune of eighty million sesterces, one of the largest in the country. He has hundreds of clients, who take turns at his table. Fifty to sixty are glad to be his guests every day."

"He must have a kind heart."

"A very kind heart. The host is served by the flower of Bithynian and Hellenic youth, the guests by hard-fisted Moors you wouldn't like to meet after dark. The host gobbles up a giant lobster, dipped in finest olive oil; the guests get cheap Tiber fish, cooked in oil smelling of the lamp. The guests drink sour Sabinian, the host Falernian of ancient vintage. The host laughs, the guests are laughed at."

"Yet they always come back?"

"They consider it an honor. Their patron is their only support in life. He is a powerful and respected member of society. His son may be a praetor or a consul. Or—the client of another rich man. Often there are only three generations from slave to pauper."

"Such people can't have real friends?"

"How could they? I have heard them complain, though, that friendships, like Orestes' and Pylades' have become rare. But Orestes and Pylades ate and drank the same."

"How do you find time to study all these things?"

Seneca smiled. "Observation is the acid test of knowledge. Did I not tell you that before? Some day I hope to be a minister of state. I have very definite ideas about the reforms I want to put through. Therefore I must know what is really going on under the deceptively brilliant surface of our modern society."

Now the drive had lasted for about forty-five minutes, and the row of houses and gardens had become thinner. Then it broke off completely. After several hundred feet of open beach a villa came in sight. It was built partly on a flat rock which protruded far into the sea. A huge park, encompassed by high walls, surrounded it on all sides, down to the water-line.

"Is it there?" Marcius asked.

"Did I help you to while away your time?" Seneca asked. As the carriage slowed down, he said, "Yes, there it is."

Marcius' nervousness began to abate as they approached the main gate. It was of wrought iron, and was surmounted by a bronze eagle, flanked by the laurel-wreathed *fasces*, the axes and faggots that were the symbols of the supreme magistrates. Outside twenty-four praetorians stood guard, unarmed.

The two visitors descended from the carriage, and the gate swung open. In the park the security service was entrusted to the Imperial German Bodyguard. The men carried their long native swords, instead of the broad, short weapons of the

Roman army. Quietly leaning on his pointed shield with the argent and azure lozenges, was Luitprant. Today he wore a golden lion rampant as helm crest. Marcius and he greeted each other with a silent gesture. "You see, the Emperor is in good hands," Luitprant seemed to say.

"The villa was built by Lucullus," Seneca explained. "He had a larger one at Misenum. The park is of the Emperor's own planning."

The landscape architects had done magnificent work. Twelve terraces descended westward toward the sea. In the evening, the gleam of the weakened sun rays could be caught in full.

The walls of the park were covered with ivy. Avenues and individual groups of mulberry trees, box wood, and rose bushes varied with beds of lilies, with oleander trees and with broad carpets of violets. A few late-blossoming almond and peach trees were still in flower, while the figs and chestnuts already bore tiny green fruit. A place of honor seemed to have been accorded to Lucullus' own discovery, his lasting bequest to civilization, the cherry trees, which he had brought back from the shores of the Black Sea. On the lower levels lemon trees, planted in tubs, lined many of the parkways.

Cascades of water flooded down over tritons, naiads and fauns, standing in their marble basins. Large balls of colored glass, fastened at the top of long sticks, caught and reflected all these pictures a dozenfold.

Closer to the sea, on both sides of the villa were groups of dark green cypress trees. "They never smile," thought Marcius.

Now he noticed that hosts of court functionaries and servants had emerged silently from the park. Six members of the Imperial Bodyguard followed their steps through the laurel grove, which led from the last terrace down almost to the main entrance.

When, at the end of the vestibule, the door opened into the atrium, a vision of Gaius Cornelius' modest house came back to Marcius' memory. He did not know that the Emperor had removed most of the pompous riches, the spoils of two Oriental kingdoms which Lucullus had carried to this place or which he had accumulated in years of leisure with more money than good taste. There was no longer anything obtrusive in this house, and quite a few of Antium's new-rich citizens might not even have considered it splendid enough for an abode.

But the impression which it conveyed was one of dazzling and dignified beauty. The atrium, about thirty-eight feet high, was more than twice the size of the one in the Villa Ciceronis. The roof around the compluvium, the open square, was supported by four columns of purple-flecked Phrygian marble. The cross-beams of the spacious hall were of Numidian ophite, a green porphyry.

The impluvium, the shallow square basin directly beneath the roof opening, was of white Phoenician stone, framed by a ribbon pattern of mountain crystal. Around it, the floor was black and white, inlaid with geometrical forms and designs.

Mosaics in subdued shades covered the walls with scenes of Greek and Roman mythology. Mosaics looked as if the artists had painted their works in stone.

Marcius was only half-aware that the hands of servants undid the silver shoulder clasp of his chlamys, and instead dressed him in a white toga. "May I carry those for you?" another servant asked submissively. Marcius handed him the two parcels wrapped in silken kerchiefs, but clung to his staff. "My guide!" he thought and pressed it against his heart.

"It has been a long way from the skull-shaped rock to this place."

Now he stood in the entry hall which led to Tiberius Caesar and over sixteen hundred miles had been traversed since the words "The Emperor" had first sounded in his ears to mark his distant goal. He could see himself setting out on the road to Capharnaum, with rain and storm closing in, while phantoms and shadows galloped on his trail. Endlessly the night had stretched ahead until he awoke in the glow of the great sunrise. Then, soon, new roads had opened, and the waves and the wind of the sea had seemed too slow and too fast. He himself had changed on his journey, as men and things, until then unknown, had begun to reveal their secrets.

But time lies in coils and folds, and there are moments when one may touch the past as well as the future, which has not yet begun. "It was only a single step," he thought. Or, if the distance was greater it did not extend beyond two nights and the dawn of a new day.

Marcius was now completely quiet. Again, as in Neapolis when he had looked toward the triangular purple sail of Capri, he felt the awe of supreme rulership. But overshadowing it, there was the awareness of another force.

"My friend, I will do my duty!" Surely Longinus' thoughts were turned to him. From his prison cell all his prayers must be for Marcius that his mission might succeed.

But it was not only Longinus whom he felt standing at his side. Almost physically he had the sensation that a greater Friend kept pace with all his steps and would guide his every move. So strong did this certainty become that he did not again ask himself, "How shall I talk, and what shall I say?" when the Imperial Secretary *ad epistulis*, the Senator Gnaeus Domitius, Minister of Petitions, approached and bade Seneca and him to repair to the Presence.

CHAPTER FIFTEEN

A SCENE OPENED before Marcius, like a realistic dream, when one sees whole landscapes with many people in them all at a single glance.

There was a floor of honey-golden alabaster. Columns of the same shade and material rose up to a ceiling richly inlaid with casings of black ebony. The walls shone in deep Pompeian red, unbroken by any ornament, save for a golden mosaic eagle at the far end of the wide hall. Beneath its wings, on a low chair without a back, sat the Emperor Tiberius Caesar. He was clothed in a milk-white toga with the broad purple hem of Roman magistrates. A wreath of golden laurels adorned his brow.

To be suddenly so near to the holder of supreme power cast a spell over Marcius' entire being. He could not formulate any articulate thought, but like iron splinters under the force of a strong magnet his feelings were grouped into a definite pattern.

From this source, as from a mighty beating heart, Power, an indefinable mysterious element, was driven into all the arteries of the world. Fast and undiluted as quicksilver, it ran to all the large and small organs, wherever they might be. Its magic force imposed obedience upon the legions in Gaul, on the Rhine and the Danube, down almost to the sources of the Nile and the border of the Garamantes, in Judea and Syria, and even beyond the Pillars of Hercules, on the never subdued waves of the Ocean, and in the foggy hills of Britannia.

From the great commanders, the proconsuls and legates, to the youngest foreign volunteer the rhythm of life was set by the same will, a will formulated under the wreath of golden laurels. Marcius himself had been part of this great body, and even though he had been detached from it, the magic force of the Emperor's mighty name had carried him smoothly through the vastness of the orbit, to the very source of power.

At Tiberius Caesar's left hand, like the future of the Empire beside its incarnate present, sat a boy, fourteen years old. His hair was the color of old gold, and in his eyes of a warm lively brown there was a golden ring. His forehead, his sensitive mouth, had the noble traits of the Caesars, of Julius, Augustus and Drusus, as they appeared on their many coins and statues. He too was clothed in a milk-white toga with a broad purple hem, but he did not wear it because he was the heir apparent and the Prince of Youth. Purple belonged to him because of boyhood's own dignity, a priestly rank, which called the young sons of Roman houses to fulfill the sacred functions of prayer and sacrifice.

One of the servants had placed the *xenia* on a table of citrus wood. Now from Gnaeus Domitius' lips Marcius heard his name. He felt the gaze of the Emperor's eyes; they were unusually wide and of a shining blue-gray. The consciousness of his own smallness struck him once more, then, as from the scroll which he had read only that morning, the words stood out before him: "Whose are this image and the inscription?" In the hands of Him, there lay, struck in silver, the effigy of Tiberius Caesar—

Freely, without fear, Marcius stepped forward. "Caesar, I am the messenger of the centurion Longinus, commander of Company D, Third Syrian Legion." He took the wax tablets from his tunic. "The Imperial Clemency has bestowed upon him the privilege of asking for a special favor, as recompense for the fulfillment of a simple duty."

The Emperor accepted the tablets and dismissed Gnaeus Domitius and the servants. Seneca was allowed to stay, but he stepped back into the shadow of a pillar near the entrance of the hall.

"I greet you," the Emperor said, and signified to Marcius that he should seat himself opposite the Prince of Youth. Then he broke Longinus' seal.

Marcius' eyes followed the movements of the imperial hands. They were strong and firm, with long sensitive fingers, made to hold a sword or a pen. In contrast to a foppish custom, widespread among men in high positions, of weighing the fingers down with rings, the Emperor wore only a single large ruby on his right hand. As a ray of the setting sun kindled the stone to bright red, Marcius' mind wandered back to the evening light which had fallen on the wax slate when his friend had written on the tablets the last time they were open.

Once more the blue-gray gaze roved over the letters. Then, with a note of indecision, the Emperor passed the tablets back to Marcius. "I have read the message. Now for the key—"

"Seneca warned me not to follow a fixed program," Marcius thought vaguely. He took the tablets and got up. "To Tiberius Caesar Imperator—Greetings!" he read haltingly, the introductory formula. "Marcius Armaghensis comes to submit to the Emperor's Majesty the humble request . . ."

His own name sounded far away, he almost stumbled over the Latinized ending. Who was this Marcius Armaghensis? As if looking at a stranger, he saw Marcius walk beside the centurion Longinus, across a wide round space on the top of a hill. "Mount Golgotha," a voice told him.

When they had reached the edge, the centurion and the young man stopped and looked back. The sun was dipping down behind the mountains of the heroes, the rugged peaks of Gilboa, and its last gleam painted the gigantic shadows of three crosses on the space behind the skull-shaped rock. Under the tallest, in the middle, stood a slender virginal figure, clothed in a sky-blue robe, covered by a veil of dark gray. When the sun had drawn its last rays behind Gilboa, she turned toward the Cross. As if she wanted to take in, once more and forever, the image marked on the blood-stained wood by the holes where the nails had been and the thin lines dug out by the sharp thorns, she looked at this most precious Tree. Then slowly, she walked down to the garden, where her beloved Son was being laid to rest.

The wax slate before Marcius' eyes blurred, and he stopped reading. But engraved in his memory, he found the words of the message as he had received it from his friend, shortly before he had left for Capharnaum.

"What is it," he had asked, when Longinus had given him the tablets, "in case I should by any chance lose them on my long journey?"

The pale haze of dusk had now covered the western sky. Only a tiny spot of rose and yellow above Gilboa still showed where the sun had set. In the east, a broad wall of dark clouds, filled with warm spring rain had thrust itself high above the horizon.

Dimly through his thoughts Marcius saw that the Emperor was still waiting. "I failed to find the key," he heard again, now with a shade of impatience. He wanted to speak, but an imperious gesture interrupted him.

"There have been rumors and contradictory reports," the Emperor said, his speech coming slowly. "Perhaps before we proceed further, I should know the truth."

"The Truth," Marcius repeated. "Caesar, did you command me to report about the Truth?"

The Emperor did not reply. "My words were clear enough," his detached gaze seemed to say. There was a moment of suspense. The golden rings in the eyes of the Prince of Youth widened, as Marcius laid the tablets down at the foot of the curule chair. It almost seemed as if the boy could perceive the light that had been born in the stranger's mind.

A prayer rose in Marcius' heart. "My friend, be with me!" His eyes focused on a distant image. "An unjust judge, Pontius Pilatus, is sitting in Judea in judgment in the Emperor's stead." There was no longer any halting; each word was straight and forceful. "He delivered a just man into the hands of His accusers. I saw this judge seated on a chair of marble. A large eagle behind him spread its wings. Later, after the earth had shaken, I saw the eagle again. It lay shattered on the ground."

Now the words flooded to him, as the waves of a river gush from a hidden spring. "I loved Him. I had followed Him through the courtyards of the Temple. I had been with Him in the streets of Jerusalem, in the land across the Jordan, and the meadows and in the orchards. Twice His eyes rested on me." He paused for a moment, and the changes his thoughts were following in time and mood were almost visible in his face. "During my last week in Jerusalem, when the Jews were celebrating their Easter feast, I was assigned to the centurion Longinus. We became friends, though he did not know Him. But he saw that the Emperor's tribunal was defiled and justice mocked. Yet Pilate had moments when he knew better. I myself heard him say 'King' to the victim; scourged, crowned with thorns, dressed in a shabby scarlet mantle; he even asked Him whence He came. This question could have only one meaning, for Pilate knew that on earth His home was Galilee. Still he condemned Him to be crucified, for he feared Caesar and the people more than he loved God and Justice."

The imperial boy had left his seat. He seized the Emperor's cold hand. "Grandfather," he whispered, "don't you see? Our guest takes us along the same path." Steadfastly he looked at Marcius, whose voice, station by station, conjured up the sorrowful train.

"They could lay hands on a King," he said, and as he stood there it seemed as if the columns of honey-golden alabaster, and the walls of Pompeian red were crumbling under the impact of the howling mob. "They could humiliate one who was sacred and came from above. They were from below. Therefore they liked His abasement, and then they hated themselves all the more. That's why they were so cruel."

He pointed to the east corner of the wide room. "There stood the Cross. It was planted in a skull-shaped rock. I saw His eyes once more before He died. Then the rock gaped wide open, like a wooden block split by an iron ax. Darkness descended on the land. It must have lasted for three hours."

The Emperor had risen from the curule chair. His finely shaped head, with the hair, according to the custom of the Claudian house, falling upon his neck, was held very straight. He stood immobile, and nothing betrayed his feelings. The Prince of Youth still stood at his side. His eyes, with their golden rings were veiled, and his childlike lips trembled. "Here, too, darkness lasted for three hours," he said, though in the presence of men he was not supposed to speak unasked.

The Via Dolorosa was long and the Cross was heavy. None of the soldiers had been permitted to help. So a man from Cyrene, Simon by name, a gardener, who happened to be passing by, helped to shoulder the terrible wood. He had been accompanied by his two young sons, too weak as yet for such a burden. "He is like one of those boys," Marcius thought as he heard Tiberius Gemellus' words. Love, like lightning on a summer night, sprang between him and this child, born to the purple, whose forehead seemed marked by early fulfillment. "Surely, he too would have tried to help," Marcius' thoughts continued.

"During the trial the centurion Longinus was in command of the Fortress Antonia," Marcius went on, aloud. "He wanted to protect the tribunal against the pressure of the mob. When Pilate betrayed justice, he felt that his own honor as a soldier had been disgraced. But he also dreaded Him—he feared that He might truly be God, and thrust the Capitoline Jupiter and all the gods of Rome from their thrones."

The Emperor's hands grasped the arm rests of the curule chair. He raised his head. Perhaps he wanted to speak, to call for his servants. But his lips, half-opened, remained mute.

"I too knew of such prophecies, I had heard them in Judea," Marcius continued. "But Longinus said that a Roman poet had also predicted the birth of a Divine Child, a great Ruler, before Whom the land and the sea, the islands and all the nations would bow, with the return of the Golden Age."

"Virgil's Fourth Eclogue—" Tiberius Gemellus said softly, but he was silenced by the Emperor, who now seemed like a lifeless figure of marble.

"The prophets said that this God would die and rise again. What was meant Longinus could not understand. Neither could I nor anyone else. He must have thought that Pilate was in collusion with a faction of the Jews and was sentencing the victim to death to satisfy the wishes of his enemies, and then have Him removed from the Cross to please his friends. This, Longinus felt, might suffice to fulfill the prophecies which he feared so much. So he set out to prevent it. The sign of shame, which in Golgotha grew like a tree, was not to eclipse the golden eagles."

Never had such words been spoken where Romans held power—words which were treason as well as blasphemy. Yet the Emperor was still motionless; to listen to the end must have required his iron will, the incarnate categoric imperative of duty, as Seneca had called it. He had promised a favor to a man who had helped to save him from grave danger. Now he had asked his messenger to interpret the request. So he was bound by his own word. Never had he broken it.

"If justice was violated, justice will be avenged," he said, his voice almost monotonous. "As a stranger has seen the violation, he may hear of its remedy." The ruby on his right hand had glowed in deep shades as he flexed his fingers. "Our Legate of Syria, Lucius Vitellius, will be instructed to investigate the matter. He will suspend the Governor Pontius Pilate from office and bring him before my tribunal."

"Lucius Vitellius is a good man!" Marcius said with boyish enthusiasm. "I know him, I have served under him!"

The Emperor did not respond. His hand dropped down. "I am still waiting for the key," he said in an impersonal tone.

Marcius withdrew a few steps, and again before his eyes the triad of black, red, and gold in the Emperor's hall submerged beneath the shadows of Mount Golgotha. But superimposed upon this vision was the small room of Gaius Cornelius' house. His host had asked for more credentials, until Longinus' staff, the only one of its kind, had satisfied him. "He once showed me how it works," Cornelius had said, but resolutely Marcius had taken it away from him. "How could I have permitted his handling it," he thought, as the scene faded out.

He raised the staff. "Caesar, the key is this!" Then, as he

had seen his friend do, he pressed two buttons. In his hands, the staff with effortless ease grew to the size of a lance. On its sharp blade drops of blood, dried on the bluish metal, gleamed brighter than the ruby on the Emperor's hand. All the light of the waning day seemed to stream up.

Deep pallor covered his youthful face, and he stood, as if above him there were the right arm of the Cross, under which his friend Longinus had stood. And from afar, unable to intercede, he himself had looked on.

"The soldiers had broken the legs of the two men who were crucified with Him," he said. "But when they came to Him and saw that He was already dead, they did not break His legs." A shudder passed over him, and he closed his eyes. Yet he could still see the bluish scintillating blade of the lance shining in all-pervading clarity. Like a bolt of lightning it flashed through the still air of Golgotha.

As if he were speaking through a dense veil, his voice was muffled in the tricolored room. "The centurion Longinus stepped forth. He seized the lance. With one terrible thrust he pierced the side of the Crucified. Two streams, of blood and of water, gushed from a great wound. They touched the forehead of Longinus and flooded down to earth. In a cavity of the rock, as in a chalice, I saw the blood flower like wine."

With a great effort, Marcius struggled back to the present. "Caesar, what I hold in many hands, this is the lance of the centurion Longinus."

The golden wreath of laurels shone on the Emperor's brow in quiet strength. The gaze of the blue-gray eyes was steady, but it had lost its unmoved hardness. "And where is your friend now?" he asked.

"Caesar, he had enemies, men who hated him because he helped you to destroy Sejanus. After what happened during the trial and on Golgotha they hated him even more. His imperial favor was his only protection. But he chose to stay, and so he sent me as his messenger. Now he is held for court martial. They say he was disloyal." Urgently he added, "But Caesar, you must not believe them."

The Emperor did not seem to hear. "Was he in prison when you left?"

"No, Caesar. I found out afterwards."

"Then you may still change the request. Officially we have not yet taken cognizance of it. Do you desire your friend's freedom, without regard to the merits of his case?"

"Caesar," Marcius replied boldly, "for his freedom my friend does not need a favor. 'The Emperor is just,' he told me before we parted."

This was unheard-of audacity. A shadow passed over the Emperor's face. But, it also was an appeal to the virtue which he cherished most. After a lengthy pause he said: "His case will be placed under Lucius Vitellius' authority. The favor is still his. You have leave to voice it."

Dusk had been creeping into the hall. From the sky the sun had withdrawn its last glimmer, and the sea behind the high window was steel-gray.

Forlorn, Marcius looked at the blade of the lance. It seemed alive with an inner fire, from the hearth of All Love, which it had touched, the sacred heart of the world, in whose very blood all men, past and present, and generations yet unborn had been cleansed.

And for the first time, dimly, he began to sense that the water, which at Capharnaum had touched his forehead, was of the same well as the hallowed stream which had flowed to earth on Golgotha.

His soul was youthful, filled with faith and longing, but still he understood the meaning of his friend's mandate. With his lance Longinus had set the seal of Truth upon the message of Him who had descended from Heaven to suffer, to die, and to trumph for the salvation of men.

"Caesar," he said, "this is the message I have come to bring you." Once more his glance rested on the glistening blade. It seemed to him, as if for the space of a heartbeat, the veils of history were torn asunder: In heaving waves numberless hosts crossed over summer fields, burned by fire. Above the heads of the men flags bearing evil symbols fluttered in a wind that was heavy with the smell of smoke and loud with the cries of the victims. Like an ocean bursting from the abyss, the army flooded forth and battered against a sacred stronghold, defended by a tiny but valorous band of warriors. Again and again, in waves ever renewed, with new banners flying, the hosts came on through endless centuries, and their numbers seemed as countless as the reflections of an archway which stands between two mirrors. Forever the old enemy marshalled his strength and jubilantly expected the fall of the sanctuary.

But within there was held in anointed hands, pointed toward the height of heaven, the Holy Lance, the Lance of the centurion Longinus. From its blade, flaming forth through layers of darkness and desolation, miraculous power came to aid the hard pressed defenders. Bleeding, dying, falling, they yet shielded the Shrine against the onslaught of evil, unbroken and undaunted though the flood would not abate until the end of time.

"This is the message I have come to bring you," Marcius repeated. "The centurion Longinus desires that Caesar may keep this lance among the sacred treasures of the State and that his successors may do the same."

He bent his right knee and held out the lance. Gently it was taken from him. "The centurion's request shall be fulfilled," the Emperor said.

Marcius was still kneeling, when once again the voice from the curule chair reached his ears. "Who was the Man, Whom you saw on the Cross?"

"Death could not slay Him," Marcius replied, taking up the thought that had come to him that night on the Appian Way. "It was He Who slew death." Cornelius' message from the synagogue at Capharnaum returned to his mind, and as he raised himself up and looked full into the Emperor's eyes, he repeated it word for word, "*Resurrexit tertia die, Deus Verus de Deo Vero, Mundi Redemptor, Altissimus Dominus, Jesus Christus.*"

CHAPTER SIXTEEN

LATER ON MARCIUS would remember that the tri-colored hall had suddenly been filled with people, and that Seneca too reëntered his field of vision.

"I shall see the son of King Marke of Armagh at my table an hour and a half from now," the Emperor said. Then Marcius understood that his mission as the messenger of a Roman centurion was completed. From that moment he was on his own, a foreign guest, whom His Majesty had graciously invited to dinner.

A Greek freedman led him to a suite of rooms. In the adjoining bath he patiently submitted to the whole complicated ritual of preparation. From the hot-air cell he moved into the steam room and finally into the chilly *frigidarium.* Only then was he free to plunge into a small pool. As soon as he left it two attendants threw themselves upon him, wrapped him in blankets, and carried him to a couch. "As if I were an old gouty Senator!" he thought. Two other men were busy with his pillow, while a third straightened out his legs, so that he could be comfortable in the prescribed way.

In spite of all this he succeeded in sleeping for about twenty-five minutes. This was a good thing, for it put a definite hiatus between the first part of the evening and the very different second part.

When it was time to dress, he was handed a comfortable robe of blue silk with silver embroidery. "A so-called *synthesis*, my lord," the head-servant explained. "The toga is not worn at dinner." Instead of his shoes, he received sandals of soft gray chamois.

"The guests meet in the atrium," he was told. But there was only Seneca. Nobody else had been invited.

"Your message may have far-reaching consequences," Seneca greeted him, with unusual seriousness. At that moment a majordomo glided up. "Gentlemen," he whispered, and signified that he would show them the way.

They crossed the peristyle. The white Carrara marble of its Ionian colonnades and the red porphyry of the architraves were flooded by the light of many lamps, reflected and magnified by concave metal mirrors. But the jet of the main fountain ascended so high that it shot up out of the light and seemed lost in the dark skies.

Many exquisite sculptures of the Greek Classic period decorated this spacious inner garden. None were more beautiful than Myron's Discobolus and a recent copy of the youthful Apollo, his chlamys over the right arm and the dreaded aegis in his left hand.

Still the majordomo walked on. At the far end of the peristyle was a narrow path, high above the sea. Following it for about two hundred feet, they reached a large vine-covered pergola built on the farthest corner of the protruding flat rock.

There, the Emperor awaited his guests. He too was now wearing a *synthesis*, and instead of the golden bays his forehead was decorated with a wreath of fresh laurels.

Three couches were arranged around an oblong low table of speckled Mauretanian thuja wood. On its open side was a chair for the Prince of Youth. On dressers of veined marble were displayed silver vessels, plates, cups, and sets of golden knives and spoons. Two large candelabra of terra cotta adorned with acanthus ornaments threw a mellow light over the sparkling metal. Each candelabrum had three branches, with twelve flames arranged in clusters. On the dining table stood two tall slender lamps of bronze on tripod bases. Above it, a wrought iron, ring-shaped chandelier with twenty-four flames was suspended by chains. Later, Marcius heard that the wicks of most of these lamps were of asbestos and that they were fed not with olive oil, but with a fuel first described by Herodotus. It came from the Western shores of the Caspian Sea, and, in a curious mixture of Greek and Latin, was now called "petroleum." Due to its high price it had not found entry into many private homes.

While the men reclined on their couches, Tiberius Gemellus said a short prayer: "Father of the Universe, look graciously upon us and upon this table, which is sacred to Thee, and bless these gifts bestowed by Thy bounty. Grant us a contented and tranquil spirit and health of mind and body, that we may live honorably and render to every man his own."

Marcius was given the place of distinction, on the *lectus consularis*, the couch at the lower end of the table. The Emperor took the couch to the left, Seneca the one to the right.

A large silver tray, surmounted by a rack holding many small plates and shells, was placed on the table. This was a so-called repositorium for the hors d'oeuvres. "I didn't forget to start with the eggs this time!" Marcius thought with satisfaction. There were a great variety of salads, artichokes in vinegar, stuffed olives, sardines in oil, cold tuna fish, oysters grown in the Lucrinian lake near Misenum, mushrooms, cold lentils, red beets, and green cucumbers. "Seneca is a good observer," Marcius reflected during this course; the Emperor left most of the things untouched, except for the cucumbers.

A white vermouth and a light Sabinian wine sweetened

with honey were served with the hors d'oeuvres. Slaves with silver finger bowls and linen napkins were in attendance.

The dinner was really very simple, though it was deliciously prepared. The Emperor, who was left-handed, reclined on his right side, thereby facing Marcius. A menu card lay before him. He named the dishes and commented on their origin. No beef was served. To slay oxen, the sacred animal of the paternal Roman farm, the Emperor said, was once regarded as sinful—and sinful it still is! But there was roast pork, mutton and various game with preserved fruits and Spanish quince jelly, black and white chestnuts, and spotted beans. Much of the food was strongly seasoned with Indian red and black pepper, Macedonian parsley, dill, Egyptian majoram and ground mustard seeds.

Asparagus stalks were the only real luxury; and they would not have appeared on the Emperor's table had they not been a present from the town of Ravenna—enormous in size and soft to the very end, so large that three of them must have weighed a whole pound.

According to the custom of the sober days of old, all wine, before being served, was mixed in large stone amphorae with two-thirds of water. Most of the brands were domestic, and the Emperor mentioned the year of the vintage and the places from which they came.

Marcius, even though the Emperor acted as a kind, attentive and paternal host, was far too shy to say much himself. When he did have an opportunity to speak, he asked somewhat awkwardly whether a message could be sent to his father by the imperial "tele-graphos."

The Emperor smiled politely. "Modern youth seems very much interested in technical progress. We shall see what can be done."

During the whole dinner there was only one direct reference to the things which had been discussed in the tricolored hall, and it was Seneca who made it.

"Caesar," he said suddenly, and Marcius noticed that he had lost his courtier's smile, "I may ask for a leave of several months."

"To visit your family?"

"No, Caesar. I should like to journey to Antiochia, as Your Majesty's courier to the legate Lucius Vitellius."

The Emperor's eyes which now had again assumed their unfathomable blue-gray gaze, seemed to express consent.

Marcius felt that a hand was gripping his heart. "The Truth," he thought. "It will conquer. It is conquering already. Of course Seneca will not want to stay in Antiochia! I must give him a letter to Cornelius." He laughed happily to himself. "Think of it! For me to be giving Seneca a letter of introduction!"

When the dishes and trays of the main course had been cleared away, a servant brought in Marcius' *xenia*. They were still wrapped in their silken kerchiefs.

"How very thoughtful of you, my young friend," the Emperor said, obviously surprised, when Marcius had explained the nature and the hidden qualities of the *te*. The pot, however, gave him as much genuine delight as Seneca had foreseen.

"An exquisite, a truly unique, piece of art, more precious than a vessel of pure gold. And certainly much more beautiful!"

"But, Caesar, it must never be used for anything else but the *te!*" His boyish simplicity got the better of him. "I was warned of the Great Dragon and his youngsters. But it would be even worse if one took the *te* with milk or cream. Only the black-skinned, low-caste Indians do."

The Emperor could not help smiling. "Perhaps one might fall prey to the dragon of bad taste? Since you know all the rules, why don't you yourself prepare the first *te* for the Ta-Tsinian brother of the Grand King of Sinae?"

Servants handed glass balls to the guests to cool their hands, and then the dessert was served. It consisted of little strawberry tarts, marron glacé, candied plums, peaches, apricots and pistachio nuts, green and purple figs and pears from Numidia, cherries, medlars, and apples. There were several large round fruits, greenish yellow, with net-like tracings. Their flesh was juicy, with a sweet, aromatic taste. "They come from the Oxus and Jaxartes rivers, deep in Central Asia," the Emperor explained, "Lucius Vitellius was successful in transplanting them to Campania. He calls them 'melons'."

When the dessert was finished, a young Greek scholar entered the pergola, and at once Tiberius Gemellus rose. "Aristides, his pedagogue," Seneca said. The imperial boy bade his grandfather and the guests good night. But when he came to Marcius, he said, "I should so much like to see you again."

The Emperor tenderly kissed the boy's forehead. "My child," he said, "you shall see your friend whenever he has the time."

A charcoal brazier, with a kettle suspended to catch the heat, was brought in. "We are waiting for our first *te*," the Emperor said. All the servants filed out, and for a few minutes nothing could be heard but the softly singing steam and the irregular beat of the waves of the sea lapping against the foot of the flat rock. But even while Marcius repeated half-aloud the rules: "One spoon for each cup, one for the pot," he began to feel restless.

Then, as he was pouring the boiling water into the dragon-patterned pot, he heard Tiberius Caesar's voice, "Your *xenia* are very precious. Won't you tell me whether you have any particular desire which I might fulfill?"

Before Marcius' eyes came the memory of Nerva's emaciated face and mockingly the words sounded in his ears: "If you desire the vanities of life, grasp the moment! Don't let the chance you have when in the imperial presence slip by!" So now the moment had come. But he could think of nothing he desired. The only thing which mattered, his friend's freedom, was already taken care of. . . . Was there really nothing he could ask of the Emperor? Yes, there was something. Now he knew and he wondered only why he had not thought of it at once.

Slowly he poured the steaming drink into the three cups. An ugly feeling of fear crept into his heart. "What is wrong, my friend?" the Emperor said, but Marcius overlooked the question. Instead of returning to his couch, he sat down on the chair which Tiberius Gemellus had vacated.

"A delicious drink!" two voices said.

"I think it's very good," he replied, and sipped from his cup. Gradually his composure returned, and the weakness of his will gave way to an almost reckless decisiveness of purpose. Still he did not speak. He looked into the amber-colored liquid and watched two *te* leaves until they settled on the bottom of the cup. What he wanted to say alternately appeared to him very easy and at the same time foolishly impossible.

The Emperor had raised himself to a sitting position. The blue-gray gaze rested on his young guest.

"What is wrong, my friend?" he repeated.

Marcius got up. His movements had the stiff assurance of a man walking in his sleep. But he knew precisely what he was doing, and because he had to do it he felt fear no longer.

Silence was around him and was in his soul. Deep down there was a voice saying, "—for the sake of Love."

From the inner pocket of his tunic he took the chrysoprase ring and, in his outstretched open hand, held it before the Emperor.

"Caesar," he said, "grant mercy to the man who owned it." His heart leapt and raced wildly. Stumbling and stammering he added, "Grant mercy to all!"

It seemed to him as if the man to whom he spoke, the table, the many slender flames of the candelabra, the whole world around him, had drawn away from him in a rapid spiral movement.

He stood again in the cavelike shop where he had first looked at this ring with its prongs of yellow gold and its Oriental emeralds. "A charm?" he had asked.

"Yes, a charm, and a deadly one too."

Now the full meaning of these words began to dawn on him. Hidden in this gem was the secret of Sejanus' friends, and perhaps also the secret of those who had been instrumental in the killing of Drusus, the Emperor's only son. Through the translucent stone of pale apple-green, as in a magnifying drop of water or in a magic crystal, could be seen all those whom the courts, the informers, the agents, the whole dreaded network of the secret police had vainly tried to track down in the last two years.

The violent and futile chase was still on. Private revenge, vile lust for gain, blackmail, and unhappiness held sway. The sword of false accusations was suspended over the heads of many, as by a thin thread. None could feel secure in his innocence.

Marcius caught a glimpse of Seneca. Under the tan, his face glowed white with terror. His friendly association with a man who had owned that ring, could be seized upon by his enemies. Surely he had many in Herod Agrippa's and Caligula's entourage.

As for the Emperor, Marcius could not see him. He only felt his presence. It was the Presence not of an attentive and paternal host, but of unalloyed power, impersonal and awesome.

Still there was no fear in Marcius' soul, even though through this ring death stared at him more closely than it ever had done on the field of battle. A word, a gesture to the praetorian guards would suffice–

But while he stood dauntless he summoned all his strength to withstand the terrific impact of the Power. It was intangible, yet it threatened to overwhelm his very personality.

"Who gave you this ring?" he heard, as from afar.

"I purchased it."

"For whom?"

"For a child. She is waiting for me on an island out in the Britannic Sea."

"What did you give for it?"

Marcius hesitated for a moment. "Twenty aurei more than anyone else would." He felt his strength growing. "I have seen gold pieces of different coinage. All have the head of Tiberius Caesar. But on their reverse, some have the Roman she-wolf. Others, minted in memory of Your Majesty's mother, have the head of the Empress Livia, and the words *Pietas et Clementia*."

The tension around him began to relax. Still searchingly, but less remote, more human, the Emperor's voice asked, "Do you know what it is?"

"It is Domna Apicata's gem."

"Did you know its meaning?"

"No, Caesar." The beach at the Villa Ciceronis lit up before him in the gay sunlight of morning. "But I saw some children at play, Caesar. And what they were playing was called the 'investigation game'—a ghastly game of cruelty. There may have been real informers among the ringleaders. A boy hardly younger than the Prince of Youth, was the main victim. Unknowingly he may have given away his own parents. To-morrow he may be an orphan." His voice became pleading; it sounded as if he were speaking in behalf of his own little brothers. "Caesar, do you see? Everywhere children may have been driven into that wicked game. Soon no Roman boy will dare to play. How can a country be happy where boys don't dare to play?" With pride he added: "At home it is different. Among my father's subjects, young and old, no one ever needs to fear."

"In your country there is no treason. No one is plotting against your father's life."

"Because he is mild and forgiving, Caesar." Tears came into Marcius' eyes, and his hand, whch had so bravely held the ring, trembled. "Caesar," he said, almost choked with emotion, "grant mercy, for the love of the Crucified."

Through the veil which covered his vision, the light as of flame broke through again. "Keep it," the Emperor said mildly and touched his hand. Then he dismissed him.

It was well after midnight when Marcius, alone, returned to the Villa Ciceronis. But before daybreak he was awakened by a courier with a letter from the Emperor. "Forgiveness will be proclaimed throughout the land," Marcius read, "You may tell the children that they can return to their play."

A draft for five hundred aurei was enclosed. "We want you to pay the former owner of the ring its real value. The balance may cover your stay and your journey to Hibernia. But we trust that you will not be leaving us too soon. Our grandson is in need of a brave and loyal friend."

CHAPTER SEVENTEEN

IMMEDIATELY after breakfast Marcius began to make a budget. It was no easy task, with such high figures and the complicated Roman numbers. He had had a sneaking suspicion recently—Cornelius must have paid him a sum much higher than the value of his gold dust.

"The *Acta Diurnia* might tell," he decided and looked up the price of gold. He blushed. "I have been spending Cornelius' money all the time. I must repay him at once."

Something else occurred to him. "Should I not return to Hibernia at once? I have discharged my mandate; that was all I was expected to do. Cornelius warned me not to undertake too much. 'Others will come,' he said."

"But the Emperor wants me to stay," he replied to his doubts. He read again the last paragraph of the imperial letter. "Perhaps the sentence only means that he is very courteous. The money for my return journey may be a hint."

He brushed his scruples aside. "I don't see what harm it can do for me to stay here for the summer." He thought of the two Cornelii whom he had not looked up yet, and of the Prince of Youth. It would certainly be an important time, not merely a pleasant one. "I can't leave things half finished," he added resolutely.

He whistled a gay tune as he went to the stable. "Everything is shaping up nicely, Pomponius!"

From the office of Titus P. Atticus he went to the cavelike shop. Somewhat incoherently he told the gnome why he had come and what he wanted him to do. Then, as if he were building a toy city, he paid a hundred and eighty aurei on the counter, piling them up in many shining reddish turrets.

"Tell the town councilor that he need have no fear," he shouted gaily and rushed out. In the street it seemed to him as if everyone looked freer and happier. He bounded along. "Even the air feels different!" he thought.

The man at Pomponius' parking place received a whole denarius, and then Marcius galloped down the coastal road, leaving the marble palaces far behind him. He did not return to the Villa Ciceronis until supper time. There he found that with his blue Macedonian chlamys the robe he had worn at the imperial table had also been sent to him. In a separate box was the white toga, and to receive it for permanent use from the Emperor's hands meant that the status of a Roman citizen had been bestowed on him.

"Our third evening under the eucalyptus tree may well be our last," Seneca said the next evening as they walked out into the garden.

It was a dark night, with pale summer lightning showing on the horizon of the sea, a somewhat anxious night, and Marcius said that he wished Seneca would not leave so soon.

"It can't be helped. I must go to Rome first. Then I'll take a through car to Brundisium. There I can get some fast naval vessel to Corinth. The crossing should not take more than three days. From Cenreae, on the eastern side of the Isthmus I take a boat directly to Antiochia. That would save a week or more, compared to your voyage around Italy."

"I must give you a letter to Gaius Cornelius!" Marcius smiled impishly. "You won't find him an old fogey, I trust."

"You are certainly not one who forgets a grudge!"

"I was only joking."

"There are no jokes," Seneca said, with a shade of sententiousness. "Jokes always express what people really mean."

They sat down on the garden bench. "The Emperor wants an exhaustive report, so Gaius Cornelius may prove very helpful." He touched Marcius' shoulder. "I understand why you did not want to talk before you had seen His Majesty. But now—could you tell me everything that was left unsaid during the audience?"

Marcius leaned back, and his eyes fastened on the few clouded stars up in the high trees. "I will try," he said, and before his mind arose the white and golden cupola of the great sanctuary as he had seen it from the height of the Fortress Antonia.

"One day I was walking through the outer courtyards," he began. "Surrounded by a group of friends or disciples, I saw a Man—"

Haltingly, his story unfolded. But though at first the inner and outer worlds seemed interlaced in his speech and his longing for the Great Garden, the tales of the priests in Hibernia, and the faint images preserved from the Promise given to all men were superimposed upon the meadows and orchards of Judea, slowly the One Whose name he was too reverent to mention emerged in ever greater clarity.

In the tricolored hall, Marcius had spoken of the trial and the consummation on the skull-shaped rock. Rapturously he had been carried along from station to station, like a wanderer through the night, who grasps for the bright ribbons which the lightning throws across his path.

Now, his feelings were withdrawn and almost unemotionally he restricted himself to the bare recital of events. He wove into his eyewitness account some significant passages from Cornelius' scrolls—the raising of Lazarus at Bethany, and the Master's words, "I am the Resurrection and the Life."

Briefly he mentioned his ride to Capharnaum. During the audience with the Emperor he had stated the facts of the Great Triumph. Now he described the entire course of the service in the synagogue. Every detail and all of Cornelius' words had remained firmly engraved in his memory.

There were long intervals between the pulse of thought and speech, but Seneca never interrupted. Finally, after nearly two hours, Marcius stopped. "I have told you everything," he said. A naive, almost helpless smile was on his lips, the smile of a young boy who has become aware that he is talking to a grown-up.

Minutes passed, and Seneca was still silent. "That the body is the tomb of the soul the Greek philosophers well knew," he finally said. "Plato spoke of the recompense of the just and virtuous, which here on earth can never be perfect. Freedom and happiness must wait until the fetters of the body are broken. The day of death is the birthday of eternity. Afterward no shadows will disturb the light of everlasting serenity."

"Did you learn that from the Hebrew Scriptures?"

"They only confirmed my belief."

"But you held it before?"

"Yes. You will find it in my writings. You spoke of the Promise given to all men. We might call it a pristine revelation. We carry within us a notion of our origin and of our ultimate goal. Some great spirits, such as Socrates, Plato and Pythagoras, may have seen more clearly still. They were illumined by the eternal Logos. But seeds of it, a *logos spermatikos*, as the Stoics say, are in every man who comes into this world."

No one else was in the garden, and the hour was so late that in the Villa the servants must have retired long ago. Yet Seneca's voice sank to a whisper as he continued. "You have heard of the Eleusinian Mysteries? Like all other rites of initiation they aim at giving to the adept a knowledge of the deathless life of the soul, by leading it through the realm of death." A deep excitement trembled in his measured words. "The candidate must submit to a three-day trial by fire, sword and water. While his body rests in deep sleep, he passes into the spirit world. There he learns that death is the one compensation for the calamity of birth. The Egyptians, Plato's teachers, practiced most elaborate rites. But no people, high or low, is without some traces. Yet all these mysteries are imperfect, and have gathered more imperfections, as time moved on. Men perform them, men misuse them. And everything is very secret, a hidden path for the happy few. There is no greater crime than to 'betray' those secrets! The poet Aeschylus almost suffered the supreme penalty, because allegedly he revealed on the stage what had been shown to him at Eleusis."

"What has this to do—"

"Don't you see? Throughout the ages men have been longing for the One, the unique and perfect Initiator, who would overcome death by his own power and throw the mysteries of life open to all."

"Do you mean the Great Garden?" Marcius asked, under his breath.

"The name does not matter." He noticed Marcius' troubled face. "You have faith, while I am a skeptic and a speculator," he continued gently. "The raising of Lazarus, in the full light of day, sounds to me like a new Mystery, but one which demands no secrecy. And the whole of your Master's life, death and triumph would seem to bear the marks of the initiate Initiator."

Marcius rallied. "You see how important it is?"

"So important that future ages may envy us as contemporaries of the unveiling. What struck me most were the words: 'I am the Resurrection and the Life.' Only the incarnate Logos could use such speech. So if there is a foundation to it, it would indeed signify the reconciliation between man and the Absolute. It would be a divine life which we receive passing through the new initiation. No longer 'I,' but the Logos, living in me, the same, in whom daily we die and rise again."

"You will report to the Emperor when you come back?"

"Of course. But, though to a lesser degree, he, too, is a skeptic, his mind is almost as speculative as mine."

"So Truth has not convinced him yet!" Marcius exclaimed.

"He wants to have it reaffirmed."

"But Truth simply *is*."

"Your young friend, the imperial prince, seems to share that view."

"What will happen if the Emperor becomes convinced?"

"He may bring the matter before the Senate."

Marcius jumped up. "It's all going to happen, I know it is!" Then he calmed down. "Will it take very long?"

"It depends on what you call 'long.' Tomorrow is the first of June. By the middle of the month I may be in Antiochia. I could leave for Italy by the middle of August. The Senate will still be in recess when I come back. Its first regular meeting is on October first."

"I had hoped that before this month was up—" Marcius said despondently. Half-afraid that it might sound childish, he stopped. "That they would beat the swords into ploughshares," he ended.

Seneca did not smile. "You would not want a conquest which overrides our most precious gift, the freedom of the human will?"

Marcius did not grasp the meaning of the words. All that

he drew from the reply was that his way of reasoning may not have been too much off the track.

"Until recently I never thought of death, because life all around us is so great. When I was a boy, I loved to run away from my father's house. I would lie in the grass for hours and watch the stars and the fireflies." Marcius' voice had assumed a dreamy tone. "I often felt sorry that I had no little brother. I wanted to show him all my friends up there." The scruples which he had had in the morning came back to him. "Perhaps I should be returning to Hibernia at once. If I saddled Pomponius tomorrow, I might reach Armagh before the end of summer."

"That is for you to decide," Seneca said, evasively.

But something must have happened to Marcius' desire to return to his father's roof. Perhaps it was not quite as strong or as genuine as he himself had seemed to believe.

"Don't you think the Emperor meant it when he said that I shouldn't be leaving too soon?" he asked, and his voice was anxious.

"I am sure he did," Seneca replied as evasively as before. He thought for a while. "Tiberius Gemellus could really do with an older friend."

Marcius breathed, deeply relieved. "But he'll find me very uneducated. With his fourteen years he probably knows so much more than I with my twenty."

"That shouldn't worry you. What he needs is comradeship and guidance."

"If I can help protect him against Herod and Caligula I'll do it gladly!"

"You must be very careful in everything you say and do," Seneca replied, obviously uneasy. "Otherwise, you may stir up a hornet's nest of intrigues."

"I won't be talking to anyone when you are gone. I'll spend

all my free time reading the books in the library, or at least some of them."

"Reading is one way to keep out of trouble. I must send you an appropriate list: Plato, Varro, some history, the better known lyric poets, and for a change some natural science, Archimedes, Strabo—"

"I have always been rather weak in mathematics."

"You should try to catch up, though in my opinion modern schools are putting too much emphasis on it. What should be an instrument of mental training, has become an end-in-itself. 'Youth should be educated vocationally' is the latest slogan of our technical age. As if we were not humans, but ants or bees! A horrible departure from paideia, the forming of boyhood through wisdom and virtue, which will lead to a general deterioration of philosophical interests."

"A bank clerk was saying to me this morning, 'Sending money by light letter will speed up business and make life really enjoyable,'" Marcius remarked.

"In a way, it really would. Think what it would mean to flash help around the world in times of distress. I am not opposed to technical progress as such, only to what it may do to our souls."

"How do you mean?"

"It's simple enough. If people gave thought to the nature of things and to their proper categories of values, new discoveries would neither shock them nor make them supercilious. But since they know so little, they may soon believe that they know too much to need the Divine. 'The Roman rules the world,' Horace could still say, 'because he walks humbly before the gods.' This is no longer true. The men of our time are little concerned because they know nothing about the source of all knowledge, the Infinite, while the knowledge of finite things has steadily increased. Soon it may be regarded as a mark of the highest intelligence to 'prove' that it is not even possible to know the Infinite. Our very souls have thereby become futile phantoms of finiteness, mirrors upon which fall—as in Plato's parable of the cave—only shadows, only phenomena—"

"Are people really coming to that?" Marcius asked, more and more disturbed.

"They are well on their way to it." He made a gesture toward the sea where the lightning had become stronger. "That is a mysterious power, dangerous and so far destructive. Yet it may be the same which Thales of Miletus has described six hundred years ago, and which the Greeks call *electron.* One day it may be tamed and put to human use. Then, and when light and sound are our servants, so that we can see and talk through mountains and across the sea, when my imaginary continent will be our neighboring land, and when our eyes may penetrate into the structure and secrets of the stars and of matter, Democritus' atoms, then, my young friend, the age of true and unmitigated barbarism will be at hand!"

"Oh no!" Marcius said with horror. "Some men would always remember that God became Man."

"I love to speculate on the question, Marcius."

"Why must you speculate? What I told you is true." He hesitated. "On our first evening together you spoke quite differently."

"Did I say that we cannot love God, and hence not know Him? Don't you understand, Marcius? I myself am torn between two feelings." He got up. "You still have a letter to write, so you had better start soon. It must be two in the morning."

Silently they walked to the house. In the atrium Marcius turned to Seneca. "I think you just like to disturb me," he said. "The more you sweep me off my feet, the more you enjoy yourself. But I'd be glad if you had time to do it again."

"Shall I return the compliment?" Seneca replied with feigned sarcasm. "You would think that I was making jokes. But remember what I said about jokes."

Marcius thought of no answer. His Hibernian wit deserted him. "I must go and write my letter," he said, "but for the spelling I won't be responsible."

"Never mind the spelling," Seneca replied, and then, warmly, they shook hands.

CHAPTER EIGHTEEN

THE OLD COUPLE who were caretakers of the Villa Ciceronis spoiled Marcius as if he were their own son. The six slaves served him gladly; he always said "please" and was neither condescending nor too intimate. But there was one man, Tiro the librarian, who soon became Marcius' trusted adviser. Of Greek stock, he was a descendant of Cicero's devoted secretary and friend, and mentor of his son Marcus during his university years. Cicero had freed this elder Tiro in his will, but later all provisions made by the hapless orator had been declared null and void. Yet, the librarian could have received his freedom years ago had he not disdained to ask for something which he considered was by natural law his own.

Tiro knew exactly what books to read and what editions were the most authentic. He noticed that Marcius could never concentrate for long; so when he was tired of reading, the old librarian would take time to tell Marcius about men and events connected with the deeds of Julius Caesar and of Augustus—a period of history of which he had many personal and family recollections. In turn, he was eager to listen to Marcius' description of conditions in Hibernia, and finally, as their friendship deepened, of the events in Judea.

The association with Tiro soon proved of a further and unexpected advantage. In the second week after Seneca's departure Marcius received word from Aristides that on the following morning he was expected at the cottage where Tiberius Gemellus was living. He was just going out when this letter arrived, so he was wearing his white toga, of which he was very proud. He was still holding the parchment in his hands when, through the high windows of the library, he saw an elegant carriage drive up to the main entrance. An instant later one of the servants brought in a man somewhat exotically dressed.

"My name is Eutychius," he said and bowed three times. "My master, the noble lord Herod, son of the son of King Herod, is waiting in the atrium. He has come to pay his respects to the son of King Marke of Armagh."

"His Highness will be glad—" Tiro replied to the amazement of Marcius, who never before had been referred to by such a title.

"I don't like this visit," Marcius whispered when Eutychius had backed out. "Quick, how shall I address him?"

"Call him 'dear cousin.' You are younger, yet he can't reciprocate. That will put him in his place."

"Cousin—that man?"

"It is courteous, and designates your precedence. Such things are important to Orientals."

"All right. Well, I am counting on you!" Marcius replied, while Eutychius and another courtier were pompously drawing the curtains aside.

Herod Agrippa was a youngish-looking man of about forty. He wore a silken gown of heliotrope blue, with wide sleeves over a loosely girdled tunic of white satin. Medium-sized and heavy-set, he wore shoes with heels two and half inches high. His flabby upper arms were covered with broad golden bands. The stones of his many rings shone with all the colors of the rainbow. A narrow black beard rimmed his face and chin, though every hair was carefully plucked from his upper lip. His mouth stood out very red, as if he used cosmetics.

His complexion was of a livid white, with spots of pink on his cheek bones.

Smiling, he paused in the entrance long enough to size up this young man about whom there had been so much talk lately. "A chip off the same block as the tetrarch, anyone could see that!" Marcius thought, and then he too smiled. It had just occurred to him that the stones of the rings might come from a shop in town which sold "genuine imitations." He'll replace them by real ones, if the Little Boot should become Emperor and make him king.

Tiro stepped forth. "His Highness's surprise is as great as his happiness," he said.

Herod smiled still more and advanced a few steps. Then, to Marcius' utter confusion, he opened his arms and kissed him on both cheeks.

"Welcome to a friend of my beloved country!"

"It's a very beautiful country," Marcius replied, and made a clumsy gesture, inviting his guest to sit down on one of the high-backed easy chairs. Tiro, meanwhile told the house slave to bring in some refreshments.

Herod sighed. "Beautiful, yes. But in unworthy hands."

"Not for much longer."

This was a clear enough reference to the expected change in the governorship of Judea, and a perhaps unintentional rebuff to any Herodian aspirations.

Herod Agrippa chose to ignore it.

"I mean the man who happens to be my uncle and the husband of my beloved sister Herodias. His influence will be felt, whoever represents the Emperor at Caesarea."

"An outsider should never take sides in a family dispute," Marcius said politely. But it seemed to Herod that his deprecatory remark about the tetrarch had caused a favorable impression.

"Family, family!" he said more warmly. "How can one still talk of a family! It was the tetrarch who incited my grandfather to put my father Aristobolus and his brother Alexander to death. Naturally, since the tetrarch's mother was a low-born Samaritan woman, while my grandmother Mariamne was of the Hasmonean house." His voice assumed a tone of resigned sadness. "Now, the last heirs of the Hasmoneans must spend their days in exile—

"My grandmother Mariamne, too, was executed upon the instigation of the tetrarch," Herod Agrippa went on, watching the effect of his remarks on his impressionable young listener.

Marcius was unable to give a reply, but he shuddered as all these bloody spectres marched before him. Perhaps Herod Agrippa had been slandered by his uncle, the tetrarch? Perhaps he was just an unhappy and haunted man, and not a shrewd schemer, as Cornelius had said was a widespread opinion—

"I can see how you feel, and I thank you for it," Herod said. "As matters stand it may turn out a good thing after all that for the last twenty-seven years Judea has been an imperial province, while the tetrarch had had to content himself with Galilee and Perea."

"He himself does not think so," Marcius replied. Now the tetrarch's behavior during the trial appeared to him in a new light. "He would do anything to become king."

"But the people?" Herod asked. "What do they think of him?"

"The people!" Bitterness bordering on contempt tinged Marcius' voice. The day on which he had met Longinus returned to his mind, a beautiful day, all blue and gold. From the height of the Fortress Antonia they had looked down on the huge multitudes in the outer courtyards of the Temple.

Thousands upon thousands, clad in festive robes, and with palm branches and flowers in their hands had gone out of Jerusalem to greet Him and to escort Him back on his triumphal entry into the city.

Then, while the trembling air of high noon had spun a haze before Marcius' eyes, a chant, ever swelling in volume, had risen to the sunfilled sky. Questioningly, he had turned to Longinus, who translated the Hebrew words of the greeting into Latin:

"Hosannah to the Son of David, hosannah to him who comes in the name of the Lord."

Yet, only five days were to pass, and in Marcius' ears there would resound the terrible cries, "Let him be crucified!" and "His blood be upon us and upon our children!" They were shouted by the same people from whose lips, so shortly before, had streamed the great Hosannah to their King and Master.

But another feeling rose uppermost. Led by venal priests unworthy of their office, torn by factional strife, a pawn in the power game of the great, the people had been driven into betraying itself and its own mission of salvation. And while thousands, pitiful slaves of darkness, had blasphemously cried out, saying that the blood of an Innocent should fall upon their unborn sons, others had stood forth in shining heroism, anointed with the signs of divine election.

From that same people had arisen the Woman who in a sky-blue robe, covered by a dark-gray veil, had stood under the Cross. The loyal Eleven, the men of Capharnaum, and certainly countless others of the same blood—they all were numbered among the elect.

"The people," Marcius repeated, now with love and compassion. "The best among them know that they have been bereft of their King."

His face was like an open book, in which Herod Agrippa could read at ease.

"I know everything," he said. "Such a king can never return." There was a sob in his voice. "All we humans can do is provide for decent administration, to safeguard the religious freedom of the country, and prevent a vile murderer from climbing still higher in the Emperor's favor."

The slave brought in trays with wine and fruits, and while the table was laid, there were a few moments of commotion. This was fortunate, for Herod's words had been too startling —they could refer only to Him. Through direct intelligence from Judea and through many channels at the imperial household, Herod was, of course, well informed. But he was the last man from whom Marcius would have expected a profession of faith. "He wants to be king one day, so naturally he will be most unsympathetic to your report," Cornelius had warned.

Tiro sensed that Marcius' feelings were heading towards dangerous cliffs. "His Highness is pondering your words, my lord," he interposed. "He wonders whether you would care to explain."

A gleam of discontent came into Herod's eyes. "There are two spheres," he said. "One is spiritual. The governor should never have dragged it into the political arena, while the tetrarch acted like a wicked fool when he looked upon the movement as a menace to his ambitions and pretensions. The other is the sphere of this world, something entirely different, even though indirectly it may serve the things which really matter. A well and justly governed people has more leisure to occupy itself with the realm of the spirit and reach the higher meaning of life."

His words continued to flow in softly undulating sentences. But a feeling of uneasiness had come over Marcius. Silently he peeled an apple, while his face was as bland as if there were nothing more important to him than to produce one single unbroken spiral of skin.

"In a way, there was a system of checks and balances that was more or less sound," Herod said. "The frictions between the governor and the tetrarch always enabled the imperial overlord to see things in the right perspective. This has changed. First we hear that these two men have become friends, and now His Majesty's justified indignation may remove the governor from office. Will this not leave the tetrarch supreme—a man without any legitimate claim to the country?"

Pensively, Marcius looked at his apple. "So the Hasmoneans would have a better claim?" he asked with his most winning smile. "Tell me, dear cousin, 'Hasmonean' doesn't happen to be another name for 'House of David'?" Apologetically he added: "I am very weak in history. But some day, with friend Tiro's help, I hope to do better."

Herod's eyes shifted nervously. He was not sure whether this was the admission of an appalling ignorance or a provocation. He decided to reply in a matter-of-fact tone.

"The Hasmoneans rose to fame two centuries ago, in the fight for national liberation against the pagan kingdom of Syria. They restored the customs of our forefathers, cleansed and rebuilt the Temple, and for generations exercised a powerful rule."

"Yes, of course! Judas Maccabeus—" Marcius said, as if his memory were returning.

"He was the great hero of the original resistance movement. The house descends from his brother Simon. Its claims passed through Mariamne to my son and me, who are the last of the line."

"But the House of David is different?"

"I just explained." He suppressed his impatience. "Today the House of David is nothing but a name. Its sons are simple people who live by the toil of their hands. They are small craftsmen, artisans, and carpenters."

"His Highness can hardly feel that outward circumstances could ever lower the status of a ruling house."

Gratefully Marcius looked at Tiro. Such an answer would probably not have occurred to him simply because it was too obvious. "My father always recognizes a king when he sees one," he had said to Longinus during the trial. He had only been surprised that a man like Pilate had not been misled by the humiliation, the scorn and the wounds inflicted upon the royal Victim.

His suspicion was now fully aroused. With his friend Pilate on his way out, Herod probably thought that the time to remove the tetrarch was now or never. The tetrarch was certainly an evil man, but the range of his wickedness was somewhat limited by his laziness and indolence. This man, his nephew, was far more clever, and in spite of his effeminate appearance he probably possessed a good deal of energy. That he so far had been guilty only of a few cases of private cheating might be ascribed to his lack of power. Should he become king, things would change, and for the people concerned the new rule might be worse than the old.

"Somewhere I think I read," Marcius said, "that the throne of David would remain forever and that of his Son's kingdom there would be no end."

"Spiritually, spiritually!" Herod replied hastily, and seemed to feel that something in the interview was going wrong.

Spiritually. Marcius considered the word. The man who had used it was the same one who had put into Caligula's head notions of a most blasphemous nature, the Emperor a divine being, a man as God! "Such a conflict would shake the foundations of the world," Cornelius had said–meaning if belief in Him were declared incompatible with loyalty toward the State. Here, then, was a terrific danger, which he so far had not fully realized. The government of the God-Emperor would bear down with its full power upon all the believers. The case of Longinus would become the general precedent, and there would be no just and humane authority to set the victims free.

The abyss of hell seemed to open before him. Cornelius, Elon, and the others, that whole small community, could easily be crushed under the weight of the most monstrous machine of power which the world had ever seen. In the blood of the witnesses the flame of their souls would be extinguished.

Then, a telling symbol of the triumph of evil, Herod Agrippa as vice-regent of the "god" Caligula, would set himself up as a self-styled divinity to rule over Jerusalem, over the hallowed meadows and orchards, even over the skull-shaped rock.

This rock had opened like the gates of the Great Garden. If all these evils should come to pass, its sides might come together again and the wide entry would close once more–forever.

But as Marcius' thoughts moved swiftly on, taking no more than a fraction of a second, it seemed to him that a new and greater mission had been laid upon his shoulders. Never must Caligula ascend the throne of the Caesars. It was Tiberius Gemellus, the high-souled boy with the pure eyes and forehead, who alone might avert defeat. And he, Marcius Armaghensis, was to be his champion and standard-bearer!

He looked at the round, whitish fingers of his guest. The rings were set in swollen flesh as on cushions of cotton. "Such a king can never return!" he had said. How false was the tone of these words! The belief of others in a restored and timeless Kingship would serve Herod's personal ends, to build up a rule of desecration against that Kingship itself.

"What exactly do you want?" he asked, his inner horror welling up into his voice.

Herod did not reply at once. His unctuous mien began to peel off, like the masks which Greek actors, in quick succession, hold before their faces. Though the changes are made before the eyes of the spectators, it may take several minutes before the audience becomes aware that the tragedian has vanished and the comedian had taken his place.

With a gesture, Herod dismissed Eutychius. Apparently he expected Marcius to do the same with Tiro. He waited for a few seconds, then he accepted the situation. Pasted upon his over-red mouth was a sly smile, the satisfied smile of a broker who feels quite certain that his deal will go through.

"The uncle-nephew relationship, of all family bonds and combinations, is the most unfortunate," he said. "I should know! And in the second generation it is scarcely different."

The implication was obvious. The Little Boot was the Emperor's grand-nephew. But he did not press the point.

"You will see His Majesty's grandson, the young Tiberius Caesar, tomorrow," he went on. "A most promising boy, as our esteemed court philosopher, Lucius Annaeus Seneca, would say. I hear that he was fascinated by your report about my little corner of the world. So perhaps Judea would profit greatly from a rule guided by a friend and by a philosopher." His eyes twinkled. "I may have to join my prayers to those who wish for his succession to the Empire."

Marcius' bewilderment had been growing. Herod changing sides? Surely he must know that Tiberius Gemellus would never lend himself to the insane temptations that were so inviting to Caligula's unbalanced mind.

"It's a very small corner in which I am interested," Herod continued quietly, "but, frankly, it is not one of the poorest. Even after paying all Roman taxes, the ruler of the united kingdom of Judea, Galilee, Perea, and Trachonitis would have an annual income of at least twelve million drachmas." Smirking, he folded his hands. "How much good one could do with this money! One could even support the things that really matter!" He licked his lips and sucked the words in, as if they were oysters on the half shell. "Twelve million drachmas! At the present rate of exchange that means roughly four hundred and eighty thousand aurei, or forty-eight million sesterces. And of course, with such expectations reasonably assured, one's credit is practically unlimited!" Softly he added: "The young Caesar of course, has all the riches of the world. Yet, his name must first have become an office. Point out any Senator you want, beginning with Claudius, His Majesty's much underrated nephew. I know most of them personally, or at least, I know their income, as balanced against their expenditures and debts. So you see, I could really be of some service."

Marcius' confusion had become complete. This was an insolent offer extended to the imperial youth. It also meant a conditional renunciation of the evil schemes of God-Empire. Had his visions of terror been nothing but the product of unbridled fantasy? But there still remained the suggestion of an unsavory pact, which would disgrace the name of the young heir.

"I can either pass it over or throw him out bodily," he thought with mounting rage.

Before he could answer one way or the other, Herod got up.

"I must be going now." He fanned his face with a little batiste kerchief. "My masseur will be waiting. Do let me know when you have time to come for dinner. I would be *so* sorry if I did not hear from you, let's say, within the next two weeks—"

"People told me about your big dish with all the surprises," Marcius replied, to say something.

"That was only for my guests!" He put the manicured nail of his middle finger to his lips. "I am a strict observer of the Law. All those nasty, impure animals without fins and scales! Why, I would never dream of touching them!"

"What a beautiful trait," Marcius said and accompanied him to the door.

Eutychius helped Herod into his carriage.

"And as I said, if this classic hut should ever get on your nerves—" He made an apologetic gesture. "Of course, I, too, live in a modest place. But—"

"I'll remember your kind invitation," Marcius replied. He swallowed. "My dear cousin—"

Exhausted, he returned to the library. Only then did it occur to him that Herod might interpret that farewell remark as a promise to inform the Prince of Youth on the half-proposed deal, and to report on his reaction.

He blushed deeply. "The scoundrel!" he thought, with helpless indignation. "Well, he can wait forever, if he pleases, not just for two weeks!"

But not until he had discussed all aspects of the matter with his faithful Tiro did he regain some measure of tranquillity.

CHAPTER NINETEEN

NOW GOLDEN DAYS of summer rolled over the shores of Latium. It was not a season when one could sleep late. Every morning before sunrise Marcius would take a shower in the backyard of the garden. It was delightful and refreshing, for the water, which in its lead pipes had retained its warmth, as the standing water was exhausted would slowly turn cooler and finally come down with tingling cold. Then, in long fast bounds, Marcius would sprint up and down the beach for forty-five minutes, and, after a quick plunge into the sea, return to the Villa for a substantial breakfast.

Sometimes, when the dawn stars were just fading, he would take Pomponius out and ride through the winding paths in the vineyard-covered hills near the coast. The rays of the sun, before its full disk climbed up over the blessed Italian land, seemed fastened to midheaven like the strings of a huge harp which resounded with the mighty accord of the new-born day. Then when the sun had risen above the horizon and the harp had turned silent, a hidden orchestra took up the harmony with solemn drums and ceremonial lyres and cytharas, with languishing, laughing, and longing reed-pipes and shalms and shepherd flutes.

Elated and happy, Marcius returned from such a day's beginning; it was the day he was to see Tiberius Gemellus.

There had been no embarrassment even during his very first visit, though he had feared that the young Caesar might be greatly disappointed in him. Aristides, the pedagogue, received him in the vestibule. He was the man who was responsible for his pupil's moral development and was in charge of his curriculum. Three or four teachers acted under his direction. A native of Rhodes, he had graduated in history, philosophy and mathematics from his university, a university which the Emperor's seven-year visit to the island had endowed with new fame. He was about thirty, a scholarly type, whose eyes had the slightly melancholy and aloof expression of the Greek race. His forefathers had experienced much of glory and defeat, humiliation and rebirth, and their thoughts had spanned the whole range of the spirit, from things human, or all-too-human, to the lofty and immortal concept of the Platonic ideas.

"His Majesty feels that you may wish to sit in at some of the classes," he said. His smile showed that learning and research had not divested him of his Attic humor.

Marcius was led into a screened porch. It had the smell of school, even though it was used only by a single boy—that indefinable smell, composed of dried ink, books, papers, and the dust of chalk and pencils. There was a large colored map of Italy and the Alpine provinces, Rhaetia-Vindelicia and Noricum. Small insets showed the whole Empire and many individual provinces. Textbooks and illustrated chronicles lay on a desk, and there was also a corner for Tiberius Gemellus' private library—mainly travel and adventure stories.

The interruption caused by his entrance was gratefully acknowledged, for the imperial boy had just been exposed to the farewell speech of the dying Cato—a very noble manifestation of Rome's love for liberty, to be sure, but nevertheless extremely boring. The *grammaticus* read it sentence by sentence, and then his pupil had to repeat the whole passage and charge his voice with impassioned defiance toward the foes of old-fashioned republicanism. It was a beautiful thing to be declaimed at street corners, and in spite of its subversive language, it was completely harmless. His Majesty's government knew that no sensible man would ever take it seriously.

After the proud champion of virtue and democracy had finally fallen upon his sword not, however, without having admonished the people to collaborate from that day onward with the victorious Julius Caesar, there followed an hour of exercises in rhetoric. They consisted of a discussion of the moral merits of insoluble cases. For instance, in a civil war, the father and the brother of a married woman were on one side, the woman and her husband on the other. The husband was killed, his wife returned to her father, who drove her from his home. It almost seemed as if the great art of public speaking had been invented only to cause head-aches to little boys.

During a short interval, Tiberius Gemellus, yawning, took his textbook, and underlined a sentence. With raised brows but with a whimsical smile, he pushed it over so that Marcius could read it. "Go your mad way," it read, addressing Hannibal. "Hurry over the terrible Alps that you may please boys as a subject for declamation." When Marcius indicated that his feelings were identical with those of the prince, contact was established; in both the conspiratorial mind of youth was exposed to the same tiresome ordeal.

The third and fourth hours were given up to mathematics and philosophy. A good teacher, enthusiastic about his subject, was in charge. His name was Serapion, and he was a Romanized Assyrian. For Marcius' sake he explained that these two disciplines should always be taught together, for they were nothing but two different aspects of the same category of thought. "Just as the movements of the starry sky and the moral law in our own hearts," he said, "form together our concept of divine truth. We may decipher the orbits of the stars with the help of mathematics, but only if we draw the heavens into our souls, and phenomena give place to reality."

Time flew by rapidly, and Marcius was greatly surprised when Aristides came in and asked whether he could stay for lunch. It was taken under a rust-colored sunshade in the garden. All sat and the food was of the simplest. When Marcius left shortly afterwards, the invitation was repeated, and from this time on the program of the first day became the standard rule. However, not all classes were so dull as the one devoted to the dying Cato; the curriculum also provided an introduction into the science of government, and a study of the fundamentals of Roman constitutional life. But Serapion's classes were always the most inspiring, whether he talked about Pythagoras' and Euclid's geometry, the wisdom of Plato, or, upsetting as it was for Marcius' untrained mind, about Aristarchus of Samos' theory, which held that the sun stood in the center of the universe, while the earth and its fellow-planets, swinging around it, were nothing but small stars, lost among the countless hosts of other celestial bodies.

Marcius never saw the Emperor during these visits to the cottage. But it was his feeling that it was he himself who, through the mouth of Aristides, arranged and supervised his grandson's entire schedule of education and relaxation.

Four weeks after Seneca's departure, Marcius received a letter from Cornelius. It was mailed from Jerusalem, where he was spending his leave. It had taken only twenty days to reach Italy. The station master in Neapolis had forwarded it directly to the Villa Ciceronis.

He felt somewhat anxious when he saw the voluminous

letter on the breakfast table. With forced calm he finished his meal and then withdrew to the library, where he opened the seals.

It was written in black ink on many individual leaves of Egyptian papyrus, one side of each sheet remaining blank. Cornelius began with a few personal messages: everyone whom Marcius had met was well and he hoped to hear soon how things in Italy had been developing. Then he wrote that so far he had been unable to find out about Longinus' whereabouts. The affair was shrouded in complete secrecy. Only this much was known: that Company D had a new permanent commander.

The style then changed, and what followed was clearly intended not as a private letter only, but as a document supplementing his earlier scrolls. "My servant is making copies of this part," Cornelius wrote. "Great things have happened since you left Judea."

Slowly Marcius' eyes followed the firm handwriting, and the library with its high windows disappeared as his mind was carried away by what he read. Like the notes of a music score, which in an artist's hands translate themselves into a dominant melody, supported by many voices and instruments, until the lifeless paper becomes one with the symphony itself, so the words of this letter transformed themselves into colors, scenes and men.

Before Marcius' mind, as he read Cornelius' letter, arose the image of Him, clearer than it had ever been since the service in the synagogue at Capharnaum. In the first dawn of day He stood in a small courtyard in Jerusalem. Close to Him was the Woman in the sky-blue robe, freed from the covering dark gray veil. Her name and who she was Marcius now could know, for as he went on reading, it seemed that his thoughts became petitions to her, all addressed to Mary Our Mother.

In the courtyard were eleven men, and further back a crowd of many disciples. Gaius Cornelius wrote that he had been among them. The leader of the eleven was a strong man with bushy eyebrows and broad hands. His name had been Simon, but now he was called Peter, which meant the Rock. Next him was a fair youth with long light-golden hair, a forehead moulded of pale ivory, and hands of slender shape. In his clear eyes was the vision of the eagle, whose flight can be equalled by none. Marcius remembered him at once—he had stood under the Cross, and in a gesture of filial protection, had taken the Mother into his arms.

"Who can he be?" he had asked himself. Now he received the answer from Cornelius' letter—his name was John, and he was called the "beloved disciple."

As the daylight grew stronger, the group began to move. Many people were waiting at the gate of the small courtyard, men and women, young and old, of many races and nationalities.

"They were going toward Mount Golgotha," Marcius thought anxiously as he read that they passed by the foot of the Fortress Antonia and descended into the dismal Tyropoen valley. He knew the way well; helpless, he had followed it on that day when darkness covered the earth for three long hours. Now, as they emerged from the valley, Cornelius wrote, the northern gate of Jerusalem was passed and the hill, crowned by the skull-shaped rock, was not far away.

Behind the Mount of Olives, east of the Cedron, the sun had risen, and for a moment the group paused at a meadow. The grass looked very green, and a full ray of light broke through the budding branches of the trees. It fell deep into an empty grave which had been hewn like a cave out of the rock.

Crowds of people had left the city and moved through the northern gate. But timidly they waited outside the garden, beneath Mount Golgotha, until the group returned. Then, with long shadows like velvet trains falling behind them, all walked toward the Cedron valley and, over several wooden bridges, crossed the stony little river.

Now the Garden of Gethsemane lay behind them, and the groves and meadows of the Mount of Olives were opening ahead. As the crowds fell back, He was walking ever faster and appeared to be enfolded by a sacred light.

The summit of the Mount of Olives was reached. On its soft slopes many hundreds of people were waiting in silent meditation. Only the Mother, Peter, the fair youth, and their nine companions stood closer. The sun had moved above the valley and the morning sky was bright. But the light, ever expanding, shone with still greater strength, though its intense brilliancy, like a mantle laid around the Glory which was Himself, looked like a sheltering shadow.

Cornelius, standing far off, raised his eyes, he wrote, only for fractions of a second at a time. Now the departing King had placed His left hand on His heart, while with His right, which in its palm seemed to hold the stars and all the suns, He gave His blessing to the human race, the dead, the living, and the generations yet unborn. When Cornelius looked up once more, another stream of light, as strong and all-pervading, had broken forth from on high. They merged in a single sea of transcending glory.

Covering their eyes with both hands, the people sank to their knees. Many lay prostrate on the ground. But when they arose again and gazed up, there was only the morning sky, arched like a dome of polished gold.

Marcius put down the letter, and an hour must have passed before he could continue reading. Again the style of the writing had changed and now there were short sentences and hammering words.

"Do you still think of our talk by the quiet pond?" Cornelius asked. Marcius remembered how at their feet, a map, drawn in the sand, had depicted the confines of the Empire.

" 'Beyond the Garamantes and the Indies . . .' do you recall how you objected to the thought? I, too, understood it only dimly. I am not ashamed of that. We all moved in terms of temporal dominion. Even the eleven asked whether the kingdom of Israel would now be restored. Until—"

Ten days after the Ascension had been Pentecost. According to the law of Moses the day was the feast of the first fruits, marking the end of the grain harvest. Thronging crowds, strangers from all over the world, had come to the city. Parthians and Medes were among them, Elamites and Mesopotamians, men from Judea, from Cappadocia, from Pontus, Phrygia, and Pamphylia, from Egypt, Lydia, and Africa Proconsularis, as well as Cretans and Arabians and visitors from Rome. There were also many Greeks, Gauls and Germans, Indians, and men from the far East.

The sound of thunder approached from the Mount of Olives, and the air was filled with light. Like a cloud, in which there is no darkness, the Power, not conceived by the senses and yet working through them, drew nearer until before the eyes of the thousands, It came to rest above the meeting place of the chosen companions.

"On that day," Cornelius explained, "the giving of the Law is commemorated."

But a new Rock had stood before the crowds, a man who spoke without the trembling awe of Sinai, yet with anointed authority. From his mouth came words that were no longer in the heavy and halting Galilean speech; on the great and luminous day of the Paraclete, wisdom and dominion moved his awakened spirit. And each man in the crowded place listened and heard the words as if they were spoken in his own tongue.

Marcius reverted to the map drawn in the sand of Capharnaum. As his eyes fastened upon them, the limits widened until they dissolved, joining together in a new orbit, made up not just of lands and seas and peoples, but composed in a globe, in a single unity. Myriads of suns and stars swung through the breadth of the uncharted and seemingly endless space. But holding its place, steadfast in the midst of the swirling universe, was the earth. Into it had entered a mighty flame, which would break forth out of the souls of men until the globe itself would be transfigured into the golden orb in God's own hand. And surmounting this orb would stand forever the Sign which had been planted in the skull-shaped rock.

Again Marcius paused in reading the letter, then he went back a few pages. There was a passage which at first had not caught his whole attention. It pertained to the founding of the realm to come. "A new mandate has been imposed upon us," he read. " 'Go and make disciples of all the nations.' " The golden orb stood firm before his mind, even though he did not understand the full import. Then he continued reading. " 'Baptize them in the Name of the Father and of the Son and of the Holy Spirit; teaching them to observe all, whatever I have commanded you: and lo, I am with you throughout all time, even until the consummation of the world.' "

It was noon when Marcius left his desk. Only then did he notice that Tiro had been in the library all these hours. "I know this is the right thing to do!" he decided quickly, and handed Cornelius' letter to the old and trusted adviser.

In the afternoon he went to the cottage. There he heard that Tiberius Gemellus would enjoy a few days of vacation, which the two of them might spend together. It was suggested that they should make the ancient town of Lavinium their headquarters. There Aeneas had first set foot on Latian soil, and since he was the ancestor of the Julian House, the place was held in high honor. One of the imperial villas would be made ready to receive the young guests, and Aristides was to accompany them as their faithful mentor.

CHAPTER TWENTY

"I AM GLAD my *grammaticus* isn't here," Tiberius Gemellus said as they rode out on horseback into the country. "He would start reciting the whole of the Aeneid!" With comic exaggeration, imitating his teacher, he scanned the opening lines:

Arma virumque cano Troiae qui primus ab oris
Italiam fato profugus Laviniaque venit–

They had halted on a hill which overlooked Lavinium. A huge oak tree, centuries old, crowned its top. It may have been a young green sapling when seven hamlets had still been perched on the Seven Hills, with cattle grazing in the valleys between them, long before a wall encompassed the rising city.

The small town at their feet also seemed marked by great age. A compact agglomeration of round, wattled houses and moundlike huts made of clay or baked earth, it evoked a picture of archaic, pre-Roman civilization. This was the way the early Etruscans had built when they had first settled in Central Italy; their language had become extinct a long time ago. Only Claudius, the Emperor's scholarly nephew, still knew how to speak it.

"The town was restored thirty years ago," Tiberius Gemellus explained. "A sort of open-air museum. But there were really quite a number of old things left to build on." He pointed toward the north. "If you should get to Rome, you must look at Agrippa's Pantheon. There you'll see the Etruscan style glorified."

Fifteen miles away, a rosy glow lay on the marble splendor of the Capitol—Roma Eterna, in which the City and the Orbit were one. From this distance it looked like a mural crown set on the helmet of a hero.

There had been many talks during the three days of their companionship, but the Prince of Youth seemed to have shied away from speaking of Rome and what it stood for. This was the first time he had even mentioned it.

Marcius had been so filled with the news contained in Cornelius' letter that he found it difficult to be silent about it. "But what will Aristides say?" he had wondered. Yet very much to his surprise, the pedagogue even encouraged him to talk. He could not have acted in that fashion without the Emperor's consent.

A grain of suspicion had entered Marcius' mind. "Politics again?"

"After Him," Aristides had said, "no one should ever be deified. His Majesty feels very strongly on this point. The Roman constitution might suffer under the apotheosis of men. For his own part the Emperor has categorically declined such honors."

This fact Cornelius had already mentioned, as Marcius well remembered. Yet, this whole approach was somewhat disturbing. Was the Emperor, for political reasons, trying to make his grandson absolutely immune to those temptations to which the Little Boot seemed to yield? Or was he using something far greater than the needs of the Roman constitution to forestall Caligula's deification, if he should succeed to the throne after all?

Marcius would have liked to ask Gemellus, but he felt that he should not speak about Tiberius Caesar. And there were in the soul of this boy many secrets which no one could fathom. He was young, his head was full of dreams, he could still play like a child; yet there were moments now and then when the glance of his eyes was far away and had a spark of the wisdom of the ages. And wisdom always is crystallized pain.

"Perhaps because he has lost both his parents and his twin brother?" Marcius wondered. But that explanation was not sufficient.

They had tied their horses to wooden posts and had sat down on the dry mossy ground under a big oak.

Gemellus pointed toward the great city. "The Pantheon is like the senate of a gods' republic," he said. "Officially its members are all equal. But there are distinctions of culture and family standing. Fortunately many of the foreign intruders, like the dog-headed Anubis and the other Egyptian animal deities have now been expelled, but it's still a strange enough crowd. Jupiter is only the first among peers, their Princeps, just as my grandfather is among Roman senators." This might have sounded precocious, even cynical. But it was only resigned, with a note of disgust. "I ought to clear out that whole gods' republic; don't you think so?" A strange gleam came into his eyes. "You and I, we must do something great, which men will remember us by!"

"Of course we must," Marcius replied. "I know exactly what."

Gemellus nodded, serious. "Absolutely! But it will be difficult, if the cause doesn't succeed in my grandfather's lifetime. You have seen how things are. My dear cousin Caligula won't be without influence."

"He won't have anything to say, I hope."

"Make no mistake, he is very popular with the army, especially the Germanic Legions. They call him 'son of the camp,' their 'chick' and 'babe.' You may be sure that he'll make a strenuous effort to survive me!" He shook his head, as if to throw off depression.

"Marcius," he said boyishly, "I am afraid you don't realize how wicked I can be. Sometimes I even lie to my grandfather." He blushed. "Or at least I don't always tell him what I know. The other day I did something very wrong."

"Won't you tell me?"

"I eavesdropped."

"Why don't you ask the Emperor for his forgiveness?"

"I can't." He drew close to Marcius. "I wouldn't want even this oak to hear." He held his mouth to his friend's ear. "My grandfather and Caligula were standing behind a curtain and talking about me, but they didn't know that I was so near. So I couldn't resist listening—" Horror came into his voice. " 'I don't trust your promises,' my grandfather said. 'I know you are going to kill this boy. But beware! If you do, soon you yourself will die.' "

"Oh, no!" Marcius cried.

"Now you'll think the worst of me!" Convulsive weeping shook his slender frame. "And you believed that I was worthy to—"

"My little brother," Marcius said tenderly. "Dear little brother!" He put his arm around the boy's shoulders. "It was quite natural that you should listen." A fit of temper seized him. "That reptile, that venomous monster!"

Gemellus smiled again. "He has his good traits. It's Herod who is corrupting him. But don't worry! I know how to fight, and I can trust my sword! They won't get me easily."

"You know what that man wants?" Marcius asked. "He is ready to drop Caligula and throw all his intrigues and influence on your side, if you will promise to make him king of the Jews."

A cool, disdainful look came into Gemellus' eyes. "I shall

never make him king." His tone was impetuous. He spoke as the heir apparent, fully conscious of the weight and meaning of his words.

"Gemellus would not be too young for the throne," Marcius reflected, and as the light of the waning day fell on the hair of the color of old gold, it seemed to him as if the youthful brow were adorned with a wreath of gilded laurels.

"You told me about the wooden tablet," Gemellus continued. "I can almost see it myself. It had His name, you said —and His title—*Rex Judaeorum*." His face became tense, and his lips trembled with indignation. "There shall be none who wears a royal crown where He wore a triple crown of thorns."

For a long time neither spoke. In the east, the silhouette of the Alban hills had become one with the sky. It looked as if a cloak of dark purple billowed up to the zenith, slowly to sink down behind the shore of the sea.

"Do you know all the constellations?" Marcius asked, remembering the desire of his boyhood to have a younger brother at his side. "The big W over there is my special friend."

"In winter it looks like an M. It's your initial. I'll think of you whenever I see it."

"But don't neglect the Great Bear! He's a nice animal."

"It would be difficult to overlook him."

"And there is the Polar Star—the hub of the whole world."

"One should really greet it with reverence."

Again there was silence. "To think that these stars were turning long before Troy was built!" Gemellus said after a while. His soul seemed to recoil before an awesome vision. "They will still turn when all this is dust." He pointed towards the Great City. Now the glow of its lights flamed high into the night. On one of the hills one could distinguish a thin streak of fire. "That is the big torch before the Temple of the Capitoline Jupiter," Gemellus explained. "Dust—" he said again. "After the battle of Pharsalus, Julius Caesar crossed over to Asia to visit Ilion. Trees and dirt and rotting wood filled the fallen houses of the kings. Brambles and weeds crept over the tombs of Achilles and Patroclus. No one knew their exact sites. Rubbish lay high where Ilion's proud castle had stood. Mount Ida, from which according to legend, Ganymede had been taken up, was wasteland. Thoughtlessly, Caesar crossed a tiny current of water; it was the Xanthus, the river of the heroes. He walked through high grass. 'Don't step on Hector's ashes!' a native guide warned. A heap of stones stood near. 'Don't you see the altars where king Priam fell?' "

"Why are you so sad tonight, little brother?"

"I am not sad. I am only wondering." He turned to Marcius. "Why don't you stay with me? I need you—"

"My parents are waiting."

"Don't go!" the boy said urgently, "Please don't go!" A new idea brightened his face. "I will make you co-regent of the Empire."

"I shall be Tiberius Gemellus' champion and standard-bearer," Marcius had thought during his conversation with Herod. Was this to become reality? A feel of dizziness clouded his eyes. "I am not Roman—" he said, haltingly.

"What does it matter? The Empire spans the world! Besides, you are a citizen already." He thought for a while. "Look, this is what we'll do. I have a sister, Julia. She is now seventeen. I know you would like her, and she would like you. You ought to get married!" He laughed happily. "That's it! Then you'll be my brother-in-law, and I could always keep you here."

"But another girl would think that I am the most faithless

of men," Marcius said, struggling with himself. And then he told the boy about the wild coast, the galloping waves, and the island far out in the sea.

"I am sorry," Gemellus said gravely, "I would never have suggested it, had I known—"

His thoughts wandered off. "On the day that the six hundred Senators convene to confirm my power as tribune and the proconsular imperium which will give me command over all the armed forces—"

"What will you do first, Caesar?" Marcius asked, caught by the spell of imperial power.

"I shall take up a plan of Augustus Caesar. He wanted to give to the local senates of the Italian colonies the right to vote for the magistrates of Rome. They were to send their votes under seal. But nothing came of it." His voice had a metallic ring, though still boyish. Yet it was the same tone which, grown a thousandfold stronger, had lived in the imperious commands of Julius Caesar, Augustus, and Tiberius, and which vibrated in the mailed might of the marching legions.

"It will not be enough," he went on. "Many of the Roman Senators are venal, self-seeking men. Quite a number are not even of ancient lineage, but are enriched greengrocers and ignoble speculators. Others made their money during the revolutionary wars. As to the Roman populace—that's a beast with four hundred thousand heads. The crowds want only bread and games. *Senatus Populusque Romanus* is a proud name for these world rulers—so long as you don't look too closely. My grandfather has tried hard to ward off the dangers of this system, but for a lone man, who is righteous and respects all ancient traditions, the burden is too great. We are headed towards Persian despotism or anarchy, unless we remodel the constitution."

"How will you do it, Caesar?"

"First, we need a central assembly, composed of the delegates of all peoples and provinces of the Empire."

"Can this be done?"

"It can. We will build it upon the provincial diets. The province of the three Gauls is the best organized. There the diet has a great share in the administration of the country. My father Drusus used to open it at Lugudunum every first of August."

"A diet of the Gallic people?"

"Yes—elected by their sixty-four autonomous cantons. Caesar gave them great rights; some even have military authority and a militia of their own. In Greece things are similar. Augustus Caesar restored the freedom of many cities and districts. They all elect their own senates and magistrates. Athens doesn't pay a single copper penny of tribute. It has sworn alliance with Rome, that's all. It even coins its own money, which is not stamped with the Emperor's head. As in Gaul, there is a national diet, which meets in Argos. Its members are called the 'Panhellenes.' Spain, Syria, Upper and Lower Germany—all have autonomous cantons and districts. If I follow everywhere Caesar's and Augustus' example in Gaul and Greece—"

"How do you know all those things?" Marcius marvelled.

"It's part of my education," Gemellus replied simply. Excitement flushed his cheeks. "You know what we must do? We must combine Roman power with the Greek federal principle. Think of the Delian and the Achaean Leagues—that was the greatness of Hellas, the manly glory of the Dorian fields, and the splendor of the shores of Attica! If the Empire could do the same—form a federation of free peoples, each composed of free men, filled with Plato's ideal of friendship and virtue, a league of nations, held in balance by the

Roman Princeps, the world assembly, by Roman law and by a common peaceful purpose–"

Marcius drew a deep breath. "If that should happen," he said, his earlier prejudices vanishing, "if that should happen, Caesar–Hibernia will not stay out." He smiled proudly. "Since Caesar landed in Britannia we have had a federation of five large and many smaller kingdoms." His talks with Seneca returned to his mind. "One day, we will sail westward. There lies another continent. It too must come into the world federation."

The imperial boy looked towards the reflections of light above the great city. "Then the whole globe will be under the wings of the Eagle," he exclaimed.

"It must be under the arms of the Cross," Marcius said in a low voice.

For a moment Gemellus hesitated. Then he replied, "It will."

The night had become deep and resounded like a great shell. Seconds purled down over the two glowing youths as if they were filled with the murmur of the future, the incoming waves of the centuries.

"I have seen a greater ruler," Marcius had said to Luitprant. Now the heir of the great Tiberius had entered the service of Him who was greater.

And while they sat side by side under their shadowing oak, their eyes roamed over the sleeping land, until they centered on the glow of the Eternal City. It seemed to them that the veils of time had been rent. Over these plains and hills, as over the face of the whole earth, many peoples would pass–tribes, kingdoms and nations, rising and falling like the waters of a great fountain. Broken stones, and fields of golden wheat, dust and brambles would alternate with the high towering splendor of marble and graceful columns; servitude and dominion would be their changing lot.

But quietly growing into a new dawn, to the light of noon without dusk and evening, and crowned by the sign of the coming and perpetual age, this city would stand forever, the great sanctuary of all men and of all hierarchies.

" 'To them no bounds of things, no terms of years I set; the Realm I gave shall never reach an end,' " Gemellus whispered rapturously. "Now I understand the meaning!" Then, with vigor, he repeated the majestic prophecy, Virgil's words in the *Aeneid*, foretelling Rome's timeless reign:

> *His ego nec metas rerum nec tempora pono;*
> *Imperium sine fine dedi–*"

A tide of enthusiasm swept over Marcius' soul, even more youthful than that of Tiberius Gemellus, for in the imperial boy there lived the awakened mind of centuries of conscious history.

"Before your glory," he said, "the fame of Alexander, of Caesar and Augustus will pale." Lines learned in his school-days returned to him. They had been meaningless then. Now they expressed everything he felt. "When your work is done," Marcius continued, "you will be able to say: 'I have built a monument more lasting than bronze and loftier than the Pyramids' royal pile, one that no devouring storm, no furious north wind can destroy, nor years without number and the seasons' flight. I shall not altogether die, for a mighty part of me shall escape death. On and on shall I grow, ever fresh with the glory of after times–' "

This was the famous ode by Horace, the poet's proud epitaph. Silently, the imperial boy had listened. But his lips moved as if he were praying for strength against the lure of *hybris*, the temptation to rise above the decrees of Providence.

Gemellus remained silent even after his friend had finished. His face looked ageless and mature, and on his forehead there seemed to stand again the mark of early fulfillment.

"A monument more lasting than bronze." He cast a final glance at the faint gleam woven around the Seven Hills. There, on the Palatine, stood the throne of supreme power. Between lofty shrines and noble statues ran the broad *Via Triumphalis*, the road open to the great of Roman history. Since the founding of the Republic countless members of the illustrious Claudian house had passed over it. In recent years it had stretched out with a carpet of flowers for Tiberius Caesar, for his father, and for the elder Drusus, who was to die in far-away Moguntiacum. But, much as he strained his imagination, Gemellus could not visualize himself, surrounded by glinting arms and drawn by snow-white horses, passing over the Via Triumphalis.

"I will tell you how the monument will look. I can perceive it very clearly." Gemellus' voice had a note of finality. "There will be a tombstone of gray granite that high—" He raised his arm. "On this stone an inscription will be engraved: 'Tiberius Caesar Drusi Caesaris Filius—Hic Situs Est.' It will give the date of my birth, and perhaps it will mention that I was still in my praetexta."

He jumped up. "It is very late," he said with forced lightness. "Aristides will be worried. I'll tell him that it is all my fault, and you'll tell him that it is all yours. Then he won't know whom to scold, and so he won't scold either of us."

They returned to their horses. "That was a bad idea of mine, trying to keep you here. I'll be glad to know you are safely in Hibernia, long before my grandfather closes his eyes." Almost casually he explained as they rode off, "You see, Marcius, I am very fond of you."

CHAPTER TWENTY-ONE

THE GOLDEN DAYS of summer still sent their cascades of light and color over the fields and shores of Latium. The sea was warm and blue, with streaks of silver, and at night the stars shone clear. Yellow and purple figs matured in dark green trees and the vines drew sweetness into the ripening grapes. On the beach, little Publius Quirinius and his friends began to talk about the teachers they might have when school opened again.

There could be no doubt that a nostalgic breath, a first foreboding of the approaching autumn, had come into the air.

Unspoken and never fully realized, this same mood now underlay the friendship between Marcius and Tiberius Gemellus—even though they might still talk at times about the great things they would accomplish. Together they would rule from sea to sea and from the snow-covered acres of the Hyperboreans to the burning sand of the deepest south! Within such a realm, the Garamantes and Indians would be inland dwellers.

Once or twice Marcius also visited the two Cornelii. He found them polite hosts, who never voiced too much personal opinion, not even when he told them what had happened in Judea.

There was no word from Seneca, but by the middle of August a letter from Cornelius arrived. "I find Seneca interesting," he wrote, "but he has yet a long way to go. He still resolves everything into metaphysical speculations. He talks about 'cosmic dialectics,' when he might say 'I believe' or 'I believe not.' "

A week later, another letter came. "The news is bad," it began, "but you are not one who will mourn without hope." Carrying the letter Marcius then fled into the library. He knew what the next sentence would say. But he was afraid to continue, as if he thought, "Until I see it in black and white, it is not true."

"You coward!" he told himself, and finally he went on.

Longinus was dead. The news had been published in the official army gazette shortly after Seneca, representing the legate Lucius Vitellius, had arrived at Caesarea. "He died of a fever," was all the notice said. There followed a eulogy which listed all his campaigns and his services to the Emperor and the people of Rome. Brief mention was made of an undefined "unfortunate error" due to which he had been detained for a short time. But throughout the obituary as if nothing untoward had ever happened, he was referred to as "commander of Company D, Third Syrian Legion."

Marcius remembered well some of the facts that his friend had told him during that memorable week. At the age of thirteen Longinus had lost his father—he too had been an officer in the Third Syrian Legion and before his son's eyes he had been killed in a skirmish with the Jews. Thereupon his mother returned with him to Latium, and on the Appian Way they were allotted a small land grant with an inn, called The Three Taverns.

"I must have passed it!" Marcius thought remorsefully.

Young Longinus had not stayed there for long. At the age of sixteen he had enlisted, and soon afterwards in the army of the great Drusus Germanicus had fought east of the Rhine, deep in the woods and hills of unconquered Germania Magna.

His whole life had been one of struggle and hardship, all

along the ramparts and the broad rivers, which lay around the Empire like a fortress moat. It had been the life of a soldier, one of the countless many who, unpraised and unsung, had built the Roman world.

Then, two or three years later, he had received his commission as an officer and his centurion's staff. Shortly afterwards he had distinguished himself in the crushing of the Sejanus plot and had been granted his special favor. New avenues of honor had seemed to open before him, had he only followed his ambitions. But there was something else, a longing for justice, and for things greater than military glory, and this finally had led him into open opposition to a wicked and cowardly superior. And so he had lost his rank, his liberty, everything he had worked for since his boyhood days.

Now he had even lost his life, but he had kept his stainless soldier's shield, and his immortal soul.

A touch of envy came into Marcius' heart. His friend's struggle was over. Even his terrible deed under the Cross had been turned into salvation. Grace had overshadowed him, and though he had died, he would live forever in the memory of men.

But as evening fell, the fullness of sorrow seized upon Marcius. What a death he must have died! Strangled perhaps by a secret executioner as soon as the spiteful praetorian chief, Flavius Sabinus, and Pontius Pilate had been informed of Lucius Vitellius' mandate. Before the Emperor's tribunal Longinus would have been one of the main witnesses against the unjust judge and all his henchmen.

Then even these feelings abated. Nothing remained but the deep pain for the man who had been his friend and whose loyalty and strength of duty had sent Marcius to Italy, while he himself stayed on to face his enemies—a simple officer, divested of his imperial favor, alone and abandoned, at the mercy of a ruthless power.

"No one even told him that his request has been fulfilled and the Lance was safe," Marcius said over and over.

He stayed up all night, praying and mourning. When the light of morning broke through the windows—a pale morning, with the first cool drizzle of the approaching autumn—he lay down and slept for a few hours. When he left the room, Tiro was waiting for him, but he asked no questions until Marcius himself began to tell him what had happened.

Later Marcius went down to the beach. A light rain still fell from low-hanging clouds. In the sand were small holes, pitted by the drops. The air was heavy and the sea was like molten lead. In the water, near the horizon, was a black streak.

Tiro followed him. "Why don't you leave for a few days?" he asked. "Perhaps you could stay at the Three Taverns? I will let you know if there should be any news."

Like a child Marcius allowed himself to be led back to the Villa. Tiro packed for him what he would need during his trip and reminded him to write a note to Tiberius Gemellus. Then he took Marcius to the stable.

While it rained for two whole days, Marcius sat in the dim-lit main room of the inn. It had a low ceiling, supported by hand-hewn oak beams. The gleam of smoking brass lamps mingled with the shine of the red tongues of fire in the open furnace. Leaping up the black chimney, they painted fantastic patterns on the stone floor.

The owner of the inn was a one-legged veteran. He had been a soldier of the Eighth Legion, called the Augusta, which formed part of the Pannonian army. He had never heard of the Longinus family, so there was no use asking him questions. But Marcius still hoped that in this room, where his friend had lived as a boy, he might catch some of his spirit. At moments he succeeded in visualizing him rather clearly, but it was nothing real—only a phantom shape.

On the third day, after the rain had stopped, he remembered that his friend had once told him about a deep wooded gully nearby. Sometimes, when Longinus had played in it, he had thought that this was the place where he would like to be buried, nobody need know exactly where.

So Marcius rode away from the inn and soon the gully was found. "My friend's grave!" he thought, overcome by his emotions. Then again he realized that this sentiment was artificial. His friend was not here, any more than he was in the oak-beamed room.

He sat down on a log, with a feeling of unreality mounting within him. "What am I doing here?" he thought. Now it was a feeling of abandonment—it swooped down on him like a bird of prey on wide gray wings. A desire to flee seized him, a wish to escape from this world of intrigue, of plots, treason and secret murder, a world where everything was twisted and even men like Seneca talked in riddles and tortuous speculations.

A certain satisfaction lay in these accusations. But they were not too well founded. Gaius Cornelius, Aristides, Tiro came to his mind, little Publius Quirinius, and even the gnome in the cavelike shop. He remembered his fellow-soldiers out on the Eastern frontier and in the Cohort Antonia. Most of all, he thought of Tiberius Gemellus.

Yes, he was unjust. Of that he was certain. Those accusations had helped him to conceal some personal failure, even guilt—

He could be in Hibernia by now. Why, then, had he stayed in Antium all summer if his longing for his paternal roof was completely sincere? There was no use denying the clear fact: life in the midst of culture and comfort was very pleasant. The palaces, the Villa Ciceronis, the whole world of modern refinement—how different it was from the hamlets and straw-thatched huts of Hibernia.

And there was something more: the lure of power, the fantastic hope, of writing, as Tiberius Gemellus' friend and co-regent, his name across the pages of history. "I have been disloyal to my father," he muttered, and thought of the wide, smoke-blackened hall, which was covered with hunting trophies of the kings of Armagh. Should it not be dearer to him than all the marbles, the mosaics, the alabaster, and the Pompeian red in the imperial residence? And the child on the wild island? For weeks he had not even thought of her.

Was this all? If it was, he could atone for his faithless vanity by renouncing all ambitions, returning to Hibernia at once, and there doing his simple duty.

But had not Hibernia changed, or rather, had not his relationship to his native island become different? He had sensed it before, but he had been reluctant to admit it, reluctant, even, to scrutinize his feelings more closely. It was not just the comfort of Italy or his friendship for Tiberius Gemellus which had caused him to tarry beyond the accomplishment of his mission. And the lure of power could not explain it fully. Things went even deeper than that. And suddenly he knew what it was.

"When I am back in Hibernia," his soul asked, shuddering, "where am I going?" He raised his head. Above the gully the clouds had withdrawn and he saw that the foliage of the trees looked bright and refreshed. But no voice replied to his question.

Undecided, with his feelings still in a turmoil, he mounted and slowly walked his horse back to the Three Taverns.

There he found two messages. One was from the imperial

chancellery at Capri. The Emperor had returned to the island and wished to inform him that word had come from Armagh; King Marke expected his son not later than spring. The other was from Seneca, mailed at Neapolis. It contained only a short greeting and said that he would be back at Antium within a week.

Even though the skies had cleared completely, the summer failed to recover from its first attack of chill weather. The vineyards and the fig trees understood the warning. Hastily they took up their work, so as not to be found wanting in their duty when their time of probation should be over and account must be rendered to the lord of the harvest.

But Marcius was again in the brightest of moods. "Seneca has been received by His Majesty," Aristides told him. "He has seen the Emperor three times since. Things seem to be going well."

It was incredible how fast rumors could fly, but a disquieting report was the most persistent and widespread of all. It held that two "parties" had been formed, one supporting the Prince of Youth, the other backing Gaius Caesar Caligula. The first was identified with what the people called "the new creed," without knowing what the words really meant.

Almost everyone had heard this story. Tiro talked about it, so did the slaves in the household. In the shops and on the streets Marcius caught shreds of the same gossip. Even little Publius Quirinius and his friends were discussing it, and of course, they sided violently with the "Gemellus party."

Marcius, inexperienced in such matters, enjoyed this development greatly. "A showdown!" he thought. "This is the best thing that could happen!" But then his eyes were opened to the possible consequences.

The day before Seneca arrived, Marcius found the cottage

surrounded by a wing of the imperial German bodyguard, under Luitprant's command.

"We were sent back from Capri to guard the young Caesar," the Suevian explained, with an unusually serious face.

"Why?"

"Because of the rumors. They fly faster than the wind. In a few days they will reach the farthest frontier posts. The attitude of the troops remains to be seen. But among the eight Germanic legions there is strong sympathy for Gaius Caligula. The praetorians are definitely against the young Caesar."

Marcius turned pale. "Treason?"

"Things bordering on it. His Majesty wants to take no chances."

"Why should the praetorians—?"

Luitprant smiled contemptuously. "I suppose because of the rumors that on Gaius Caligula's accession the pay would be higher."

"Spreading those rumors must have been Herod Agrippa's idea!"

"It was. But he has been taken care of. He was arrested yesterday by order of the Emperor. Eutychius reported a conversation; during a carriage drive at Misenum Herod Agrippa said to Gaius Caligula, 'May the old tiger soon depart from this life so that I may greet you, so much more worthy, as the lord of the world.' "

"Eutychius reported it? His own freedman?"

"What do you expect? That's the way things go."

"With Herod in jail, there shouldn't be any immediate danger. Caligula can't do much left on his own."

Luitprant looked uneasy. "There is another powerful group, the augurs. They are wicked men without faith in anything. But they wield terrific influence over the people.

When they are alone they chuckle together because the crowds are so credulous. Of course, they don't want to lose their livelihood; so they have spread the story that the young Caesar wants to destroy the gods of Rome. For the last few days frantic masses of people have been crowding the temples, yelling, screaming and shouting, 'Don't take the gods away from us!' "

"I am the one who compromised Gemellus," Marcius thought, with self-condemnation. "It was irresponsible of me to stay. Of course, Herod's and Caligula's informers were all around us."

Luitprant noticed his disturbed expression.

"Don't worry," he said proudly. "We are here now! We stand by the Emperor. We'll stand also by the Greater King, if the Emperor so desires."

"I must tell your more about Him."

"I wish you would. When you return home, why don't you stop with my people?"

"I'd like to." His immediate worries did not, however, leave his mind. "Your force here wouldn't be strong enough in case of a revolution," he said.

"The Emperor has ordered the Second Syrian Legion and the Eighth, the Augusta, to Italy; he commanded the Eighth in person during the Pannonian campaign."

"It will take weeks for them to arrive."

"That does not matter. The news of their arrival was released today. It will have a sobering effect."

Inside the cottage slaves were busy packing.

"The Prince is leaving for Capri tomorrow," Aristides said with a sad smile. Depressed, Marcius went out to the screened porch. There the radiant face of Tiberius Gemellus reassured him somewhat.

"There is no school today!" he said. "As soon as I am in Capri, I'll ask my grandfather to send for you."

"I am returning to Hibernia, little brother."

"But not before spring!"

"Long before that." He sat down, despondent and longing to hide his face. "I am the cause of all the trouble. I should never have talked with Herod. Of course he guessed that I reported to you and that he hasn't a chance. That is why he started this whole intrigue."

"Would you want him to think that he had a chance?"

"No, no!" Marcius replied violently. Then he went on brooding. "I must have blundered somewhere." He stroked his forehead. "Cornelius warned me not to undertake more than I could do. 'Others will come,' he said."

"*You* didn't do anything wrong. It's just that you got into the midst of all these intrigues. A moment ago I talked with Aristides about it. He says it's quite natural that the prefect Naevius Sertorius Macro should be against you. After all, the centurion Longinus was your friend, and he helped to destroy Sejanus. Then, after you made your report, the Emperor ordered an investigation, just when Flavius Sabinus thought that things were going his way."

"I see what you mean. Praetorians always stick together. Traitors or loyal men, they are all the same."

"Yes. I would dissolve the guard and rely on the civil administration and the regular army," Gemellus said. "But listen! Next comes the story of the ring. You'd think that the praetorians would be glad about the amnesty for Sejanus' friends. Far from it! Now they can't go on destroying their own enemies, whoever they may be. Finally, says Aristides, both the praetorians and my cousin were afraid that you might get an official post." Shyly, but with boyish directness, he added, "They soon found out that you were my friend."

"Thank you, little brother!" He thought of the hour in the wooded gully. "What you say confirms my feelings. I should have left immediately after the audience."

"And what would have become of our friendship?"

"Had I gone then, I could always have come back. Now it may be a departure for good."

Gemellus' eyes filled with tears. "Oh no!" He turned his face away. "Let's go into the garden!" he added quickly.

Marcius cast a last glance at the colored map, the text-books, the corner with the travel and adventure stories—the whole small realm of a boy, wider and more his own than the Empire, in which his House was supreme. Then they left the screened porch.

On the grass, by a stream which, from one of the ponds, ran down to the sea, they found a seat. Gemellus was the first who broke the silence.

"I have heard that the Second Syrian Legion is coming to Italy. If Gaius Cornelius should be with it, you must tell him to look me up, and Aristides too. It's Aristides who made it possible for us to meet so often."

"Wasn't it the Emperor who arranged our plans?"

"Indirectly." He tried to hide his embarrassment. "Aristides did the actual planning. He knew how much it meant to me." He lowered his voice. "Also, he wanted to hear more about Him."

He made an effort to change his tone. "You know, I have given more thought to the Roman constitution." But this was not what he wanted to talk about. "Do you remember the end of *Phaedrus?*" he asked abruptly.

"I have never read it."

"Then let me tell you! Socrates asks whether it wouldn't be proper to render thanks. 'Of course!' Phaedrus replies. And so Socrates prays for their own souls, for a satisfied and tranquil mind. It is a beautiful prayer, simple, strong, and not like the sweet, flowery stuff of the augurs." He paused. "When friends part, perhaps never to meet again–Marcius, don't you think they should pray?"

"They certainly should, little brother." Under the confident glance of Gemellus' eyes, Marcius forgot his sorrow. All his feelings were submerged in his love for this boy, born to the purple, whose fate swung dangerously between supreme power and utter abandonment–a fate which would not overwhelm him. Whatever might come to him, his clear soul, the spirit of a youthful hero, had freely accepted it.

"I wanted to be his standard bearer," Marcius thought. "Perhaps I really am."

"Yes, we should pray," he said aloud. Words which he had read in Cornelius' records rose to the surface of his mind. Only now did he begin to understand their true meaning.

He looked straight toward the sea, and as the boy at his side waited in complete stillness, slowly, uncertainly at first, he told him of the new prayer which established the sonship and the brotherhood of all men:

"Our Father, Who art in heaven, Hallowed be Thy Name; Thy kingdom come; Thy Will be done, On earth as it is in heaven. Give us this day our daily bread; And forgive us our debts, As we also have forgiven our debtors. And lead us not into temptation, But deliver us from evil."

Gemellus' gaze had rested on Marcius, and his lips had moved, as if he were trying to form the words for himself.

"We shall pray it together," Marcius said, when the *libera nos a malo* was spoken. Then, with a firm voice, they repeated the filial invocation, from the *Pater Noster* to the Hebrew *Amen.*

"Now we are in the same community," Gemellus said joyfully after a long pause.

Marcius did not reply at once. He left the grass and walked a few steps to the edge of the stream. "A new mandate has been imposed upon us," Gaius Cornelius had written. The prayer was like the preamble to a constitution, not of imperial dominion, but of the Kingdom. It applied to all who would like to see this dark earth transfigured, as by a mighty flame, into the Golden Orb.

"You can enter it," he said, when his little friend had joined him, "if you believe–"

"With all my heart–so that I may understand," Tiberius Gemellus replied, and inclined his head. Both bent down, but Marcius more deeply. With his right hand he took up water. Its silvery drops hallowed by the Triune Name, would touch a youthful brow before these drops could return to the stream and mingle with the waves of the sea.

CHAPTER TWENTY-TWO

THE WHOLE of the following day had been passed in waiting. But when Marcius, after dinner, was sitting in the atrium, Seneca suddenly emerged from his suite, nonchalantly, as if he had just returned from a short walk through the town. His welcome was equally surprising.

"Three more months," he said with a faunish smile, "and you would qualify as magister of liberal arts."

"That's very exaggerated," Marcius replied, bewildered.

"I am sure it isn't. According to Tiro you have been doing the work of a full-fledged summer course." He made a little gesture. "But what about me? Do you notice anything special?"

"You don't look tired."

"Why should I? I had a very comfortable trip." He sighed. "Oh, vanity of earthly honors! They impress not even one's own friend."

"Your tunic perhaps—" Marcius said, uncertain.

"At last!" He folded his hands over his breast. "Sooner than one could legitimately expect, these beloved stripes have grown to the right size."

"So you are a Senator now?"

"Since the day before yesterday. But as the social ascent is rapid nowadays, my nobility may soon be among the most ancient in the Empire." He bowed as if he stood before a full-length mirror. "In recognition of my completed duties as imperial ambassador-at-large extraordinary and plenipotentiary." With mock pompousness he sat down. "My station in life has definitely moved upward. I don't have to girdle my tunic any longer. I may wear red shoes, with high heels and thongs up to my knees. Why, there are simply no limits! If I ever went to public games, I could sit in the front row. My official title has been advanced to *clarissimus* and my bank account shows an increase of one million sesterces."

"My sincerest congratulations!"

"Never mind. Except for the high heels; those are a gratifying addition for a man of my stature. Since they come with duty, no one can accuse me of vanity."

"What's behind all this flippancy?" Marcius wondered, baffled. He tried to penetrate the feeling behind Seneca's front. "How is Gaius Cornelius?"

"He's all right. He gave me a letter for you, but he didn't know at that time that he would be coming to Italy so soon."

"I'll be gone by the time he arrives."

"I am sorry to hear that. No chance that you may change your plans? No? That's too bad."

Marcius' uneasiness grew. All this had been said in one breath, too fast to allow him a reply. He heard soft steps behind him.

Seneca looked up. "Thank you!" he called to someone across the atrium. "I had my supper in town!" He turned again to Marcius. "Very conscientious servants in this villa! Which of the six would you say has been most intent on your daily comfort?"

"I wouldn't know. All of them—" He stopped. "What do you mean?"

"Nothing, my little collegian. Or just that in June the atrium and the eucalyptus tree were splendid places but that on the last day of August I prefer a drive in a two-wheeled carriage. I bought a nice one today." He bared his white eeth. "I am not too good a coachman, though. Well, you'll now how to handle it."

Seneca's new acquisition was a nimble contraption with ne double-seat, drawn by two light Numidian horses. "I'd ke to buy a couple of them for my father," Marcius said, s he took the reins.

"Why don't you? They are not very expensive."

"I have quite a few things to take home already."

"An imperial passport is waiting for you in my room. It llows you to ship everything by mail to one of the North ea ports."

"That's wonderful. So I'll take with me just what I can ack on Pomponius." He remembered an advertisement he ad seen in the office of Titus P. Atticus. "Perhaps I had etter insure my property?"

Seneca glanced at him with a shade of irony. "I see! A tudy of our modern conveniences also goes with a summer ourse!"

The streets looked emptier than usual. Some of the big ouses had begun to close up. "There's Herod's place!" Marius remarked. "Remember when you showed it to me for he first time?"

"Let's turn left!" That was all of Seneca's reply. Soon the ray-blue water, lying under a thin haze, had disappeared ehind the groves of olive and pine.

"Where are we going?"

"Nowhere. Just drive on."

Translucent clouds, like patches of frosted glass, marked he course of the half moon. Marcius shivered a little and was fraid to ask further questions.

"The story is," Seneca finally said, "that even our indisensable prefect Macro, when desirous of privacy, conducts his conversations in a moving carriage. There he is compara tively sure that he will not be watching himself through th medium of his own agents."

"Oh, that is why—"

"Don't jump to hasty conclusions." His sarcasm left him "His Majesty's plans have been greatly upset by some recen leakages or indiscretions."

"I hope the Emperor is not angry with me," Marcius sai defensively.

"Your puerile feelings of self-importance get on a man' nerves!" exclaimed the new Senator. But the next momen he regretted his rudeness. "Nobody reproaches you. Th Emperor says that he himself did not foresee what emotions prejudices, and resentments would be stirred up by you presence. Many religions have come from the East, but non which poses such fundamental problems."

Marcius dropped the reins. "So you are now convinced o what I told you?"

"I have gained full knowledge," Seneca replied evasively

"I mean did you convince yourself?" Marcius asked wit growing excitement.

"Our convictions are mostly subjective," Seneca said "When we state that the sky is blue, we are using conven tional terms. But while we may assume that the impression which we receive are identical, there is no way to prove it Blue is a category of our individual perception, not of th sky."

"Now you talk like those whom you once criticized— Plato's cave, our mind as a mirror, on which there fall onl shadows, only phenomena—"

"Not quite. I never said that self-evident ideas, or th categories of good and evil, of divine and human, possess onl subjective existence. I am not a moral anarchist."

Marcius picked up the reins and drove the carriage past an orchard. There he stopped the horses. "Why doesn't he give a clear answer?" he asked himself.

"You have been in Judea," he said aloud. "So now you must know the Truth."

"The Truth, Marcius! Haven't we talked about that already?" He drew his cape closer around his shoulders. "What is truth?"

A chill passed over Marcius. "Please, don't say that! It's a terrible question. I have heard it before."

"Where have you—? Yes, of course, I remember. I certainly would not want to be associated with that man, not even in my speech."

"Has he been ousted from office?"

"Not yet. His Majesty felt that reasons of state necessitate patience."

"Patience towards an unjust judge?"

"The Emperor is very prudent. Prudence is a virtue no ruler can afford to neglect." Thoughtfully he caressed his pointed brown beard. "Would you like to contribute to Pilate's removal?"

"I?" His pent-up nerves broke out in a flurry of excitement. "You want me to go to Caesarea? Arrest the scoundrel? Drag him in chains to Rome? When shall I leave? Tomorrow?" Hectically he leaned over as if he wanted to seize the reins.

Seneca stayed his arm. "Imperial policy is not a game for growing boys," he said severely. "I had enough authority vested in me to arrest him. But right now Pilate is popular with certain influential Jewish factions."

"I can quite see why!"

Seneca ignored this. "Judea is a very touchy problem. Every riot may kindle the flame of nation-wide revolt."

"The four Syrian legions could cope with it."

"One legion is on its way to Italy. Two are stationed on the Eastern frontier."

"One legion could certainly do the job!" Marcius said obdurately.

"Perhaps, perhaps not. Anyway, the Emperor thinks differently. He does not want a fight which would serve no useful purpose, especially while there is danger of defection among the Germanic legions. He remembers too well their mutiny at the very opening of his reign. The legions wanted to make Germanicus Emperor, but loyally he refused."

With significant emphasis he added, "Germanicus' wife was Agrippina, the granddaughter of Augustus, a most remarkable woman, very popular among the soldiers. Their son is Gaius Caesar Caligula, whom the legions have known since his earliest childhood."

"Have the commanders given any sign of disloyalty?"

"No, but if they are not very determined to resist the pressure of their soldiers—"

"Pressure, due to those rumors?"

"Yes. As matters stand, the position of the Emperor's grandson is very insecure. So far the legions have not known much about him. If now he should incur their hatred—" He seemed to hesitate. "I may as well mention it, it is more or less public knowledge. The daughter of the legate of Upper Germany was engaged to Sejanus' son, who was executed together with his father. The legate himself had been denounced by an informer. The Emperor paid no attention to it. He even reinstated him in his command. Yet the legate's feelings may not be of the friendliest."

Marcius was startled. "That legate you are talking about —that's Gnaeus Cornelius Lentulus Gaetulicus!"

Seneca almost smiled. "None other! And the legate of

Lower Germany is his father-in-law, Lucius Apronius. Together they command almost eighty thousand men."

"Now I understand! You want me to go there as imperial messenger."

"Not quite. His Majesty only wondered whether you might want to visit the legates—privately, so to speak, just as a personal friend of their cousin Gaius Cornelius. You can tell them that he has been made lieutenant-commander of the Second Syrian Legion."

"If I ensure their loyalty, you'll get rid of Pilate?"

"As soon as the Emperor receives a free hand, Pilate's days are numbered. But remember: nothing is official! The legates would rightly consider it a grave insult if they were told 'The Emperor expects you to be loyal!'"

All the feelings of inadequacy which had beset him during the last few days returned. "I don't know whether I ought to undertake such a mission," he said. "I am not trained for it."

"Just tell the legates what has happened in Judea. Talk to them about Gaius Cornelius. The Cornelii are a very loving family, deeply devoted to each other. So you should mention that the new lieutenant-commander shares your faith. You needn't worry; you are very convincing in matters in which your heart is involved." Into Marcius' startled silence he interjected, "Isn't your belief also the faith of the Prince of Youth?"

Marcius nodded with a happy smile. "It is!" In his mind the legates, the Germanic and the Syrian legions, Pilate, the whole intricate game of imperial policy, had completely vanished. "That means," he said, stumbling over the words, "that the Emperor and you are siding with the Faith! So you did convince yourself, you and the Emperor—"

But again he waited for a clear answer.

"We have left the thread of our conversation," Seneca

replied. "Otherwise my little discourse on subjective an
objective realities might have led us to a positive result." H
paused for a moment. "Shall I illustrate my views with
concrete example—the one which I have studied during th
last few months?"

So this was the moment. Through labyrinths of abstrac
terms this strange man had finally reached the answer whic
he could have given in straight and simple language. Thoug
Marcius could not suppress a creeping uneasiness, he prepare
himself for happiness.

"I told you about the Greek concept of the Logos," h
heard Seneca's smooth voice flowing on. "On my wa
through Greece I met a man, a member of the Areopagus o
Athens and a great philosopher. Perhaps under the influenc
of the Hebrew scriptures he explained the Logos as th
Mediator between God and the world. Plato and the othe
thinkers, he said, helped to educate man for this concept
they worked in the light of the Logos, though not in it
fullness, as men work during the hours of dawn before th
sun has risen."

His voice lost its sententiousness. "The meeting with th
Areopagite was a good preparation for the main part of my
journey. It taught me that even though we cannot fathom
the Divine, due to an original knowledge embedded in ou
memory, we can determine what falls short of it. Take Soc
rates as an example, or Pythagoras, Plato, the great artist
of the Periclean age. Exalted as they are, they are all men
Their very lives would show a thousand imperfections
incompatible with the objective concept of the Divine. Wha
these men present to us simply does not agree with ou
original perception of the Godhead. There is none in all th
world who would force us to a different judgment. Bu
One—"

"He–" Marcius said, shuddering.

"Yes, He. I have talked with His friends and disciples. I have also talked with His enemies. There was no praise and no detraction which would have showed the slightest stain. You have been witness to the final phase of the drama, but I have diligently enquired into all known details of His life, His signs, His work, His teachings. In all aspects of His personality there is a concord without spot or shadow, such as there has never been in any other man. Necessity freely willed, and freedom, necessitated by Himself, transcended His every word and action."

One of his earlier thoughts returned to Marcius. "Even the sun and the stars conformed to His harmony," he said.

"I willingly agree. When the Emperor asked me for my opinion, I summarized: one of His disciples actually referred to Him as the incarnate Logos, the Son of God, through Whom all things have been created. All asserted that He was both God and Man, in hypostatic union. The enemies I talked with said that this had been His claim, in which, however, they did not believe; but none was able to prove that on such lips a lie, or so weighty a self-deception, could be found. Neither did I myself discover any evidence by which that claim could be nullified."

In wild elation Marcius seized Seneca's hand. "So you do believe," he stammered. "It was May when I arrived–I hoped that by its end the swords would be turned into ploughshares. Then I waited–waited patiently, until my hope almost left me." Tears welled up in his eyes. "But now everything will change, the whole world–"

Seneca withdrew his hands. "Please understand me correctly," he said, visibly moved. "My knowledge tells me that the divine self-consciousness, should it ever become flesh, could well appear in such historic manifestation. There is

nothing in it contrary to our reason and its concept of the
Supreme Idea."

"I don't care how you put it!" Marcius exclaimed with
a happy boy's delight. He thought of Cornelius' letter. "A
you're so fond of terms which nobody can understand, you
may even speak about 'cosmic dialectics.' There's only one
thing which matters–"

Seneca's embarrassment grew. Once more he made an
effort to explain his position. Then he realized that it would
be of no avail.

"Now listen," he finally said. "There are many things to
be discussed. After all, you are being sent on an importan
mission, even though it is a confidential one. You too are now
an imperial ambassador-at-large."

"Just tell me what to do!" Marcius replied obediently.

Seneca lowered his voice. "His Majesty at once remem
bered Captain Thamus' report. The coincidence, to say the
least, is certainly remarkable. He also mentioned that from
time immemorial hope for a Mediator had lingered on."

"The Great Garden–"

"The Golden Age, as we call it. There is a beautifu
poetical description of it in Ovid's *Metamorphoses*."

"I don't know it," Marcius admitted.

"Oh, you must read it! No summer course is complet
without Ovid!" Then he quoted the opening verses: " 'The
Golden Age was first founded, which without any avenger
of its own accord, without laws, practiced both faith an
rectitude. Punishment, and the fear of it, did not exist, and
threatening decrees were not read upon the brazen tables
open to view–"

"The return of such age has been foretold for a long time,
he continued. "The Emperor thought of it at once. He quote
Virgil's Fourth Eclogue about the coming of a Divine Child

nder Whose scepter the iron brood would first begin to ail, and a new generation of men be sent down from the eight of heaven."

"He is turning towards the Greater King," Marcius said, is emotions rising to high pitch. He stood up in his seat and hrowing back his shoulders, he looked over the heads of he horses, as if he were driving them along a track with nbridled speed. "And I brought it about—I—as His ambassa-lor, not only the Emperor's."

"Go slowly, little Phaethon, go slowly!" Seneca said, almost vith a note of fright. "Suppose the chariot were given to ou; what could you do? Could you proceed, opposed to he whirling poles, so that the rapid heavens should not carry ou away?"

"What do you mean?" Marcius asked, an uncanny feeling iounting in his heart.

"I was still thinking of the story of young Phaethon who vanted to drive the chariot of the sun."

"He didn't succeed though, or did he?" Marcius said, ncertainly.

"The horses were too fast and the heavens too high. He vas struck down and fell in flames into the Eridanus, now alled the Padus river. There, where its waves bathed his urning face, his sisters mourned for him night and day, ntil they were changed into weeping poplars, and their ears into amber."

"That's a fable, isn't it?" Marcius asked with forced light-ess. He sat down again. "No man can drive the chariot of he sun!"

"It may be a fable. But it is educational. I must give you copy of Ovid. Remind me of it." In a matter-of-fact tone e went on. "The Senate reconvenes on the first day of)ctober. His Majesty will use his constitutional powers as

Princeps and Pontifex Maximus to introduce a motion pertaining to the religion of the State. It is the imperial will that by this law, should it pass the House, further deifications would be excluded for all time. Immediately after the session is over the Prince of Youth may be given the toga virilis."

"Isn't he too young for it?"

"Not necessarily. His father received it at the age of fifteen. So did Caesar Augustus."

"That is a good portent," Marcius said, as if to himself. "He had such gloomy forebodings that he might never outgrow his praetexta." He forgot that not so long ago he had been scandalized at the thought of political considerations being mixed with religion. "It should also dispose of the Caligula question!" he added.

"It will," Seneca replied. But he seemed not too happy that his young companion had gained so much insight into a carefully laid plan. "You may truthfully tell the legates that His Majesty's grandson is in no way at variance with the sanctioned religious practice of the Empire."

"Thank you," Marcius said warmly. "Now I know what to do." His face was serious like that of a young student who has received permission to solve a set task in his own independent fashion. "Don't you think I ought to have another talk with the Prefect of Rome and the Senator before I leave?"

"That's a very good idea. I told you that the Cornelii are a very loving family!"

"You will let me know the outcome of the meeting of the Senate?"

"Of course. If we time everything correctly the news will reach you on your way north." He was not entirely at ease when he asked: "Are you very anxious to see Rome?"

"Well—I had hoped—"

"May I be entirely frank? You have been His Majesty's guest for too long to visit the capital unnoticed. And you know how excited the people are there just now. We must avoid any incident which might cause unrest and sharpen the crisis."

"If the Emperor thinks so—"

"I knew you would make this sacrifice." He took a map from his tunic pocket. "It's too dark for it," he said, with artificial gruffness, "but I think I can explain. There's an old proverb: 'All roads lead to Rome.' It isn't quite correct though. There is always a way to by-pass the city. If you ride along the coast to Ostia, and then for twelve more miles—" He gave Marcius the map. "Just keep it. You can study the details at some other time. At Alesium you reach the Via Aurelia, a very beautiful road. It leads you through Pisa up to Luna. There you turn right, over the mountains to Parma and then across the Padus river."

"You have worked it all out beautifully," Marcius said with some surprise.

"I am an old schemer," Seneca replied jokingly. "I'll write you at Verona, in care of the place commandant. My letter will go by fast mail. That should leave you a few more days in Antium."

"I had better go tomorrow," Marcius replied coldly.

Seneca paid no attention to this. "Take your time. The second day of September is the anniversary of the Battle of Actium, the greatest feast day of the imperial house. All shops and offices will be closed. Most of them won't even be open tomorrow. And you still want to do some shopping, arrange for your insurance, perhaps write a few letters and see the Cornelii. There is ample time if you leave on the sixth or the seventh."

“The sixth will be a good day.” He fought down his resentment. “Where shall I go from Verona?”

“Up the Athesis river to Tridentum, then to Bauzanum and over the Brennus Pass to Rhaetia.”

“And from there?”

“Down into the Aenus valley. Then you can cut across to the Rhine, along its left bank, until you reach Moguntiacum. Both legates may be there from autumn till spring.”

“Moguntiacum, where the elder Drusus died? Luitpran told me about it.”

“The story about the Germanic maiden? It doesn’t frighten you, I hope?”

“Why should it? I am not going as a would-be conqueror.”

“Besides,” Seneca said, “since the exploits of Germanicus the Eagle has dealt rather effectively with trans-Rhenish magic and prophetesses.”

“But there are still no legions numbered XVII, XVIII, o XIX in the Roman army,” Marcius retorted impishly, gla to have found an outlet for his mounting temper.

“Are we getting irritated with each other?” Seneca asked and suggested that they return to town.

The moon had set completely as the carriage rolled along the raised promenade. Silently Marcius watched the horse and gazed at the dark houses along the beach. His mind wa again at peace, but in spite of Seneca’s efforts, the conversation did not continue, not even when they had returned to the sleeping garden of the Villa Ciceronis.

CHAPTER TWENTY-THREE

FIVE WEEKS after Marcius had left Antium, he reached the southern embankment of the Padus river. Shortly before it came in sight, the name of Verona had begun to appear on the road signs, like so many other places during his long ride. Each place had been a distinct goal as he drew near, but had later sunk back into the pattern, like the colors on a wheel which turns faster and faster.

Verona would be different. It marked the end of the first real lap of his journey, and it would bring order into the chaotic succession of places, every one of them only a stepping stone to the next. And with the end in sight, the beginning of the trip again stood forth in sharper contours.

He could have crossed the last broad barrier on his way north by the bridge at Brixillium and gone on to Betriacum. From there the main Italian artery, the Via Postumia, a continuation of the Via Julia Augusta, would have brought him straight to his goal at the Athesis river, the capital of the region of Venetia.

But as if by a magic power the wide stream seemed to hold him to its bank. He rode eastwards for a whole day, while the smoothly flowing waves changed their colors with the steadily fleeting hours.

An inarticulate feeling of anxiety was in his heart. "This is the water that extinguished Phaethon's blaze," he thought. A group of weeping poplars had come into sight. "And here are his sisters!" He stopped, and for some minutes looked up at their tops. The leaves trembled in the still air of the late afternoon.

"Let's rest, Pomponius!" he said, and sat down on a patch of turf close to the spotted black-and-white trunks of the mourning trees. "We've both been a bit sad since we left Antium!"

It was the first time that he had thought of their departure. Yellow and purple streaks had come into the waves. A tired dragonfly dipped its wings in the water, and then returned to the shore. With eyes veiled by memory Marcius followed its course, until his gaze glided back to the rainbows lazily gleaming in the river. Here, on its southern bank, he still moved within a world which had meant so much—

He tried to find a note of comfort. "But shopping was fun, wasn't it, Pomponius?"

Seneca had not only given him an imperial passport, entitling him to free transportation on all the land and waterways of the Empire, and free room and board in all government-owned *mansiones*, but had also given him a draft for two hundred and fifty aurei! Now he could really go into town and buy presents for his parents and all his friends at home. Silverware, linen, capes, mantles, shoes, furs, in addition to all his previous purchases, were packed by expert hands. The firm of Titus P. Atticus arranged for shipment, storage and insurance. Tiro, the caretakers and the six slaves also received appropriate gifts, and after everything was paid, he still had a sizable balance. Sixty aurei, and a checkbook, he took along on his journey, while the balance would be held for him at Titus P. Atticus branch office at Iuliobona, the port at the mouth of the Sequana river, where his belongings would wait his arrival.

The final conversation with Luitprant had taken place shortly before the Imperial German bodyguard was recalled to Capri. What Marcius told him he accepted, just as he himself would have accepted it, had he heard it from a trustworthy man.

"They too must have had knowledge of the Great Garden and have known that it would open again," Marcius pondered, forlorn in his memories.

Luitprant's blue eyes had flashed with indignation when he heard about the traitor Judas Iscariot.

"Selling his King—of all Kings the most gracious!"

"Judas must have been blind."

"He must have been! But why did he not implore the mercy of his King?" There was complete confidence in his voice. "The greater the King, the greater also his forgiveness."

"When you come to my people," he had said in parting, "tell them about the twelve legions of angels who were waiting at the King's command. Tell them about the eleven followers, those keen blades, who loyally stood by Him." His eyes had shone with warlike fire. "Tell them about Simon the Rock, who drew his sword for his King, when so many were arrayed against so few!"

On the day after Seneca's departure a parcel had been delivered at the Villa Ciceronis. It contained a beautiful edition of Ovid's *Metamorphoses.* The leaves were of purple parchment. The text was written in gold and silver ink. The margins were richly decorated with allegoric figures and ornaments, and there was a portrait of the poet with many other illustrations.

Marcius was so fascinated by this present that he almost failed to notice a small slip of paper. "These are the horses I want you to drive!" it said. On the reverse was a receipt, signed by Titus P. Atticus Heirs for two light Numidians and a carriage with one double seat, to be delivered to Marcius Armaghensis at Iuliobona. The firm acknowledged that all expenses had been defrayed by the Senator Lucius Annaeus Seneca.

"That was good of him," Marcius thought, jumping up from the patch of turf. "I hope you'll get along with them, Pomponius. I want you to be at your best when you meet them. You are a Belgian, so we are practically neighbors. But they are strangers! They come from a very warm country, close to the Garamantes!"

Now the waters were turning to a dull gray. But he still rode eastwards.

"One can feel that it is October!" he thought. When it was almost dark, he came to a boathouse. A lean old man, with a flowing beard of faded red lived there.

"Can you take us to the other side?"

Wordless, the ferryman showed them into a large flat barge. The craft groaned beneath their weight, and through its seams came a flood of marshy water.

A thin drifting mist mingled with the veils of fear arising in Marcius' soul. To his eyes, as to his mind, the crossing seemed endless. "There may be no other side," he thought vaguely.

When they had finally reached the northern shore, he just had time to pay his coin before the silent boatman and his barge vanished into the shades of the slumberous night.

The mouth of the Mincius river was near. A good road followed the course of that stream, but after such a crossing the beating of Pomponius' broad unshod hoofs sounded almost unreal. During those two or three hours, until they reached Mantua, it was once more the good stallion who was in command, while Marcius plunged ever deeper into his memories.

The imperial villa, the cottage of Tiberius Gemellus and most of the houses by the beach had been closed when

Marcius was finally ready to leave. In the windows of the more expensive shops posters announced that the seasonal sale had begun. Instead of the elegant carriages, oxcarts rumbled through the promenades and the main streets, bringing vegetables and meat to the market for the use of the local population.

The whole town was ebbing away, making ready to slumber for many many months. Finally, during his last two days, Marcius hardly left the Villa Ciceronis at all. He spent hours secluded in the library, again reading Cornelius' letters, especially the last one, which he had entrusted to Seneca. Of all that he had received, this was the one which moved him most deeply.

Teaching with compassion and authority in the Temple courtyard, on meadows and in orchards, as the sovereign leader of souls, the One, to Whose harmony the sun and the stars must conform—this had been the image which his eyes and his mind had indelibly beheld.

Through all the sufferings and humiliations, to the death on the Cross, and finally in the Great Triumph, and in the Ascension in glory to the throne of the Eternal Father—it was the Master, the anointed King, the Divine Conqueror, God's only begotten Son of Whose deeds and graces Marcius' knowledge had steadily increased.

But though he had met Him, clothed in flesh as a true man, so far he had never asked: "What was He like before His ministry began? Where was He born? How did He live as a child among children, a youth among youth?"

Now it was the earliest part of His earthly life, hidden so far or never thought of, that he was told of in Gaius Cornelius' letter.

"A decree had gone forth from the Emperor Caesar Augustus," Marcius read, "that a census of the whole world should be taken. This first census took place while Cyrinus was governor of Syria. And all were going, each to his own town, to register–"

It was the time of the year when the days are shortest. A light frost covered the trees, and whiteness stretched across many of the meadows. Shallow little holes in the country road to Bethlehem were covered by a film of thin ice. With compassion Marcius' inner gaze followed two figures–an elderly man, tired, walked with weary feet beside a mule, on which sat a young woman.

"As inspired prophets had foretold–" the letter continued, "a Virgin will conceive by the Holy Spirit and bring forth the Saviour."

It seemed to Marcius that the young woman on the mule was looking up–and while his heart missed a beat, he recognized the features of Her whom he remembered so well standing on Mount Golgotha, her sky-blue robe covered by a dark-gray veil.

Dusk was coming in a steady fall of large soft flakes, and still the group moved on. "Will they find quarters for the night?" he wondered anxiously. Here were the first houses of Bethlehem. With his staff the faithful guide knocked at their doors, but there always came the same answer. There was no room for them in the inn. But then they found a stable, and stillness and peace spread over the face of the whole earth.

Now, as a feeling of joyous elation began to fill his soul, it seemed to Marcius that he too was out in the fields, where shepherds kept watch over their flocks. From there, admonished by a great voice, and guided by a brightness from on high, together with the shepherds he went again to town and to the stable. In a manger lay a newborn Child, Who recognized His mother with a smile.

There was little he could write in answer to the letter. So he only asked Cornelius to get in touch with Tiro, Aristides, and of course, with the Prince of Youth. Pride in his mission dictated his closing sentence: "Now I'll be off soon as an imperial ambassador, and as a royal one too!"

"Where will this letter reach Cornelius?" he had wondered. "Perhaps I should give it to one of the Cornelii." Only then did he remember that he had almost neglected one of his main tasks.

The Senator had left for Capri, but the Prefect of Rome, fortunately, was still at Antium.

"Marcus Cocceius Nerva was consul-designate for the balance of the year," the Prefect said. "Now His Majesty has nominated me in his stead. This means that I shall preside over the October session of the Senate. My brother has been asked to take over the other functions of the late Prefect of Campania."

"This puts the Cornelii pretty well in control of the State," Marcius thought with delight. Excitedly he told the Prefect about his forthcoming journey to Moguntiacum and what he hoped to achieve. To all this the Prefect listened without voicing his personal opinion.

"I wonder whether I didn't talk too much?" Marcius had asked himself afterwards. "He looked somewhat pained. Oh well, I could never be a tight-lipped Roman gentleman, even if I tried." Yet, he could not quite suppress a feeling of uneasiness every time he thought of the interview.

By now the first lights of Mantua had come in sight. On the Mincius river were a few barges with paper lanterns. His spirits picked up. "There's the town, Pomponius! You can't miss it." And then his thoughts returned to his journey.

At Lavinium he had made a short stop. The oak tree had

a few yellow leaves, and in the clear September air Rome's mural crown seemed within reach of his outstretched hand. Wasn't that the cupola of Agrippa's Pantheon and there, more to the right, wasn't that the Senate meeting house, where at the feet of the statue of Pompey, the founder of the Julian house had fallen under the daggers of Brutus and his wicked accomplices?

"Don't worry about treachery!" he said, as if Tiberius Gemellus were again at his side. "I am bringing you eight of the best legions!" A feeling almost of triumph seized him. "Now I know! The King Himself must have commanded Longinus to send me to Italy!"

Joyously he galloped down the hill. "Didn't I tell you, Pomponius, that everything was working out well? Soon you'll find yourself walking alongside the golden chariot of the Emperor Tiberius Caesar Gemellus!" His thoughts ran wild. "It isn't either the one or the other–it's both, the Eagle and the Cross!"

Over the Tiber, always along the blue ribbon of the Mediterranean Sea the good broad stallion had carried him northward. Every evening the sun had set a shade further south, and the nights had become more autumnal. At Luna, where his path turned sharply inland, he bade the sea farewell. It had been his companion ever since Tyrus. "But don't worry, Pomponius," he said. "We'll soon be back again!"

Of course, when a young man is on his own for so long, there are many thoughts which whirl through his head. These thoughts had started coming when he had passed the Tiber on which many ships from all parts of the Empire were going up to the capital.

"What a great task to share in the duties of government!" he had thought. But Tiberius Gemellus was so young! "What does it matter? He is of the race of the Caesars!" But he has many opponents, came the counter-argument, and gigantic prejudices must be overcome. "A friend and a philosopher," as the sly schemer Herod Agrippa had put it, would not be enough. The young ruler would be in bitter need of an active loyal helper.

"You are a Roman citizen already," Tiberius Gemellus had said. Now Marcius remembered it. "Even an imperial ambassador!" he added in his thoughts.

"We have been ruling rather well in Armagh!" he reflected, proudly. "And men grow in stature with the growth of their duties!"

Thus, slowly, certain parts of the conversation under the oak had emerged ever more clearly. "Another girl would think that I am the most faithless of men," he had replied when Tiberius Gemellus had spoken about his sister Julia.

But was the child on the wild island really still waiting? And even if she was, she might understand that the call of duty . . . "No, no, I mustn't think that! It's wicked—wicked!" Yet, once the thought had crystallized in his mind, he could not help returning to it again and again.

It was almost midnight when Pomponius brought him to Mantua. That was Virgil's birthplace, and throughout the year it attracted many sight-seeing tourists from all parts of the world. The *mansio* was full, so he went to an inn by the Mincius river where it broadens out into a lake. Prices were accordingly high, five denarii for the room, but the bed had a large mosquito net, a very good thing. Tired as he was, though, he found that his plans and speculations kept on coming, and so the night was not quite so restful as he had hoped after his eery ride along the Padus river.

When he continued his journey on the following morning,

haste spurred him on, a feeling of restlessness, almost of fear, completely irrational and only half understood, such as he had not experienced since his ride from Jerusalem to Capharnaum.

The great plain with its countless fruit trees—olives, figs, apples, plums and pears—lay under the glare of a cloudless sky. Lonely cypresses stood between the orchards like folded sails. "They never smile," he had thought in the garden of the imperial villa at Antium. Now it occurred to him again.

The road was covered with deep dust. As far ahead as one could see, it was lined by poplars. From stubble fields peasants brought in the last harvest, turnips and sheaves of rye and wheat. In some villages he noticed that the people had Celtic names.

The shadows of the poplars were lengthening when he perceived that a wide-stretching gray-blue bank of clouds was thrusting up over the northern horizon. It took him several minutes to realize what it actually was. The clouds were no clouds, but instead the Alps, which at one point directly behind Verona protruded deep into the wide basin of the Padus plain.

"Where have I—?" he thought, and then the scene returned. There was the screened porch with the big map and the corner with the travel and adventure stories. A dull class hour was dragging on, as the imperial boy, his hair looking like old gold, bent over a textbook. He underlined a sentence, and with a whimsical smile pushed the book so that Marcius could read it.

"Go your mad way," it said. "Hurry over the terrible Alps that you may please boys as a subject for declamation."

A painful longing for the past summer that had waned far behind the Padus, down by the now deserted shores of

Antium, took hold of him. Pomponius, always alive to his master's moods, slowed down and then stopped.

From the east, shadows had begun to drift across the land. A sea gull from the Adriatic Sea, which had followed the course of the Athesis and had now lost its way, circled with anxious cries above the trembling summits of the trees. In the north the mountains had assumed clearer shape.

"The roof of the world!" Marcius thought. He pulled himself together. "Rely on me, little brother! I am not going there for the sake of declamation."

Pomponius started on again, slowly at first, and then at a fast trot. One hour, two hours, and Verona was reached. It lay in a loop of water formed by the winding of the Athesis. One could approach it only from the west.

Now Marcius saw the city gate. It was a simple arch, with one passage, flanked by Corinthian columns, dedicated to Tiberius Caesar and his brother Drusus in honor of their Germanic and Pannonian victories.

Blazing torches, held by iron rings, were fastened to the wall on both sides of the gate. The horse halted abruptly, and Marcius heard the challenge of the watch. In the semidarkness he saw glistening spears barring his way.

He sat erect and drew his sword. With a gesture, which was like a command, he pointed toward the town. "In the name of the Emperor!" he said in a sharp voice, and the gate swung open.

CHAPTER TWENTY-FOUR

THE *mansio* of Verona, the main road hub of northern Italy, was a spacious four-story building. From here the Via Postumia ran to Aquileia, and on to Byzantium, almost twelve hundred miles away. Another all-weather highway connected the town with Mediolanum and with the passes over the Graian and Cottian Alps to the Rhone valley, Geneva, and Lugudunum. To the southwest, the Via Postumia extended to Cremona, to continue as the Via Julia Augusta down to Genoa and along the coast to Massilia. Somewhat further east of the second-class road to Mantua, still another highway went to Bononia, where it linked up with the Via Aemilia to Arimium at the Adriatic Sea and with a branch of the Via Cassia, the great north-south artery to Florentia and Rome. Finally, there was the hard-surfaced road along the left bank of the Athesis, up to Tridentum, Bauzanum, and the Brennus. It served as the main supply route for all garrisons in Rhaetia, on the upper Rhine and Danube, and throughout Vindelicia, with its fast-growing capital, Augusta Vindelicorum.

The *mansio* was filled up, but as soon as the station master saw Marcius' passport, he bowed and led him to the third floor. There was a suite, bedroom, dressing room and bath, set aside for special guests. That Pomponius would receive the best of care was a matter of course.

"This is the most comfortable place I have been in yet," Marcius thought, as he washed the dust off. "Why not enjoy it? Tomorrow it's goodbye, civilization!"

He opened a window. The night was not too warm, but it

still had a southern depth. Somewhere a young man was singing a sentimental serenade, and the disjointed thrumming of his lute awoke Neapolitan memories.

"It seems like years since I stayed at the Taverna ad Vesuvium! I have learned a lot since then!" He turned to a mirror and scrutinized his face. It was deeply tanned; the lines were sharper; and because he had lost weight, his blue eyes, with their lively green spark, appeared somewhat larger. No doubt there was more maturity in their glance, though not quite as much as he might have thought.

He thrust out his chin. "Don't I look like a Senator already?" He puffed out his cheeks. "Perhaps I'd need more of that!" An irresistible urge to throw himself into postures came over him. He crossed his arms and focused his eyes on the tip of his nose. "This is the way old Cato must have looked!" He stepped back and raised his right arm in the Roman salute. "*Patres Conscripti, ceterum censeo*—" Planting his feet straight on the floor he sat down on a chair. He looked grim. "Oh, wicked Casca!" With a gesture as if to catch the arm of a would-be assailant, he added: "*Casca, quid agis?*"

He grew sober. "One shouldn't make fun of Julius Caesar's death," he thought shamefacedly, and backed away from the mirror.

The night outside was still filled with murmurs. Behind the loop of the Athesis the darkness seemed more intense. "The terrible Alps—" the phrase came back to him. But because he was too tired, or because he felt sorry for his behavior, he did not assert that he was not going there just for the sake of declamation.

Well rested and in good humor, Marcius was awakened by the noise of heavy hammers and screeching stone-saws.

"It sounds as if they were breaking up whole mountains," he thought, and rushed to the window. Something like a huge oval crater was taking shape. As far as he could judge, it was an arena, about five hundred feet long and four hundred broad. Three tiers of arches were under construction.

"An ambitious town, I must say! I had better dress carefully." Anyway, he reflected, it would not be proper to appear at the place commandant's office in anything other than the citizen's toga.

It was nine o'clock when he finished his breakfast. In the waiting room he looked at the *Acta Diurnia.* It was the issue of the last of September. The official column reported that on the calends of October the Senate would reconvene to discuss a written recommendation by His Majesty the Emperor, to be presented to the Conscript Fathers by the presiding consul, Corsus Cornelius Lentulus. This recommendation, according to a semi-official spokesman, who would not permit direct quotation, pertained to the religion of the state.

"The spokesman is Seneca!" Marcius thought, delighted at his inside information. "But why on earth doesn't the paper say so?"

Far more prominence was given to the arrival of the Second Syrian Legion. Three cohorts had disembarked at Ravenna, two at Brundisium, two at Misenum, and three at Ostia. Several columns of the sheet were dedicated to detailed descriptions of the popular rejoicing caused by the sight of the legionnaires. They had been away from home for a long time and had filled Eastern nations of all kinds with trembling fear of the Eagle and of the Emperor's and the Roman People's sacred majesty.

Marcius repeated the names of the debarkation points. "They make Rome pretty well their center," he concluded, pleased. The Eighth from Pannonia must have arrived already.

This is a language the most stubborn augurs and Herodian and other schemers will understand."

Humming a gay tune, he stepped out into the sunny streets. Many were lined with arcades, their groined vaults spanning the whole breadth of the sidewalks. Peddlers, schoolboys, shopkeepers, servant maids, were swarming everywhere. At one corner there was a delicious odor of freshly roasted chestnuts.

"The town reminds me of Capharnaum," Marcius thought, "only the types are different." Instead of Egyptians, Indians, and Jews–though there were some of them around–one could see many people with Celtic and Germanic blue eyes, dark-haired Gauls and Helvetians, fair Marcomans and Hermunduri from the rim of the Hercynian Forest, called the Sudeti Mountains, and tall Suevians from the Upper Danube. Even a few Vandals, Goths and Burgundians, who dwelt at the mouth and along the banks of the Vistula had followed the trade routes out of the mysterious plain of Germania Magna. From the outer fringes of the known world the men of this throng had brought precious amber and furs, and to the anger of the wholesale tradesmen, they seemed well informed about the real value of their choice products.

On the main forum was the well-known statue of the ruling Emperor; the august Prince rested on his curule chair. Marcius greeted him with joy and shy reverence. "In Antium he had the same expression!" He visualized the tricolored room. "Over there sat the Prince of Youth. And here stood I, delivering Longinus' message and the sacred lance."

At the north end of the forum stood a large building which housed the offices of the collector for Transpadanian Italy, where the five-percent inheritance tax was paid. Passing it, Marcius came to the oval excavation, the big crater which he had seen from his window.

The headquarters of the place commandant were near by. Scribes in civilian tunics stood before high desks. The rooms were badly lit and buzzing with flies. Unarmed soldiers and untidy city guards strolled yawning through the corridors.

At last Marcius noticed a junior officer who looked more alert than his comrades. "May I see the place commandant?"

"He has gone to Ravenna to meet the Syrian cohorts."

"Oh, but that's terrible!"

"Why, if I may ask?"

"Because I want my mail."

"For that you don't need the place commandant." A suspicious gleam had come into the officer's eyes. "Your name—"

"Marke de Armagh." He produced his passport. "By order of His Majesty!"

"At your service!" He saluted. "Please follow me."

The officer brought him to a waiting room and bade him sit down. Ten minutes later he came back. "I am sorry, sir. The mail has not been sorted yet."

So Marcius waited. People went in and out, talking rapidly in a harsh Venetian dialect; bristling and shaggy in its words and accents, it was difficult to understand. "The whole of life is waiting," Seneca had once said. "But today everything was to be different!" Marcius thought. Time seemed endless. Repeatedly the officer returned, only to apologize. The air became sticky and the flies buzzed.

It was almost noon when the officer brought him the letter. It was carefully closed with several seals. "Sorry to have kept you waiting," he said, and asked to be excused.

"I must read it quietly," Marcius thought, and put the letter into the sinus of his toga. A bell rang, and clerks, scribes, soldiers and city guards, bursting from all the rooms, pushed their way through the narrow crowded corridors. In their stream Marcius was swept along, but immediately in front of the building, the people dispersed. It looked as if they were swallowed up by the countless small taverns and bars all around.

The shops under the groined arcades were closed, the sidewalks and streets were deserted. Over the empty forum glided the Emperor's glance, as of living marble, detached, and with a shade of disdain. His wreath of gilded laurels shone bright in the autumnal sun.

"They eat and take their naps, while I am carrying the destiny of the world," Marcius thought. He came to the Athesis. Its current was strong, and as if the waves had not been told yet that the mountain valley lay behind them and that they could now more freely expand, they rolled and tumbled over each other, like packs of tiny gay shepherd dogs.

Close to the river bank, on a square covered with cobble stones, stood an old playhouse. Washed-out marble stairs led to the water. Grass and moss grew out of their joints and in the many cracks in the stones. There Marcius sat down and opened his letter from Seneca.

All he noticed at first was that it was long. "Why does he waste so many words? Oh well, cosmic dialectics!" He smiled happily. "That's his way of saying simple things."

"My dear friend," the letter began. "I wish you were not leaving the Empire without having seen the city from which it derives its name!"

"It's not of my own choosing–" Marcius thought involuntarily.

The letter flew off into a somewhat chatty description of official pageantry–"I realize that our costumed ceremonials may look strange to our modern, matter-of-fact age, yet they still retain a beauty of their own. The reopening of the Senate, after its summer recess is a unique sight–"

There followed a caustic picture of the members of this illustrious body. "Some Senators always remind me of the Barbary apes, which populate the southern tip of my native Hispania. They scratch their backs and wag their heads and pretend to be very philosophical. But they only wait for their peanuts. If you dressed them in togas, they could easily pass as *clarissimi.* Others among our elder statesmen look more dignified. They are intelligent and well educated, yet they are just as malicious as my long-tailed fellow-countrymen around the Pillars of Hercules."

"That's all right, my friend," Marcius thought, amused. "You are still very glad to be one of them!"

All the six hundred were present, but for four or five. "They would never attend any public function, not even their own weddings, or their own funerals."

The cohorts of the Second Syrian Legion had formed the guard of honor. In shining armor they had lined the path up to the Capitol and its slopes down to the Via Sacra on the great Forum. An air of expectancy and of subdued excitement filled the whole city.

"Our Conscript Fathers looked decidedly preoccupied. Some seemed to have received quite a few pieces of mail relating to the forthcoming session. The display of armed public security, staged by our valiant Syrian veterans apparently failed to cheer them up. While piety is always a beautiful trait, it looked to me as if incense was burning rather ostentatiously before the altars of all the main shrines, the Temples of the Jupiter Capitolinus, of Castor and Pollux, of Julius Caesar, of Augustus and of Venus and Rome. Of course, the other participants in the senatorial procession noticed it too."

"What is he driving at?" Marcius wondered, and felt a slight pressure in the pit of his stomach.

Suavely the text continued. "Legally the Senate is nothing but a body for consultation, whose advice is sought by the presiding magistrate. 'What is your opinion?' he asks the Senators, beginning with the ex-consuls and continuing all the way down the list of former office holders, to the ex-quaestors. Then come the rest, those who wear the plain white toga and have never yet sat on a curule chair. They are called 'pedestrians,' and they may never get a chance to speak up at all. I am still one of them, as you know. When all the '*Quid censes?*' have been put, the chairman, from the mass of opinions expressed, chooses the one he likes best, and submits it to the judgment of the house."

"I can see why it is so important to have the right chairman," Marcius commented.

"The Senate was in sulky mood. The consul Corsus Cornelius Lentulus did little to dispel it," the letter went on. "Even his reading of the Imperial Message was rather listless. I add the main points, for I know that they will interest you. Meanwhile the full text has been inserted in the records of the Senate, which are kept in the archives of the State."

So this now was the measured voice of the Imperator Tiberius Caesar, Princeps Senatus and Tribune of the People, speaking through the mouth of the presiding consul: "Conscript Fathers, while it is well attested that the Founder of our city, Romulus, was transported to heaven, and heroes and favorites of the Immortals, Heracles, Ganymede, and others are said to have been chosen to dwell in abodes exalted above the realm of the shadows reserved for ordinary men, the intelligence that has reached us surpasses everything that the chronicles of by-gone ages have been able to tell. Since the original chaos was molded into the form of the earth, and of the celestial spheres circling around us, it has never been heard that any man by his own power has been able to reassume his body, a body which died on the cross, as proved irrefutably by the thrust of the lance of the late centurion Longinus, a body, finally, which by order and under the authority of the Governor Pontius Pilatus was guarded while lying in its grave. We have satisfied ourselves as to the veracity of the reports pertaining to this event, unique in the annals of the world's history, just as we have received proof of the exemplary life and power of the same, a power that has transcended the limit, which in the days of old Tellus was set for even the most beloved friends of the immortal gods. Therefore, Conscript Fathers, we wish to elicit from you the following opinion: does your conviction correspond to my own, that the Divinity of Him, Who by a miscarriage of justice was put to death and Who rose again on the third day, be recognized herewith by the Senate and People of Rome. Furthermore, do you agree with your Princeps and Pontifex Maximus that by the same advice of the Senate, pertaining to the Divinity of Him, Who is called the Christ, the list of the deified should be closed for all time? Conscript Fathers, it may not be inappropriate to remind you that I for my part, even though of the line of Divus Julius and Divus Augustus, have long ago declined such honors as would surpass those accorded to a mortal servant of the commonweal who has satisfactorily discharged all duties imposed upon him by the obligations of his sacred trust."

When reading this part of Seneca's letter Marcius forgot his surroundings. It was no longer the Athesis that splashed in quick, white-green waves up to the mossy marble stairs. Before his inner eyes another river wound its gentle course between groves of olives, oleanders, and figtrees with tender twigs. The briskness which drifted down from the mountains behind Verona gave way to the soft perfumes of the orchards and meadows of the Land of Promise.

"Tiberius Caesar professing the Greater King!" He dropped the letter into his lap. "So it has really happened—" His thoughts went on chaotically. "I shall go to Rome tonight. There is no longer any reason why I should not! No, first I must complete my mission to the legates! Or I shall stay here until the *Acta Diurnia* carries the news—or until the place commandant is back. I have full power now; my ambassadorship has become official." He drew his finger through the air. "The map of the Empire—it's outdated. A greater one has risen. 'Under the wings of the Eagle the Cross will grow up like a tree,' Cornelius predicted." He laughed. "How right he was! Over the sea lanes from Tyrus, along the Via Appia, the Via Aurelia, over rivers and country roads I have carried the Message—and I am carrying it still! Now northward over the Alps, to the Rhine, and over the German Ocean to Britannia, to Armagh!"

A new thought thrust itself into his field of vision. His mind was hurrying in unbridled course and this was like a hurdle, which suddenly confronts a rider who careers across a field; it frightens him, because it is so high, but it also tempts him, because it is so dangerous.

"Am I not one of the 'keen blades,' as Luitprant called them?" He stopped as if in midair, his daring jump not yet decided. Then, closing his eyes, he went over the top. "Let them watch my sword strokes, to see whether I cannot do better than they."

At once, fear and a sense of grievous guilt gripped his heart. "I only meant—" he muttered. His hands quivered as he took up the letter again. It still ran on for two more pages. Had not everything already been said?

"The *Quid censes?* was first put to the ex-consul Memmius Regulus. 'The august will is never without foundations in fact,' he replied. Lucius Domitius was next. 'The prudence and political foresight of our Emperor are well known,' he said. These answers were irreproachable, though not too illuminating. Neither were those that followed. 'The Pontifex Maximus is entrusted with the preservation of the state religion.' 'Was the miscarriage of justice referred to in the Imperial Message not based upon an alleged rebellion against the Emperor's Majesty? All hail, that we have so lenient and unselfish a Prince!' Then, another note was inserted, somewhat acrimonious, I should say. 'Oh, greatness of Rome! From the conquered Greeks it accepted its philosophy; from the conquered Jews it will accept a God.' This the consul should never have allowed to pass. It was unrelated to the subject, and only a means for the Senator to voice his spite. But our good Corsus Cornelius had grown restless, as soon as the words 'political foresight' had been uttered. He grew more restless still when another Senator—of the type of the toga'ed monkeys—said, 'How wise of our Pontifex Maximus! Religion too must serve the welfare of the State and make the reign of his grandson secure and ever more auspicious!' "

"That was a wicked and sneering answer," Marcius reflected, with burning cheeks.

"The next to be asked was His Majesty's own nephew, Claudius Tiberius Drusus, a younger brother of Germanicus and uncle of Gaius Caesar Caligula. A great scholar, though some disrespectful people have dubbed him 'the most learned fool of the Empire.' He has written a book about Latin orthography and some valuable works about the Etruscans and Carthaginians. Usually when he takes the floor, his fellow Senators flee to the recreation room. He is apt to stage an involuntary filibuster till sunset, when business must be suspended.

"It was a great blunder to call on him at all, even though he contented himself with a two-hour excursus on the Roman constitution. He may have been prompted solely by the fervor of the scientist, but perhaps he is more malicious than appears on the surface. And he is an intimate friend of Herod Agrippa. The two were brought up together.

"The gist of his speech was that, according to an ancient law from the time of Numa Pompilius, who established the Roman state religion, no god should be consecrated by the chief magistrate till first approved by the Senate. Nor did the initiative in such matters belong to the magistrate; the motion had to come from the floor of the House.

"The consul could have cut him short, time and again, but he just sat and waited. 'What is your opinion?' he automatically asked one of the Senators when Claudius was finally through. 'What can it possibly be?' the Senator answered in the most unctuous of voices. 'The Emperor is the protector of the laws. Who am I to depart from them?' He bowed to the consul. 'Out of respect for the Emperor's sacred majesty, my opinion is—the Lex Numa Pompilius stands.' At this moment, hundreds left the benches and came over to him, nodding, cheering. Then, with the exception of Memmius Regulus, Lucius Domitius, five or six others and myself, all bowed, mumbling, 'Out of respect for the Emperor's sacred majesty,' adding more loudly: 'The Lex Numa Pompilius stands.'

"Now the consul committed his biggest blunder. Instead of telling the Senate that the Lex Numa Pompilius was a matter alien to the debate and altogether obsolete, he declared that while he was certain that His Majesty held to his view, he would now invoke the imperial prerogative to withdraw the motion already before the House. Thereupon the Senate applauded, and following the suggestion of one of my togaed fellow countrymen adopted a vote of loyalty: His Majesty was to be thanked for having upheld the ancient prerogatives of his faithful servants. It was the devoutest, the most submissive, the most malicious, and the most perfidious thing I have ever seen."

"The Emperor held to his opinion," Marcius repeated. "That's all that counts." He read the passage over, but again he failed to get its meaning. Then, slowly he felt his hands turning clammy.

"I—I don't want to know," he stammered. A temptation to find cheap escape seized him. "I'll throw it into the water!" He dropped the letter to a lower step, but there was no wind. The bundle of leaves lay completely still. "You coward!" he said to himself and picked it up again.

The tone was no longer chatty. Neither was it flowery. It was straightforward, as he had heard Seneca talk before.

"There is no use denying that His Majesty's government has suffered a major setback. The consul has handed in his resignation. So has his brother. You may have sensed that I had misgivings about the whole procedure—from many angles. Months ago I told you, 'You would not want a conquest which overrides man's free will.' The wording may have been different, but the meaning was the same. It was the force of circumstance which necessitated bringing the matter before the Senate. The Emperor, too, would have liked to wait; but as the Prince of Youth had become identified with the new creed, we had to try to legalize it. To proceed by decree is alien to the Emperor's whole practice of government and to his constitutional convictions. Nor would it be wise. It might lead to a state crisis. I need not explain. You know the reasons as well as I."

"What now?" Marcius asked, choking, and immediately he read the answer.

"This incident must be lived down. Its importance must be minimized. The *Acta Diurnia* will pass it over completely.

In a few months nobody will even remember it. The Romans are that way! I could almost wish that His Majesty would permit gladiatorial games, banned a few years ago. They would be the best distraction."

"The silken-bearded goat!" Marcius thought with mounting indignation. "The brown-skinned satyr! He was never honest." He visualized Seneca baring his white teeth. Revulsion seized him. "The social climber, the politician! He wants to be minister of state; that's all he ever cared for." With a feeling not unlike grim satisfaction he finished the letter.

"You need not go to Moguntiacum. In fact, you should not go. The legates will be told by an official courier that everything has been greatly exaggerated. With this matter you must not interfere—not if you really love your little brother. The toga virilis will be withheld from him for a few more years; this will protect him from further criticism. As long as he is wearing his praetexta, his views have no official weight. So you will proceed, I assume, to Mediolanum and then perhaps to Genoa, and from there by ship. You know that all transportation facilities are at your disposal and that Tiberius Caesar remains your gracious Emperor. Nor have my feelings changed. *Vale—*"

There was a curious postscript. "Two cities our mind beholds. But only one has its foundation in the sacred mountains." This he hardly saw. "I have been their pawn—a try-out for Seneca's windy doctrines. Now I am dismissed." He walked through the busy afternoon crowds, feeling that all eyes were fastened on him, mocking, laughing, malicious. With a feeling of nausea he looked at the expensive shops. As at Antium, they were filled with rare and exotic merchandise. "All this must go!" he thought, a primitive lust for destruction welling up in his heart.

Only by the austere statue of Tiberius Caesar did he pass in shy reverence, and he avoided the dispassionate glance of the imperial eyes. "With the Emperor as His champion, why could the Greater King not—?" But blinded as he was by what he felt to be his own utter disgrace, he had not sunk so low as to think the terrible blasphemy through to its end.

Then, when he had reached the *mansio*, with his white toga, of which he had been so proud, burning on his shoulders like the shirt of Nessus, something else began to dawn on him: it was Herod and Caligula who had triumphed, while the cause of Tiberius Gemellus, who would never outgrow his praetexta, had been irrevocably lost. And when the blood-red sun had set behind the distant Padus river, with its lazy waters and the weeping poplars, it seemed to him as if the gates of the Great Garden were closing.

CHAPTER TWENTY-FIVE

THROUGHOUT the night demonic spectres had sapped Marcius' soul like a wasting disease. Now, as he rode through the arch of triumph, the morning shadows of the city wall still slanted deep into the great road, leading westward.

Impassively the guards presented arms. "Why do they look at me so?" Marcius wondered suspiciously. "Perhaps they know that I have had to change my route." Afraid that he might detect a grin on the stolid faces of the soldiers, nevertheless he glanced back. The inscription above the passage, flanked by Corinthian columns, lay in darkness. Only the words "Tiberius Caesar Triumphator," were clearly discernible. They had been engraved years ago, after the great soldier and statesman had pushed the boundaries of the Roman orbit to the banks of the Danube.

"Cornelius told me about it." Pain and resentment haunted his thoughts. It was the imperial name which was driving him away, so far away that he would never return. The gate, the goal of his long ride, had shut behind him forever.

He tore himself loose, and, undecided, his gaze wandered over the many road signs. "Mantua, twenty-eight miles." His heart contracted. "That was a long time ago!" Another arrow pointed toward Betriacum. Straight ahead the road ran to Arilica at the southeastern tip of the great Benacus Lake, and from there to Bergamum and Mediolanum.

"Where am I going?" he said aloud, with a lost expression in his eyes. "Well, just anywhere! What does it matter?" He leaned forward. "You know, Pomponius, that now you are my only friend?"

The day had become warm, as it does in North Italy early in October, when the air is of a clear blue though the trees and plants have lost some of their bright coloring.

"No more terrible Alps!" He had been prepared to venture into their ravines, guarded by turrets and battlements of jagged ice, and to ride his horse over the ramparts of eternal snow, through glacial deserts and across the path of the dreaded avalanches. In his mind he had already taken leave of the summer and its faded glory, because behind its veils of light and sweetness had emerged a task that was filled with greater happiness.

Now summer had been given back to him. Here it might still be tinged with the breath of the north, but soon the hours, weeks, and months would reverse their course, as if in the clock he had bought for his father the water should drip upward. From Mediolanum the road ran due south to Genoa. There a comfortable ship would set sail to pursue the sun and catch up with its chariot. During the winter months this ship would lie in port at the foot of the big rock which marked the southern tip of Hispania or, rounding the square peninsula, would winter in the wide basin of Osilipo in Lusitania, at the entrance of the Tagus river. On the tenth of March navigation would be resumed, and by then, along the Atlantic coast with its mysterious warm currents, spring would be at hand.

Many months would be his under azure skies, with waving palms and all the deepness and the perfumes of the south. But the thought had nothing alluring. It was even repellent, and as the warmth of the forenoon grew, he shivered as if from a chill.

"I don't want summer!" he murmured. The tamarisk

hedges by the road bore small pink and white flowers, and vines, half-pruned, hung on leafy elms. Red elder and black juniper berries could have refreshed his parched lips, but he did not notice them. Neither did he respond to the sweet air streaming from the benign sun. Its reflections made the smooth rounded surface of the road look black, as if a sudden cloudburst had passed over it. Pomponius was often deceived by it, and his master did nothing to urge him on. "He'll know best," he thought, while his mind shiftingly moved about.

"Nothing is lost!" He whipped himself into an attitude of defiance. "Tiberius Gemellus is still heir apparent. One day—" The slender boy with the golden hair, the strong forehead of the Caesars, and the sensitive mouth, stood almost visibly before him. "When he talked about his great concept of government, I saw him as he really is. What does age matter? That is of no importance. Never young, never old, the Emperor never dies."

Was it not a ghastly mistake to ride westward? "I am responsible, there's no use denying it! The consul was hamstrung, because I had let out the political secret. This is clear from Seneca's words. I must put things straight. I must go to the legates after all!" But at once he knew that this could not be done. The fullness of power, the mysterious element which pulsed through the world and held the legions in obedience, still resided in Tiberius Caesar. The "Emperor," the impersonal essence of rulership, transcending time and men, had not yet passed to Tiberius Gemellus. For his sake one could not break an imperial command, for no cause can be served by discarding the laws upon which it is built.

"It's the same in Armagh. I am nothing. It is my father who is everything." But even while he thought of this, he perceived the true proportions. The Roman Empire towered high as the pyramid of Cheops. From its base of nations and provinces it ascended to the lofty summit of the imperial office, exalted over all hierarchies of public servants and magistrates, and rising far above those who were related to the Emperor by mere ties of blood.

Compared with this pyramid, Armagh was like a little pebble. If the Romans ever cared to take it, they would not waste a legate or a proconsul on its administration. Not even a propraetor.

"And I thought that I could be co-regent, because I had some knowledge of rulership!"

Rulership . . . "The Romans would station one company at Armagh, under a place commandant with the rank of a centurion!"

Shame, humiliation, a helpless rage, engulfed him. "They have so much, yet they always want more!" he said. But he felt at once that this reproach was completely beside the point. He was the one who had wanted much of them. "No, I didn't!" he weakly defended himself. "It was Tiberius Gemellus who first talked about the co-regency." His face flushed. "And about Julia," he added. "Of course, he never mentioned her again after I told him about the child on the wild island. It's I who made the plans."

"I." More of the colored veils of fancy fell from his soul. Now it was almost naked, and his shame deepened.

"I? Who am I?" An ignorant young man, with delusions of self-importance, who has dabbled in high politics, indiscreet, garrulous, ignorant even of the damage he was doing, tarrying in the modern comfort of Antium beyond his appointed time, the son of a small chieftain from a half-civilized isle, who had thought that he could shape the future of the world. Now he had been cast out, left to himself to find his proper station in life.

"My sword strokes were to be better than those of the

'keen blades.' " The consciousness of a still greater guilt was knocking at his heart. "An imperial ambassador, and a royal one, too—that's what I wrote to Gaius Cornelius." Yet, only twenty-four hours after he had seen himself as the charioteer of Triumph, he had felt doubt of the greatest of Kings.

"Go slowly, little Phaethon, go slowly!" Seneca had warned. There had been a note of sincerity, even of fright, in the suave and mocking voice. "What do I reproach him for?" Marcius asked himself. Almost against his will his hate began to subside. "Seneca was not untrue. He said that he had knowledge." He paused for a moment. "Knowledge!" he repeated. "He never said he had faith."

"Phaethon—a pitiful imitation!" With self-punishment his thoughts continued. "Not even deemed worthy of a bolt of thunder."

So it was really an undeserved grace that he could go and hide his face. "My little brother, dear little brother! I am no suitable companion. You don't know that I even played with treason against my love—"

"Did you hear, Pomponius?" he asked. "Do you still want such a master?" Tears came into his eyes, but he felt no relief. There was one other veil still, dense and opaque, and his soul could not yet pierce it.

His horse stopped to allow a large herd of flat-nosed goats, under the command of a small boy, who proudly swung a switch, to cross the road. While waiting, Marcius saw that the tamarisk hedges had yielded place to long lines of marigolds. Behind them, on gently sloping meadows, were endless rows of pliant hyacinths. The air was filled with their nostalgic fragrance.

The fable about the origin of these flowers came to his mind. It was the jealous Zephyr who had turned the course of Phoebus Apollo's quoit so that it struck the forehead of the beauteous youth Hyancinthus. Out of the blood-tinged ground sprouted the flowers which were to bear his name. The word AI was inscribed in their chalice—a sigh of mourning for the beloved of the god.

But in his eclogues Virgil had called them the flowers of the Prince, for the AI showed in truth the initials of Augustus Imperator. Ever since, as a symbol of homage to the Julian house, they had been spreading over all the gardens of Italy.

He had to think of the youngest of the Caesars. Would the imperial monogram revert to its original meaning, a sigh of sorrow for the imperial youth and his too early fulfillment? A great sadness came over Marcius and kept him from thinking only of his own misfortune. He awakened to his surroundings.

"I shall take the lead now," he said, when the herd had passed. To his right, a bit of the lake was emerging behind a chain of rolling hills. On the summits, between white villas, were forests of chestnut trees. The bay trees in the unfenced parks stood high, and the myrtles were quiet.

He reached the upper course of the Mincius. Shortly before the bridge there was a sign: "To the Brennus road, ten miles. Ride carefully, slippery when wet." Almost amused, he shook his head. "This government behaves like a nurse. They'll tell you next how fast you may go!" It was a dirt road, running toward the northeast. Apparently a short cut, it formed a triangle with the main highways to Mediolanum and to the Brennus. His eyes followed it for a few moments, then he guided his horse along the left bank of the Mincius to the estuary of the river, and over a bridle path along the shore of the lake. He had to go a whole mile before he found a meadow and a stretch of beach which did not belong to one of the white villas.

"Don't go too far, Pomponius," he said. These were words

of friendship rather than of warning. The meadow, with a few plane trees at its edge, was small and, of course, the good stallion would never leave it.

Marcius threw off his clothes and waded into the lake. Where the reeds ended, the water was deep enough to reach his chest. With astonished eyes he looked at the huge blue expanse. He had never heard about this lake, even though it was the largest in Italy. Favored by a delightful climate, it served deep into the winter as a resort, not for the very rich alone; small cottages, surrounded by palms and olive groves also stood on the shore.

Towards the north the lake seemed to become narrower, and while he still wondered where it might end, or whether it was some inland sea, he perceived, drawn in soft gray and brown shades, its mountainous setting. "These, too, are the Alps!" he thought. They looked like indomitable breakers, seen from a great distance, the vanguard of an inexhaustible ocean, halted and turned into stone by a mighty hand.

The water was warm, but not so warm as the sea at Antium. "And it doesn't carry you so well!" he thought. With long strokes he swam away from the reeds until a cleansing and refreshing coolness vibrated through his whole body.

The sun stood at noon, when he returned to shore. He lay down on the grass until he was dry, then he took some bread and cheese from Pomponius' saddlebag. But when he had dressed, and sat down under one of the plane trees, his spirits slumped again.

"I am going to Hibernia, and to safety, while they stay behind. . . ." This was the thought of horror which had first struck him during that ill-fated afternoon, when Herod Agrippa had visited him in the library of the Villa Ciceronis.

"Last night, my feelings were wrong. The Great Garden

can't yet have been closing. But soon it may—" He looked up his earlier reflections, like a man who, unsure of his memory, must reread his own writing. "When Caligula is Emperor—God-Emperor—and Herod Agrippa is reigning over the skull-shaped rock, then the flame of Cornelius, of Elon, of Jairus, of the 'keen blades' and of all the others will be extinguished in their own blood."

But while he thought thus, for the first time he consciously became aware of a oneness which surpassed the bonds of friendship and all feelings of personal attachment.

"What does it mean to say 'safety'? There is no such thing. With them I too am being killed." He struggled with his thoughts, trying to clarify them. "If they were killed, I, too, would be dead, even if I lived." Longinus' face came back to him; he had looked so happy, yet he must have known what fate awaited him. "My friend lives, even though he died —because he died for Him."

He picked a dandelion and blew its winged seeds towards the lake. "Why did I have to come here? Why could I not die together with Longinus?"

There was Italy. He saw it like a big colored map, from the southern coastline, which he had watched from the deck of the *Neptune*, the roads and rivers, Neapolis, Rome's mural crown, the villages and people up to Verona and the point where he now was.

"A barren field." Never would it be broken by the ploughshares in which he had so fervently believed. His thoughts stopped abruptly. This was blasphemy; he felt its dark wings, and fear and agony seized his heart.

"My sword strokes were to be better than those of the 'keen blades,'" he repeated, his lips trembling. "Now I have betrayed my King, for Whom Longinus died." He passed his hand over his eyes. "My King—Who died for me." His contrition grew. "I am a faithless boy," he thought, haltingly. "I am not worthy to be called His servant." And then, sorrow and shame overwhelmed his very being.

Time passed, and no voice was permitted to tell him that even now, over the sea lanes from Tyrus, along the coasts, over the highways of Syria and across the Hellespont, the Word was traveling irresistibly as light itself. Soon it would bring Italy into the dawn of the awakening day. Nor was he to know that he had indeed prepared the way for those truly sent forth into the vineyards, and that for the sake of Tiro, the servants, Aristides, one day he might hear the Verdict: well done.

Even of the boy with the golden hair he was not to think in his cleansing abandonment. This boy, hardly four years later, would kneel before the Throne of Grace, drying his eyes with God's own wide blue mantle. Instead of the Caesars' gilded laurels, on his head would rest the crown of life, and faithfully he would watch over Marcius, who once had called him "little brother."

In that same year—but this too remained hidden to Marcius —at the close of Tiberius Caesar's righteous government, the last scion of the Julian-Claudian house would be born. In him, Lucius Annaeus Seneca would see the Prince, whom he might guide to be the philosopher-ruler of Plato's great ideal. But soon the disciple would yield to corruption and vice, and would force his teacher to seek death by his own hand. By then, however, the skeptic speculator, whom Marcius had known, matured by years of thought, would come close enough to Truth to be counted by many among the Word's elect.

Under that same reign of the Emperor Nero the dark of the imperial gardens would glare with living torches, and the sand of the circuses and amphitheatres would be reddened with the blood of the witnesses, the precious seed of new believers—

This too young Marcius could not know, but a whisper of the wind of history may have brought to him a faint foreboding of those future feasts of passion, pain, and fortitude. It was like a breeze, kindling the fire of his repentance to greater flame, until the voice of grace, silenced by his vainglorious desires and ambitions, could speak once more.

"The Golden Orb," he heard—surely, it could not be wrested from the all-merciful Hand by the doings and plottings of even the most evil among men. Nor could the hour of transfiguration be hastened in its coming by a human command. "Conquest must come from within." He thought it hesitantly, as if he were afraid that the tender texture of his new insight might dissolve like the threads of a dream.

There again, lit up before his eyes, lay the wide Italian land. The ploughshares would not fail to pass through it—they would draw broad furrows for the sowing of the grain. But until the tender green ears could break the ground and mature towards a never-ending harvest, time and the rain and the sun, and the wind and the dew of Grace, would have to stream into the hearts of many generations.

". . . none which imposes greater obligations," Seneca's words came back to him. "The greatest of all is the Cross!" he said aloud. "This they do not know." A deep wonder came into his voice. "How could they, if even I, who was present, did not remember?"

He took Seneca's letter and leafed through its many pages, until he reached the postscript. "Two cities our mind beholds. But only one has its foundations in the sacred mountains."

"I see what he means," he said, and his eyes focused, as if he sat under the oak on the hill of Lavinium, looking at the distant reflections of the mural crown. "They reproached the

Emperor for using his office as Pontifex Maximus for political purposes." He nodded as if in new understanding. "Of course, that was a pretext, but it struck him where he was vulnerable." The conclusion was evident. "How much less can one dare to use Him—"

A smile passed over his face. "But if the Senate had yielded, it might have helped the conquest from within." He had said it like a question, and his blue eyes opened wide. Somewhere there must be the answer. Dimly he could perceive it, like a man who has been blind and who must learn to comprehend what he is seeing.

"Just another niche in Agrippa's Pantheon would have been filled," he said aloud. "That is not the way! We must be patient and wait—wait—wait—even if He should decide to withdraw." His thoughts broke off. And even while he tried to summon all his strength, fright seized him again.

"But then the Great Garden would close," he whispered, his mind overwhelmed once more by the vision of horror which had stared at him during Herod's visit: the abomination of desolation standing in the holy place, mocking laughter predicting the fall of the sanctuary, while around its Rock the jaws of the abyss opened. And his shuddering soul was permitted to taste from the chalice which can never pass away from any man who follows his King.

Yet it is also ordained that peace and certitude should flow from this same cup. While Marcius still felt it at his lips, it seemed to him that words broke forth as from the hollow of a great shell, in which the murmur of the ocean is captured for all times and places, even up in the high mountains, never touched by the wind of the sea.

Breathless, he listened. The words, carried by the rushing waves of his blood were the same which months ago he had found in Cornelius' records—he had read them, but had failed to understand their import.

"Upon this Rock I will build my Church and the gates of hell shall not prevail against it."

Then it happened that the last veil covering his soul was torn asunder. The words were made vision, and his faith became a firm and unshakable trust. "The Pantheon—" His youthful heart flared up as if with a jet of fire. "It must crumble—the whole Pantheon must crumble!" With triumphant enthusiasm he added, "So that the King may reign over all."

His glance withdrew, and he sat silent, until his turbulent breast had become placid and calm like a lake in midsummer. Slowly the images began to pale, and like the sound of evening bells the words faded away, each leaving in its wake a trail of silver.

Marcius raised his head. Another voice seemed to speak to him, mildly, the voice of a father who knows the frailty and the limitations of his son and is aware that the young strength might give out if too much were imposed upon it for too long a time.

"Now you may go!" this voice said, and like great doors the eyes of his soul were closed. There was the meadow again and the plane trees, the reeds, the lake with its mountainous frame; he was young and forgiven, life lay before him, and at his side was his faithful companion.

He jumped up. "Pomponius, everything will be all right, everything!" Laughing, and with tears, he put his arms around the neck of the horse. "And mind you, Pomponius, we are never alone, no matter where we are!" With a tender caress he parted the horse's mane. "Promise me, Pomponius that you'll never desert me! I am not your master, I am your friend!" Hastily he put on his shoes and leaped into the saddle. "Have I ever told you before that I love you? Well, no harm in doing it again!"

When he reached the estuary of the Mincius, he felt as if years had passed. Smiling he looked at the signpost. "Good-bye, Brennus! I won't see your name again." A thought glided through his mind. "What would happen if I turned left . . . ?" He shook his head with decision. "It's against the Emperor's command. And it might endanger Tiberius Gemellus."

Yet, the thought persisted, and it was pleasing to toy with it. "Still, the ambassadorship?" he asked himself searchingly. He halted, then wanted to cut the matter short, to say, "Let's go, Pomponius! There's daylight for fifteen more miles!" He seized the whip rein, and again hesitated. "I must make up my mind about the route. Why not right here?" With his left hand he took his road map from the saddlebag.

There was no need to go down to Genoa. From Mediolanum he could ride due west, then along the upper Padus to Augusta Taurinorum, or Turinum, as the local people seemed to call it. Cutting across the Cottian Alps should bring him into the Rhone valley, to Vienna in Gaul, and to Lugudunum. "That's the town where everything started!" he reflected.

He nodded. "I am glad I got this straightened out." Yet he still felt undecided. "I needn't be in Hibernia till spring. I have time to see Luitprant's people. Where they are, my people are supposed to have lived before they moved to our island. I could spend the winter there. It's well within the confines of the Empire. On my way back I might stop at Moguntiacum."

But the Emperor's command? "The legates are Gaius Cornelius' cousins. He told me to look them up. Of course I am not going as an imperial ambassador. That's positively finished." His hand on the whip rein relaxed. Then he dropped it.

"The Emperor can't object. It'll take months until I get to Moguntiacum. By that time everything will be settled. The special courier, whom Seneca mentioned, is on his way right now. Surely the Emperor will understand that I was anxious to see my people's former country." His face became serious. "And even if he did object—I am carrying the Message to the Danube and to the Rhine. This cannot endanger Tiberius Gemellus. I won't even dress as a Roman. I'll go as Marcius of Armagh and as nothing else." An intoxicating feeling of youthful adventure, of happiness, of a legitimate task was welling up. "As Marcius of Armagh!" He repeated. "To the very borders of the Roman world!"

The horse went forward a few paces. "You're rather skittish for your age!" Marcius said. Already the unshod hoofs were beating the dirt road. "Stop! I am not yet through with my thinking!" But he did nothing to enforce his command. He gave Pomponius his head for half a mile, then he seized the reins with both hands.

"All right, Pomponius! Through the terrible Alps into the heart of Germania Magna!"

When he reached the Athesis, broad bands of sunlight slanted across the gay white and green waves. He greeted them like old friends. "I like you much better than the Mincius!" A precarious wooden bridge brought him to the left bank and to the great northern road. Oak trees filled the valley and palms and olive trees had become scarce.

"There it ends!" he thought with amazement. A mile distant, dark-reddish mountains pushed into the valley. "Did I get on the wrong road?" At a slower pace he rode on. "Or is there a tunnel like Nerva's through Posilipo?"

Horse and rider threw gigantic shadows before them. It seemed as if they were moving ever deeper into their own shade. And the wild waves of the Athesis, with frothy foam, were leaping up more furiously against the rocks, which tried to block their path towards the Padus plain.

When Marcius came closer, the reflections of the sun on the towering mass of stone almost blinded his eyes. He hesitated. "Where am I going?" he asked, uncertain, and once more with a feeling of anguish bordering on awe. The road did not end, but like some fabulous stream it seemed to submerge itself in the bowels of the earth, perhaps to return to the surface hundreds of miles away. Slowly he raised his eyes. In dark-blue shades a yawning gate rose up to the sky which glimmered in yellow and soft pink.

"Are you ready, Pomponius?" he asked, and with his knees pressed the broad flanks of his horse. One leap carried him through.

Purple veils seemed to rain down on him, while tingling coolness descended from the high walls on both sides of the valley like drops sprinkling from a fountain. Trusting the vision of the good stallion, he went on for several hundred feet. Then, without halting, he raised himself in the saddle and looked back.

A curtain of translucent gold closed the gate. Behind it lay the illustrious garden of imperial Italy, the whole of the waning summer, and his three greatest years. Somewhere, far away, there was a forgotten grave, in which rested his friend Longinus. His own youth–it too remained behind that same curtain. Now he had entered into manhood, to face, in life's proper station, the tasks that lay ahead.

His thoughts and emotions gone silent, he continued his ride. The road before him became steeper. Surely it must be leading up to the roof of the world. Then turrets and battlements of jagged ice and the dreaded avalanches would surround his path.

But not yet had these zones of solitude been reached. Yellow pears and apples, chubby as the cheeks of little country boys after the first snow, weighed down the branches, and beeches and oaks displayed their fantastic tapestries in all the shades of red and bronze, of copper and pale green. When leaves drifted down from the trees high up on the rocky slopes, it seemed as if they carried with them a final gleam of the expiring day.

"Now we are on our own!" Marcius said to his horse, and then once more he glanced back. The golden gate had vanished but for a tiny spot of fading brightness in the deepening solemnity of the autumnal dusk.

CHAPTER TWENTY-SIX

A YOUNG MAN on a dapple-gray horse had passed the last chain of posts outside the fortified town of Moguntiacum. He was wearing Celtic-Germanic dress, a Damascene sword, leather breeches, and a short Gallic mantle. "Marke de Armagh, what a name for a Roman citizen!" the outpost commander had remarked. But as the young man's imperial passport, stamped by the legate of Upper Germany, was found in order, he could not be detained for further questioning.

Now Pomponius was carefully descending a steep lane. "He knows that we must follow the stream," Marcius thought, when at the bottom of the embankment the horse turned into the broad road which led to Bingium, Bonna and Colonia Agrippina. This was to be Marcius' last ride over Roman soil, and his heart was heavy with the pain of parting.

After an hour at a swift trot he dismounted. The day was not yet quite born, and the air of spring felt like cool wine. "You have drunk from many waters, haven't you, Pomponius?" he called after his horse, who was making for the rim of the river.

A milestone of gray granite stood by the road. "Imperator Claudius Tiberius Caesar, five times consul, Pontifex Maximus, Tribune of the People," the inscription read. Beneath it was a small arrow: "Confluentes, sixty miles." A larger one pointed southward, "Mediolanum, three hundred eight miles, Rome, eight hundred seventy miles."

"Soon I will be as far from it as I was a year ago at Capharnaum," he thought.

Hewn out of the stone and gilded, an eagle spread its wings over the imperial name.

"I won't see many more like you!" he said to the stone. The flowers at the roadside were still closed, and the grass was wet with dew. He sat down on his mantle and looked at the gray-blue waters of the Rhine. Over on the right bank were the Taunus Mountains, their round and cone-shaped summits covered by endless woods of virginal green. Pointed columns of smoke from the hearth fires of a few villages, hidden there, rose high into the quiet air.

Marcius laid his arm around the stone, and his gaze, forlorn, followed the waves: moat of the Roman world, frontier of the Empire, two thousand miles long from the German Ocean to Tomi on the Black Sea.

"It's farewell for good," Marcius thought. The legate Cornelius Lentulus Gaetulicus had arranged that at Bingium he could board a ship of the Rhenish merchant fleet, sailing down to the border of the Batavi. There a canal, built by the elder Drusus, connected with the Flevus Lake and, cutting through the territory of the Frisians, with the sea. Coasting along, the ship would pass the narrow strip of water between Gaul and Britannia, and would finally bring him to Iuliobona, where, under the good care of Titus P. Atticus Heirs, his two Numidians and all his other belongings were awaiting his arrival. In Moguntiacum he heard that for the last year boats had been making regular runs to Southern Hibernia. So it should not be impossible to reach Armagh within four to six weeks.

"It was a strange winter," he thought as his mind began once more to survey the last few months.

There had been snow as soon as he had reached the Brennus. On the north side of the pass big ploughs had been at work to keep the main highways open. On the Aenus, flat barges, laden with salt and iron ore had pushed their way through cakes of floating ice.

From Veldidena, which was the terminus of the Brennus road, he had gone eastward. After a day's ride he had reached the camp of Massiacum. "That's where the good honey came from," he remembered. A week later he had been in Augusta Vindelicorum, an ambitious frontier town, the trading and market place for the whole north.

"I won't need my toga any longer," he had thought, and so, together with much of his Roman equipment, he had sent it to Iuliobona. Instead, he had bought his Celtic-Germanic outfit and woolen mantles and underwear for the winter. In the waiting room of the *mansio*, which had been cosily heated, he had written to Gaius Cornelius.

"And Seneca? Shouldn't I write to him too?" Finally he had overcome his reluctance. "It is out of respect for the Emperor! It would be dicourteous not to let him know that I have changed my route. After all, I am still enjoying his hospitality."

When he had reached Luitprant's people on the right bank of the upper Danube, it was the beginning of November. A thick blanket had shrouded the world. Little fir twigs, renewed every day, had marked the narrow paths. Life had been slumbering, with deep, regular breath.

Then the houses of the Suevians, of stone and logs, simple, but not without some Roman conveniences, had been opened to him. He had been received not as a stranger or a guest, but as a son. There had been Luitger and his wife, and Luitprant's little brothers, a crowd of yellow-haired youngsters, crouching on bearskins by the fireplace and eagerly listening to the tales of faraway southern lands.

Though under the wings of the Eagle, and part of the Province of Rhaetia-Vindelicia, the land of the Suevians enjoyed great autonomy. Sometimes Marcius would accompany his host into the people's assembly. Luitger was the chief of the tribe, but to the assembly he could not dictate. He could only try to persuade. Jurisdiction was vested in the priests, and they opened and closed every meeting. During the debate, each member, according to precedence of nobility, age, and fame had to be heard. A division of power marked the whole of their primitive government.

Another thing had impressed Marcius greatly. "They share this trait only with the Jews," he had reflected. "So for my comrades of the Cohort Antonia the Germans too would be atheists." No images or statues told of their gods. "We dare not," Luitger had explained. "To represent them as humans would be contrary to their majesty." The places of sacrifice were woods and groves, and there was belief in the One, the All-Father, the Wanderer, to Whose power all nations should bow.

"The memory of the Great Garden," Marcius had thought again, and then he had enquired further.

Handed down from time immemorial, hope persisted for the coming of a redeemer greater than the law of fate. They called him *Heliand*, a word meaning the healer, the saviour of mankind. A hero in shining armor, he would slay the old dragon, coiled in poisonous rings around the ash *Yktrasil*, the tree of life. At his advent, Valhalla, the proud hall of the intermediary gods would crumble, burying them in its gushing flames.

This Luitger had told Marcius in the family circle on a long winter night when the sun had set at its most southerly point, a faintly glowing disk, wrapped in the hovering clouds of approaching snow.

"I bring you His Message," Marcius had said firmly, when his paternal host had finished. "Foretold in the Great Garden, the *Heliand* has already come." And as even the spinning-wheel in the women's corner had paused, and the men and the yellow-haired boys grew silent in absorbed listening, he had begun to talk.

"Indeed, the greatest, the mightiest, the most gracious of Kings," said Marcius, "Who, loyally followed by His keen blades, has wandered over the land, healing the sick and raising up the dead.

"The Light of the World, which darkness could neither behold nor extinguish, the truly Anointed, the Son of the Eternal Father and of the Virgin Mother, the Creator of Life, the gentle Lord of Youth, the Redeemer of all flesh, Who would not quench the glowing wick, nor break the slender reed.

"The faithful Ruler, for Whose command the legions of the angels were waiting. He handed the keys of His kingdom to Peter, whom He has called the Rock, Peter, who drew his sword in defense of his Master, when so many were arrayed against so few.

"The Lamb of God, at Whose death on the Cross, the great sun went blind and the earth was shaken to its very foundations.

"The Hero Triumphant, Who slew the old dragon, and on the third day rose again, hurling death itself into the burning pitch of the abyss.

"The Sovereign Lord, Who ascended to heaven, whence He will come again with great majesty, to judge the living and the dead.

"The Invincible Guardian of His people, Whose Church, built upon the Rock, He guides by the power of the Holy Spirit. Against this Church the gates of hell will never prevail, so that His Reign, His Kingdom and His Glory may endure forever.

"I have seen Him myself," Marcius had ended. "I was near Him when the Cross was planted on the skull-shaped rock. Three times He looked at me." He stopped. "Now He is looking at you and me always."

Outside the snow had been piling higher and higher, drifting down softly like the gray feathers of wild swans. Now it had almost covered the small windows with their leaded panes.

Luitprant's mother had been the first to speak. "When did He come into the world?" she had asked under her breath.

"Perhaps on this very night thirty-four years ago," Marcius had replied. "In Bethlehem in Judea, the town of king David." His glance withdrew inwards. "A decree had gone forth from the Emperor Caesar Augustus that a census of the whole world should be taken—"

When he had spoken about the Virgin Mother, whom later he was to see under the Cross, her sky-blue mantle all covered by a veil of dark gray, subdued weeping could be heard in the women's corner. But then he had told them about the shepherds in the field, who, guided by the star, came to the stable, where in a manger they found the Child of Promise. Weeping gave way to a movement of joyous compassion. With happiness the yellow-haired boys had looked up, and the men had laid their hands on their long swords. "We too want to be His vassals," Luitger had said, and a faint ringing of metal went through the room.

There had again been silence, but through their souls, and visibly over their faces had glided a dream of wondrous things, which soon would overflow the boundaries of the mysterious south, the land of the milk and honey of the Redemption.

Slowly, Luitprant's mother had risen. A tall woman, she had walked with firm steps to the hearth. There she had knelt down, and from a pile of wood seized a dry branch. She had held it into the dwindling glow, and when it caught fire, had withdrawn it and held it high—

Seconds long the light of the bright flame had flared through the room, almost too strong to be borne. But even after the shadows of the winter night had again risen up to the low ceiling and in purple waves had passed through the snow-covered windows, there remained a light, which was almost like a glory.

With the coming of spring, when the ice was breaking on the Danube, Marcius had sadly bidden his hosts farewell. But they had kept him until the first rhododendrons were blossoming under the melting snow and the white and blue anemones, the yellow primroses, and the blue bellflowers and, by the awakening brooks, the buttercups and the violets were breaking through the ground.

When he had come to the big lake, through which the young Rhine flows, spring had been more intense. A southern mildness had greeted him on his ride along the left bank of the river. Noble columns, villas with wide peristyles, fountains, and mosaic-covered atria rivaled the beauty of Italian homes. And again, as so often during his long journey, there had been many a place where he would have liked to stay, but to see and to leave were always one.

Then he had reached Moguntiacum. In the forum, with sovereign quietness, with eyes of living marble, Tiberius Caesar rested on his curule chair. Shyly and with reverence Marcius greeted the august Prince. With free pride he looked into the detached glance of the imperial eyes. "Caesar, I am fulfilling your will."

Moguntiacum was the general headquarters of the legions of Upper Germany, a sounding board for the attitude of the entire German army. Sensitive to such things, Marcius noticed at once that there was perfect calm, the morale of the soldiers was high, and quite obviously not a spark of insubordination was in their minds.

This impression was confirmed when he visited the two legates. He found them more cordial than the Cornelii at Antium, perhaps because they stood at an outpost of the Empire, and they rejoiced in personal messages from their cousin, whom they had not seen in a long time.

Carefully Marcius avoided speaking about politics, yet it was inevitable that he should mention his audience with the Emperor and his friendship with Tiberius Gemellus. Finally there was an opportunity to talk frankly of what was in his heart. "We have heard about these events through some of the soldiers," Gaetulicus remarked. "News travels fast these days."

There had been letters for Marcius. A short one from Cornelius told that he had seen Tiro, and still hoped to see the others before his return to Judea.

And, with a much later date, there was a long letter from Seneca. The decision to open it was not easy.

"My friend," it said in part, "your letter from Augusta Vindelicorum, which reached me several months ago, pleased me greatly. I was glad about your decision to go north; in fact, I had expected it. Celts, if not softened up by court life—as I am, for instance—are stubborn people. Nor does the Emperor resent it. He feels that you must have grown and that you have learned many things. The door to him will always be open.

"Gaius Cornelius and the Second Syrian Legion have returned to their garrisons. There were no longer needed in

Italy. Now His Majesty's hands are free, and accordingly, he will give his instructions to the legate Lucius Vitellius. It is not impossible that I will again be sent to Antiochia."

It was a very friendly letter, almost without irony. "I am treading a perilous path, my friend. To be Phaethon to Princes is as great an adventure nowadays as it was to drive Phoebus Apollo's chariot in the days of old—even though I may first have to climb to higher honors and to greater fame. *Vanitas Vanitatum!* I would envy you, if envy were not the silliest of all human foibles. How can one desire another man's destiny, without wanting to become the other man entirely? But I can thank you. And the fact that you can hardly know how much you gave me makes your gift more valuable still."

The last sentence of the letter Marcius had read so often that he now knew it by heart.

"Believe me when I tell you from the very bottom of my soul: in all the differences and adversities of my life, this is my guiding principle; since it is God's will, I not only obey, but also assent to it, nor do I comply out of necessity, but out of inclination." Then came a surprising twist. "Don't you think this is too good a sentence to die tucked away in a letter to a young Hibernian? I may write a whole book on the theme, and if my publisher has any sense at all, it should have a wide sale. *Vale*—"

"Now he is stroking his pointed beard and baring his white teeth. A cynic never changes!" But he smiled as he thought this. "Well, I won't see him again, nor any of the others. It's goodbye forever, Capharnaum, Antium, the roads, the Alps, the Suevians." His heart became heavier still. "The whole of life is waiting, Seneca once said. There is something else too—a continuous farewell."

And as he had so often before, Marcius asked the anxious question, "But where am I going?"

He looked up. Behind the vastness of unconquered Germania Magna the watchful Aurora was opening her doors, and her halls were filling with roses. As if touched by a magic wand, the waters of the Rhine were changing from gray-blue to a golden green, with the gold becoming ever more luminous. Then, in an opening between two high waves of trees, on the farthest horizon, the sun began to rise like the crest of an illuminated fountain.

A feeling of elation thrilled through Marcius' body, and his whole being was drawn toward the ruddy east. All along the Rhine he had seen the resurgent vernal sun, yet it seemed to him as if this sunrise were the first since the translucent gate at the Athesis had closed behind him.

At the kiss of the reborn light, the uncharted ocean of trees and the gentle hills, which were so fondly embracing the wide stream, awoke to life. Larks and finches, blackbirds and crested titmice, set up their chant of praise, and the strings of the great harp, fastened to midheaven, resounded with mighty accord.

Mirroring the colors of both sky and water, a flight of silver herons circled over the waves, as if moved not by their long curved wings but by the harmony of light and song. Now the sun had lifted itself up above the distant tree tops, it was strong and mild, as it can be only in spring, when morning is almost like an early noon.

"Capharnaum," Marcius thought, and he shuddered under the returning memories. "Today, one year ago—"

Superimposed upon the Roman-German land he saw the lake of Gennesareth, and the demons and shadows, which had galloped behind him, had dissolved with the receding veils of the night. It had been the hour of the Great Triumph, and his soul had responded to it, though his mind had not yet known.

"All chains were broken so Longinus, too, was free," he thought vaguely, and then it seemed to him as if between the two sunrises there had been only one single beat of the sacred heart of the world, just long enough for him to mature to manhood.

For an instant he closed his eyes. Then, as the stations of his journey and what he had left behind at each of them returned to his thoughts, he knelt down and bathed his face and forehead in the Rhine's sparkling waters—the frontier of the Empire, yet soon to be frontier no longer but an inland stream.

His vision still veiled by the drops which clung to his long lashes, he vaulted into the saddle. The horse returned to the road. There Marcius stopped and looked at the milestone.

The gray furrows which marked the Emperor's name were filled with light and, resplendent under the rapidly ascending sun, the eagle was shining in scarlet and bright gold.

"Under its wings the Cross will grow up like a tree." His mind paused, and then another thought arose.

It was the great breath of Time, the storm wind of history, that moved these wings and they, moved in turn by their mighty beating, would carry the seeds along all roads of the world, spreading them out across the rivers, the moats of the Empire, the seas and the mountains of the universal orbit, and even beyond the limits of all future generations. Wherever those seeds touched the ground, small crosses would sprout from the blood-drenched field of the perennial combat, never lost, yet never victorious until the end—rows of crosses without number, a precious belt girdling the seamless robe of Man.

In a new farewell his eyes fastened again on the symbol of dominion and on the name which stood for the fullness of all temporal power.

"Born under Caesar Augustus," he thought, and inclined his head, "crucified under Tiberius Caesar, risen from the dead and ascended to Heaven, whence He will come again in Glory."

And firmly, joining his testimony to the Magnificat of nature, he added: "*Mundi Redemptor, Altissimus Dominus, Jesus Christus.*"

Slowly he turned his horse. "Now we must go," he said, and the great road, the last stretch of his long journey, opened again. With him went the waves of the Rhine, the flowers at the wayside, and the silvery herons, their long wings almost motionless, gliding swiftly over the green and golden stream.

"Just you and I, Pomponius," he whispered, and, anxiously he gripped the mane of his good horse. "I must not look back, Pomponius, I must not!" And, as the broad unshod hoofs began to beat the road in the rhythm of a slow, and then a fast trot, he heard the voice of a friend telling him within the solitude of his soul that from farewell to farewell he was going forever homeward.